Mortal Instruments

Mortal Instruments

JOHN MALCOLM

This edition published in Great Britain in 2003 by
Allison & Busby Limited
Bon Marche Centre
241-251 Ferndale Road
Brixton, London SW9 8BJ
http://www.allisonandbusby.com

A catalogue record for this book is available from the British Library

ISBN 0 7490 0652 8

Printed and bound by
Creative Print + Design, Ebbw Vale

JOHN MALCOLM is the author of numerous crime novels, including the popular Tim Simpson series. A former Chairman of the British Crime Writers Association, he lives in a Sussex village with his wife. He is also the author of non-fiction titles on art and antiques and is a regular contributor to *Antique Collecting* magazine.

By the same author

A Back Room in Somers Town
The Godwin Sideboard
The Gwen John Sculpture
Whistler in the Dark
Gothic Pursuit
Mortal Ruin
The Wrong Impression
Sheep, Goats and Soap
A Deceptive Appearance
Burning Ground
Hung Over
Into the Vortex
Simpson's Homer
Circles & Squares

For Nick and Sam

Between the acting of a dreadful thing
And the first motion, all the interim is
Like a phantasma or a hideous dream:
The genius and the mortal instruments
Are then in council; and the state of man,
Like to a little kingdom, suffers then
The nature of an insurrection.

Shakespeare
Julius Caesar

Tableau: a picturesque presentation; dramatic situation suddenly brought about.

Concise Oxford Dictionary

She stood on my front doorstep, carrying an old-fashioned black leather briefcase low down at the end of her arm, like a legal weapon. She had brown wavy hair and wore a grey linen suit with a white blouse under the jacket. A stocky man in his thirties peered at me from behind her. He wore an open herringbone jacket and red tie with a buttoned-down blue shirt above grey worsted trousers. He was tanned, with short fair hair and a broken nose above a wide mouth. His eyes, as they took me in, were blue and calculating.

My heart sank.

"Mr. Barber," she said factually, holding out a hand. "I'm Frances Parks, DTI. I think we spoke on the phone twelve days ago. This is my colleague, Barry Henshaw. Sorry we've arrived at such short notice. May we come in?"

Since she had the courtesy to ask the question I took the hand, said "Mrs Parks" in a neutral tone, shook it briefly and smiled. A man without much choice might as well observe the niceties. Then I stood back, shook the stocky Henshaw's powerful hand, wondered whether rugby or pugilism had done the nose, and led them into the sitting room.

"Good view," she said, looking out to sea as she put her briefcase down in the middle of the carpet. Her skirt came just over the knee, her stockings were medium brown and her shoes black, not too high-heeled but smart. An efficient, executive image. She handed me a card, which told me nothing except that she was from the DTI. No function was defined. Just the cold fact of her name, then her London office address at the Department of Trade and Industry in Victoria Street.

My heart sank further.

"Not bad, in good weather," I responded modestly, as we took in the choppy water across the stony shingle. "What can I do for you?"

"May we sit?"

"Of course." I managed to grin, waving at the settee and chairs. "Going to be a long job, this, is it?"

She smiled back politely. Good teeth, pleasant smile, which softened a rather stiff expression, crinkling round the eyes, which were blue, and widening the mouth, which had looked a bit small in repose. "Not so much that. Quite a tedious journey, we've had, from London."

"I've had quite a tedious journey, too. From São Paulo. I'd just showered and changed when the bell rang."

She paused, nodded without expression, and sat down in one armchair, clutching the briefcase to her body as she crossed her legs and showed a knee. Henshaw took the other chair, leaving me the settee. I tried to relax on it but my posture wouldn't go anything but tense.

"I gathered that you'd been away," she said, factually.

"Doing some DTI work. For which, despite a previous agreement, your colleague Graham Robinson isn't prepared to pay very much."

"Ah." Her face was impassive. "Perhaps I should explain. I'm not from Graham Robinson's branch."

My God, I nearly burst out, how many branches has your tangled thicket got? But I didn't, because I wasn't feeling natural. Something told me, some tiny voice inside, to say as little as possible.

So I just said, "oh", and waited.

"It's kind of you to see us off the cuff, as it were."

Oh come on, I nearly burst out again, you've come down all the way from London without any prior notice of any kind. A civil servant like you is not supposed to know whether I'm in or out but somehow you knew I'd be in. Do you think I'm a fool? You've either had me followed or you've got amazing lines of communication. This must be a panic telephone job, a call that told you I'd be back from Brazil right now, despite efforts to nobble me on the way. I've not been back more than an hour, yet you are here. You knew I'd be tired and generally knocked up, pretty distrait, quite apart from getting nothing by way of compensation from your mate Robinson in the 'other' branch, whose same phone you use. But I'm not responding, not letting you rattle my cage.

I didn't burst it out; I just waited.

"We 're looking into one or two matters concerned with Lawrence Edwards' dossiers."

Oh Lord, my reactions continued, surely you can't say that and pretend Graham Robinson isn't anything to do with you? He's the one who took over all that material straight after you'd been allowed, in your own parlance, to deal with Lawrence's desk. Or dossiers.

As though desks and dossiers have a life of their own.

But I just kept schtum.

"In certain circumstances, you see, there has to be a different source of checks and balances from those applied by the department in question. An outside view, as it were."

I liked the voice, though. It was light and pleasant and not demotic in any way. Home Counties, I supposed.

"That's you then, is it?" I asked. "The outside view, I mean. A check and a balance all in one?"

Her smile was polite again, not amused. "Yes it is."

"And he – " I pointed at the broken-nosed Barry Henshaw– "isn't a DTI man, is he?"

There was a pause. Then Henshaw spoke.

"No sir, I'm not."

The 'sir' gave it all away.

"You're a policeman?"

"Yes." Frances Parks intervened quickly. "Barry is a sergeant in the Metropolitan Police. Forgive me if I seemed to be concealing that fact."

"You're forgiven. Although you did. What branch? No, let me guess: Fraud?"

Catch them? I could almost hear Lawrence whispering in my ear. *Of course they won't catch them. Get killed? No one is going to get killed.*

15

Poor old Lawrence.

"We call it the Business Investigations Branch, actually, Mr Barber. The BIB. My bit of it, anyway."

For a Met man, Henshaw's voice wasn't Cockney or even estuary. He too was rather well-spoken. I decided that the broken nose might have been a rugger job.

"So what can I do for you?"

"We're looking into certain aspects of Lawrence Edwards' operations." Frances Parks took up the story once again. "I'm afraid much of it is very confidential. When a sudden death occurs, it's important to make sure there are no loose ends. Basically, we want to get the timings right." The briefcase was opened and she took out a stiff pad of papers. "When was it exactly that you met Lawrence Edwards to discuss your—your project with him?"

I told her the date of my fateful Northumberland Avenue café meeting. She nodded cautiously, making a note. She reminded me of one of those so-called customer service ladies you find in banks, blandly seated behind a smart desk with a PC monitor on it, asking owlish personal questions of indigent people whilst pretending they find the resulting banalities important. So far everything seemed much too distant, too uninvolved, to relate to violent death or my chases round the teeming streets and dusty highways of São Paulo.

"And would you mind telling us exactly what was the brief agreed between you?"

My heart soared back up several notches. I chuckled and sat back on the settee more comfortably as I grinned at them both. Their faces went still.

"Have I said something droll?" She managed to sound curious but the irritation underlying the query was clear. Her face had set.

"You don't know, do you?"

She frowned. "I'm sorry?"

"You don't know. None of you. None of you know exactly what the hell Lawrence was up to. Not you, not your Mr. Robinson, or the sergeant here. He didn't record it, did he? My 'project' as you call it: you don't know what it was."

Her tone went very formal. "I rather think we do. This may seem an oblique way of proceeding to you, Mr Barber, but it is necessary for us to have your version of events quite independently for cross-checking, you see."

"If Lawrence didn't record that he'd agreed to pay my club class return fare and two hundred and fifty quid a day consultancy charges, to cover all travel and subsistence costs inclusively, up to a maximum of fourteen full days, which is what your chum Graham Robinson says he didn't, then I'm willing to bet that he didn't record what he actually asked me to do, either."

She was scribbling on the thick pad as I shot through this sentence. "Could you just repeat those figures? The figures you say he offered you?"

I did so. It is incredible that a civil servant can find figures for agreed daily expenses of high importance when investigating possible murder and malpractice of a major order. But there it is: the devil is always in the detail, as someone said about the Northern Ireland peace agreement.

"What else did Lawrence Edwards undertake to do, from his side?" She was still writing carefully, head down, with a fine, fibre-tipped pen. I wondered whether she wore contact lenses, decided not, began to find her attractive – what age must she be? In her forties, without doubt. What sort of man would Mr Parks be?

"Nothing," I answered. "Except to pay up."

"And you: what did you promise?"

"To look into the market for high frequency microwave moisture sensors with particular reference to coffee bean analysis."

Her expression didn't flicker. "That's all?"

"That's all."

"Tell me, Mr Barber," she looked up from the pad straight at me now, "how did Lawrence Edwards come to be using your services? Why you? You're not on any list of DTI-approved management consultants or researchers, are you?"

I smiled. "Certainly not. I'm no gash DTI man. Catch me. It was a question of back history. A funny deal in South Africa a year or two ago. I knew a man who knew a man who had the details. Lawrence was trying to find a missing shipment, using the International Maritime Bureau. Eric Ellen's lot. There were false bills of lading, the usual sort of scam, the most common successful form of robbery there is. As it happened, I'd shipped a machine to South Africa on the same vessel as the dud consignment. Lawrence came to see me about it along with every other shipper he interviewed—found my consignment was absolutely kosher, of course—but I was able to steer him in the right direction. After that, he took it on himself to call me from time to time."

She raised her eyebrows. "And it was convenient for you to know a tame DTI man?"

I frowned. "I'd say the boot was on the other foot."

Henshaw stared at me curiously while this was going on, then spoke as she made another note.

"When did you hear of Lawrence Edwards's death, Mr Barber?" he asked, seemingly without much curiosity.

"The week after it happened. I was in Cartagena."

"Cartagena? In Colombia?"

"Yes."

"But you've just returned from Brazil?"

"Yes."

He cleared his throat. "Are you intending to go back?"

I paused. What did he know? How would he know it?

"To Brazil? Or Colombia?" I asked, to give my brain time.

"Either."

I licked my lips. Always a sign of nervousness. I must try to avoid it.

"It depends," I said.

2

In the summer of 1939, shortly after he arrived on a business visit, my father set fire to an hotel in a small town in Rio Grande do Sul. The building must have been wooden, so once he'd started a blaze upstairs it wasn't difficult for the flames to spread but in outrage he acted instinctively, without the slightest hesitation.

He was a hard act to follow.

In those days, hotels out in Rio Grande do Sul didn't have rooms with en suite bathrooms. You might have a washbasin if you were lucky but the loo was usually at the end of a passage where everyone could use it. My father needed the facilities immediately on arrival. Travel often affected his digestion, just as Horatio Nelson was habitually seasick.

"Typical," he used to relate, taking his pipe out of his mouth and stabbing the air with its sticky stem for emphasis whilst holding the smouldering implement in his big fist, "of Latin plumbing. Absolutely useless. They'd connected a two-inch soil pipe" – the relatively thin briar stem would be indicated–"to a four-inch outlet"– its junction with the gnarled bulbous bowl, a putative lavatory pan, served as second example– "so no wonder the thing was clogged."

My father was an extremely practical engineer. It was natural for him to be demonstrably technical about things. My mother often found him difficult that way when in company.

"The flush was totally out of action as well," he would go on. "Ball cock lever—a flimsy thing—snapped. People had thrown used lavatory paper all over the floor. In that hot climate. A great pile of it. Revolting. The stench was frightful. I dealt with the matter instantly. Instantly."

My father smoked a pipe like a small alto saxophone and had a big metal lighter to go with it, a wind-proof, petrol-fired giveaway from the Caterpillar Tractor Company. You could turn the adjusting screw up to get a four-inch flame quite easily. He played the flame on the heap of used lavatory paper and in no time the heap was burning brightly, the dry walls ignited, the fire brigade had to be called out, guests were evacuated and general panic was rampant.

They put him in jail, of course.

My father was a big man. He wasn't frightened of Brazilian jails or anything much else, having survived the First World War as a Bristol Fighter pilot. He was robust, with a truculent but humorous philosophy on life. Back in 1939 he thought that being English was something special and didn't like being neglected. When not travelling, he had a hearty appetite. After a few hours he banged on the cell door and shouted until the jailer came.

"When do we eat?" he demanded.

"Senhor," the jailer said with a grimace, "this is not a restaurant. This is a jail. Eating there is not."

My father stared at him in appalled disbelief. My father belonged to a generation that believed an average of three meals a day is absolutely essential for survival. Down in the churrascarias of Rio Grande do Sul he had been pleased to find beef eaters who could leave him far behind when it came to trencher work.

He had an affection for Rio Grande do Sul. I remember him rolling its name around his mouth like a schoolboy savouring a gobstopper.

Rio Grande do Sul; I think he found it romantic, too.

"I can tell you, however," the jailer said, half-closing an eye – he was a big man himself, not very well shaven, with a much bigger stomach than my father's – "that the Governor of the jail has not yet eaten."

The jailer stared at him steadily and with great meaning. My father understood at once. He had not been in South America for very long but he was never slow.

"In that case," he said, passing an American two-dollar bill through the cell door grille, "perhaps you would be good enough to convey my compliments to the Governor and ask him if he would care to be my guest for dinner at any restaurant of his choosing?"

The jailer smiled, creasing his black stubble into waxy folds. He put the banknote away carefully and disappeared.

Soon, accompanied by two large minders, my father and the

Governor of the jail went to the best restaurant in the town. The Prison Governor was a small, portly man with a goatee beard in the old Portuguese style, something of a natty dresser. They ate everything, my father said, from soup to nuts whilst conversing amiably enough on irrelevancies like politics and football. Then they sat back over coffee and large brandies to light Brazilian cheroots, watched enviously by the two minders, who had to remain at the restaurant door throughout, and with curiosity by other diners.

"Tell me," the Governor said after a while, puffing contentedly, "what on earth is this all about? A professional man like yourself, an Englishman to boot, setting fire to our hotel? What on earth for?"

"It was disgusting," my father answered, explaining the circumstances to him through wreaths of fragrant blue smoke. "I had to act quickly. In the interests of hygiene. Revolting. A danger to public health. Especially in this heat, when diseases flourish. The stench was execrable. Speed was essential. Not only that, but such neglect of hygienic facilities, apart I am sure from being illegal, could occasion a distinct slur on the name of this growing and pleasant town." He paused pensively and examined the end of his cheroot. "Think what would be the case if the knowledge of such a thing got out. As a businessman, I can tell you it would affect your reputation here. Badly. Not only here: the name of the whole of Rio Grande do Sul might be besmirched." He flicked a fine disc of ash into a saucer. "Possibly even Brazil itself."

The Governor's eyebrows shot up. He put his brandy down. He took his cigar out of his mouth.

"My God," he said. "You are absolutely right."

He gestured frantically at the two minders by the door, who came over rapidly, supposing him to be under threat from my father. The Governor waved at them peremptorily. He was flushed of face. His beard bristled forward aggressively.

"Arrest the hotel proprietor," he bellowed, "at once!"

My father left the town very rapidly on the next local flight, not caring to bother about its destination. He did not go back, even though he travelled extensively in South America for many years and told the story rather frequently.

I never found out where it happened. He was a difficult act to follow. I try, as must many sons, to put him out of my mind, not to give him too much space, but even though he has been dead for some years his memory often comes crowding back to me. He was a great raconteur and even his most extravagant stories usually turned out to be true. I have often wondered whether, despite his upright and ethical stance on life, he also had to deal with similar situations to mine.

When South America beckons, he comes readily to mind.

I, too, have places I will not revisit. That's why my reply to Henshaw was a prevarication.

3

"Depends?" queried Henshaw. "Depends on what?"

"How events turn out."

"What events?"

"Business matters."

He frowned, wondering whether to press the matter, then changed his tone to a more overtly interrogative style. "You say you were abroad at the time Edwards was killed?"

"No, as a matter of fact, I don't think I was. I tried to phone Lawrence just before I left but got a lady at his office – it was, I now realise, Mrs Parks here, who I hadn't spoken to before. She said he wasn't available and that his calls had been transferred to another extension. Although –" I looked at her briefly – "she was authorised to deal with his desk. She also told me of the – the fatal accident that had happened to William Pulford. Then asked what I wanted. I was concerned for security and my call wasn't important enough to explain. I was shocked at the news, so I thought I'd get through to Lawrence later, once I was en route. I guess Mrs Parks here was covering the gory facts up until someone knew what to do, maybe had to work out what the hell I was up to."

Henshaw's face didn't change much but I realised that almost certainly I'd just confirmed what he already knew.

Did they think I'd done for Lawrence? Or William Pulford? Or both? Surely not?

"So what were you up to?"

"I've told you: I was doing some market research for Lawrence into the application of an electronic, high frequency microwave moisture sensor with particular reference to the detection of toxins in coffee beans."

Mrs Parks scrabbled through her papers. "This is to do with the man Keane down here in Sussex? Who made the sensor that was stolen?"

"The very one."

She wrote something down. "Thank you. You had no other brief?"

"No."

"It is your duty," Henshaw said, without any aggression in his voice, "to withhold no significant information of any kind from an enquiry of this sort. Indeed, it is a serious offence to do so."

"I dare say it is. I'm not."

He sighed slightly. "Mr Barber, you may have us at a disadvantage but it is one which doesn't put you in a very good light."

I refrained from correcting his grammar. A disadvantage, surely, cannot cast light. I just said "Oh?"

"No. Shortly after you agree your project, brief, remit, whatever you want to call it, with Lawrence Edwards, and whatever you say it was, he is killed. While, on your own admission, you are still in the country."

"So his death is suspicious?"

"It is currently being treated as suspicious. Until facts prove otherwise."

"And what about William Pulford? Blown to bits in his caravan?"

"There appears to be no connection between the deaths of Lawrence Edwards and William Pulford."

"Oh, come on! Even I know there was. I met them together."

Henshaw blinked. "When?"

"At the café in Northumberland Avenue. Lawrence said that Pulford was assisting him but didn't want to explain how."

"They worked for quite different branches." There it was again: as though no branch of the DTI ever communicated with another. "Pulford had been to a pub, late, before he went back to his caravan. He was on holiday. It seems he was careless with his gas cooker."

"*Ultra vires,*" I said, dryly.

"What?"

"*Ultra vires.* Lawrence said that Pulford was collaborating with him on a sort of *ultra vires* basis. You know what *ultra vires* means?"

For the first time, Henshaw was put out. "Of course I do. It is a term used legally to describe something which is outside the powers – *ultra vires* – of the court."

"Correct. So what Lawrence meant was that Pulford was acting outside his official powers. Clandestinely. Now I think that Lawrence felt he was being watched himself. Hence his use of Pulford and me."

"I'm afraid we only have your word for it." Henshaw gave me a longer version of his assessing stare. "You have to see our problem, Mr Barber." He leant forward to emphasise what he was about to say. "Not only is Edwards killed while you are here, you immediately rush off to Colombia, to Barranquilla to be precise. You disappear from sight, then register at an hotel in Cartagena under a false name – Gonzalez. You reappear in Barranquilla and Bogotá as yourself, travel to Brazil, and gatecrash an official Government reception under another false name – that of Richard Keane, whose business card you maladvert. During the reception you misrepresent yourself to a senior UK Government Minister. You then make wild and unsubstantiated accusations about an important member of the Brazilian business community with whom the UK minister is in negotiation over very important and discreet trade contracts of a sensitive nature."

"My goodness, someone has been busy, haven't they?" I looked at him donnishly. "Maladvert? Is maladvert really a word? I think you mean malvert, don't you? As in malversion, possibly?"

His expression didn't flicker. "You don't deny any of this, then?"

For a moment, I almost made a defensive retort. I was tired. I was worried about Katie Gonzalez, who had lent me her name in sheer mischief. People had tried to kill me. Richard Keane needed my help. Betty didn't answer the phone. The DTI was a nest of vipers. These two might come out with almost any accusation about the deaths of Lawrence Edwards and William Pulford, quite apart from my other, clandestine interests. But it would have been a mistake to appear defensive; I managed to steady myself and sit back, cool faced, on my settee as I answered.

"Never mind me, Sergeant Henshaw. I'm irrelevant. From what you've just said, there are more important fish to fry than mine, aren't there? Discreet trade contracts of a sensitive nature, indeed. Nasty smell there somewhere."

"Is that what Lawrence Edwards asked you to check on?"

I grinned at him. "No, he didn't. But if you put a ferret down a rabbit hole, all sorts of floppy bunnies do come rushing out, don't they?"

"I'm afraid the analogy is lost on me."

"Look, I didn't know Lawrence Edwards all that well but I think he saw me as a ferret. And himself as a poacher but a poacher on the side of the law. He used to phone me about all sorts of odd business practices."

"Why did he do that, do you think?"

"Because I'm sure the DTI is a bit of a bureaucratic hothouse and he wanted to make sure he was keeping in contact with reality. He was a pedantic old fart but he knew that he was a pedantic old fart and when it came to South America he was a bit lost. He wasn't lost about his end of things, I'm sure, things like Swiss bank accounts and Cayman Island companies, but he knew he was no Vernon or Cochrane, let alone Drake or Morgan. There was nothing naval or piratical about Lawrence. So I assume he used people like me for inside knowledge."

"Like you, you say." He gave Frances Parks a meaningful, conspiratorial look. "We did wonder what the attraction was."

I felt myself colouring. "Oh, did you? I suppose you did. And did you wonder, too, why it was that a man like Lawrence Edwards, pedantic, meticulous, bureaucratic, addicted to procedural niceties, could have set up a project without recording, *anywhere*, what he was doing, why, and the budgeted cost for it?" I stared at him thoughtfully. "There must be strict rules about such things. What deep concern, or fear, or possibility of internal betrayal, could have led a man as predictable and obedient as Lawrence Edwards to depart from everything he held dear, do you think?"

For the first time a slight smile came to Henshaw's lips. "We were rather hoping you could tell us, Mr Barber," he said.

"I wish I could. But he didn't confide in me. He lied to me. He told me at our meeting that my investigation was in no way dangerous. Since when he and William Pulford have been killed and I have been attacked twice, in Brazil, by people aiming to prevent me doing something connected with this enquiry."

Henshaw frowned. "Attacked? By whom?"

"Some extremely nasty professionals. Almost certainly in the pay of Carlos Guimares. Who, as I'm sure you know is the, quote, 'important member of the Brazilian business community with whom our minister is in discreet, important negotiations'."

"But you have no evidence to support this? They could just have been muggers?"

"They were no muggers. Muggers don't pursue you the way mine did me."

"Unsuccessfully, though, evidently." His gaze took in my freshly changed, neat appearance like an accusation.

Frances Parks decided to intervene. "Tell me: Lawrence sent you to see Richard Keane?"

"He did."

"Which is where you got the business cards?"

"Richard gave them to me. Wanted me to spread the word. He'll confirm that to you. My use of them was perfectly legitimate."

Henshaw grimaced. "Maybe. We'll check that. You did, however, say that you were Keane, not yourself, at the reception?"

"I did."

"Why? Why misrepresent yourself? Fraudulently?"

I smiled. "Let's just call it a precaution. Partly because the news was making me nervous. Partly to ensure entry. Electronics are so attractive to trade officials."

"Whereas Johnny Barber, uninvited machinery broker, middleman and rather dubious fixer, might not be?"

I bit back a retort. "I was acting in the interests of my late client, Lawrence Edwards, and hence the DTI, to whom I still believed I had a responsibility. Quite apart from Richard, who is suddenly being treated very shabbily, it seems to me."

"In what way was your fraudulent impersonation in the DTI's interest?"

"In the elucidation of a too-convenient coincidence. To be precise, our Minister's sudden presence in Brazil."

"But you had no facts to go on? No connection between this perfectly normal, planned international trade event, not a sudden presence, and the theft of the instrument, nor Edwards's brief to you which, according to your story, was a perfectly straightforward piece of business research. Just your own hunch? Who are you? Sherlock Holmes? Or is there something more we should know?"

"Look, Lawrence was on to something. And so was William Pulford. The theft of the instrument was too fortuitous. It must have been taken for a purpose."

"What purpose?"

"I don't know. I've racked my brains but I've no idea. Don't any of Lawrence's papers indicate anything to you? Or any other circumstances that might explain his death?"

Frances Parks shook her head. "We've been through everything else he was dealing with. There's nothing else that fits. All of his work is very neatly documented, exactly as you've said his method and character would indicate. He was extremely pedantic and meticulous. The only uncharted thing which we've got left to follow up comes from your telephone calls. Everything else draws a blank."

I stared at her as she paused for a moment. I opened my mouth, then closed it again.

She sat back and crossed her legs as though settling in for a more comfortable session. Her thighs swelled against the pressure of skirt as she moved them. "So you can see why these sequences of events have led us straight to your door, Mr Barber," she said. "There are no other leads. Just yours."

They both looked at me expectantly. There was more than a modicum of accusation in their stares.

My heart had returned to its normal position and had stopped fluttering. I stared back at them without the slightest blink.

"You've had a long journey. I'm sure you'd like some coffee, wouldn't you?" I asked them, smoothly, just to rub in my newfound calm as I got up from the settee. "Best Brazilian, for strength, with a dash of Colombian, for flavour?"

How appropriate it felt to offer them those particular coffees as their expressions, despite attempts at self-control, became suffused with suppressed dismay.

Their quarry wasn't breaking into a run. They didn't know, you see. They'd scanned the surface but knew nothing of the depths. Like a relief force bristling with ammunition, arriving at a metaphorical Fort Zinderneuf, they were bewildered by the fatal tableau confronting them. They didn't know what it meant.

And I certainly wasn't going to tell them.

4

Narrative: tale, story, recital of facts esp., in fiction, story told in the first person.

Concise Oxford Dictionary

It started, like so many things, with a telephone call.

"Johnny?" the voice queried. "Johnny Barber?"

My heart sank as I recognised it. Lawrence Edwards was a spooky civil servant in Victoria Street who worked for some sort of fraud squad concerned with international trade. He liked to 'keep in touch' as he called it, and for his own reasons felt that we should be on Christian name terms. I had never been easy with the familiarity. Lawrence had an eye about as warm as that of a cod on a wet marble slab. He behaved as though he had been all the way somewhere nasty and back only to be bitten by his own dog at the garden gate.

I'd much rather have avoided him but I take the view that it's better to know where the sharks are than to have to quit the ocean.

"Why hello, Lawrence." Feigned heartiness has never been easy for me but I do try. "This is a surprise."

"How are things, Johnny?"

"Fine, thank you." Did I sound enthusiastic enough? I raised the euphoria level a bit. "Just fine."

"Good, good."

"And you?"

"Oh, one mustn't grumble," he murmured back modestly. "Overworked, of course."

There was a pause. I didn't take the bait and say 'underpaid as well' because in my view no one with an inflation-proof pension is ever underpaid. People with inflation-proof pensions are not my scene, not at all, mainly because I used to pay for many of them and indirectly still probably do.

I compromised and said, "Busy, eh?" in a sympathetic sort of tone.

"My goodness, yes. One's masters are very demanding just now. Very demanding."

"Oh dear."

"One simply hasn't enough hours in the day. The mendacity of the human race has no limits, Johnny."

"Indeed it has not."

"But I'm sure I don't have to tell you that."

I bit back a sharp retort. Edwards had a habit of inferring that I'm steeped in illicit lucre, constantly in company with would-be Maxwells arranging to hoodwink the World Bank or plunder unwitting charities intended for helpless invalids. Perhaps, in technical terms, there was something in his suspicions, although my Maxwells are mostly small fry. There was nothing, however, that Edwards or more assiduous investigators could pin on me, not in England. At home, my steps are cautious. Someone would always provide the services I provide. It's not a moral issue with me; just business. And patriotism, of course; why should foreigners hog it all?

"Something particular causing all the activity?" I demanded, shortly.

"Oh, one has problems all over just now. But there are concerns in an area which I feel is likely to bring yet further tedium and toil, an area which I seem to recall is one of your specialities."

"Oh?"

"South America. You've got quite a track record in South America, haven't you, Johnny?"

"I do visit from time to time, Lawrence."

"You were there in your youth, surely, quite apart from current occupations?"

"Yes." His knowledge of my past history always got right under my skin.

"Fond memories, and all that?"

"Some. Certainly much happier ones than those of my boarding school, when I had to return to England. All porridge, chilblains and Puritan sentiment."

"Ah. Of course. To the enterprising, I think you once said, South America offers a life of applied hedonism."

"So I did. *Carpe diem* and all that. I'd forgotten."

Edwards had an old-fashioned liking for Latin tags. He and I belonged to a generation that had 'O' level Latin more or less imposed on it. Not that *carpe diem* – enjoy the day – requires 'O' level Latin for its cognisance; merely an education.

"Had you? I remember it vividly." His voice took on a sort of moral tone, like a BBC newsreader announcing another scandal. "Not for everyone, that hedonism, however, is it? That's one of the reasons it's difficult, I suppose, for we in Britain to take anything to do with South America very seriously."

"Not for some time, Lawrence. Not since it became an American province, or sphere of influence if you want to be pedantic. Before that, we took it seriously. Very seriously indeed on occasion. But since 1945 the only bit of South America we've woken up to, apart from fantasies produced by Graham Greene and Bruce Chatwin, has been the Falklands. On the other hand, the South Americans haven't regarded the British as serious material for some time either, have they?"

That nettled him. There's no one more defensive than a cynical, London civil servant faced with outside criticism of Britain. They're nothing like the Foreign Office lot; they gave up on their country soon after Suez. Mrs Thatcher sussed that out; that's why she gave them the bird.

"I think," his voice moved from morality into a slightly nasal, debating-chamber tone, "that South Americans are hardly in a position to cast stones at European societies. Or their financial systems."

"Now there you may have a point, Lawrence. Financial systems, in South America, are not regarded highly by the South Americans themselves."

"With good reason. Good reason with which I am sure you are familiar."

"Oh?"

"I do not need to dilate, on the telephone, on South American economics or business practice to you. You are far more experienced, I think, in such matters. I just wondered if, perchance, you are planning a visit in the not-too-far-distant future?"

That stopped me. The pedantic Edwards had never asked, up to that point, anything about my movements, never proposed any coincidence of my travels with some task or information that he might want. I always feared he would, one day. Now it had come.

"I have no immediate plans right now," I answered cautiously. "No. Why?"

"But it could happen?" His voice sharpened interrogatively, like a teacher or parent addressing a child.

"It is conceivable."

"Even if you do not have a specific reason," he was still sharp, "it might be quite normal for a businessman to, er, *prospect* a market with a view, say, to establishing potential?"

"Of course."

"It would be very useful if, in the not-too-far distant future, indeed quite soon, you might arrange such a visit to coincide with a particular, er, requirement, we are anxious to conclude."

"Can one conclude a requirement, Lawrence? Is that grammatical?"

"Don't be so bloody pedantic, Johnny! You know damn well what I mean."

I grinned to myself at having piqued him. "Don't you have lots of your own people to, er, to conclude requirements for you?"

"Of course we do." His tone dropped from sharp to confidential. "But this is somewhat extra mural, if you follow my drift."

"Oh dear. No, I'm not sure I do. It doesn't sound very safe to me."

"It is absolutely safe." Now he was becoming testy. My experience was that he often did when he was lying, or at least being economical with the actuality, as the late Alan Clark put it. "We just happen to need someone outside our usual range of contacts to conduct a discreet enquiry for us. Someone unknown to certain parties. We would pay handsome expenses. And our gratitude would be recorded."

I nearly said "oh dear" again. There wasn't an overt threat in what he asked, nor even an appeal to patriotism, but in the ensuing silence both hung heavily over the line. Why would a decent citizen refuse to do something so safe, if needed? Businessmen must have been used on many occasions to assemble evidence, especially businessmen who wanted their own businesses to proceed without let or hindrance, without a sudden descent of the Inland Revenue or Customs and Excise, the VAT man, to complicate life. I was almost certain I kept impeccable books but you never know what they might trump up, what they could do to put me out of action, answering queries, for long enough to do damage or frighten my contacts.

Life, on the other hand, was a bit empty just at that moment. A bit dull. I wasn't short of money, not at all, but there were no particular deals on hand that would take much time to arrange. No wild adventures were beckoning, nothing to set the pulse athrob. A pretty dim prospect, excitement-wise.

"I would," Lawrence Edwards's voice resumed in almost a polite, almost a supplicant tone, "count it as a personal favour, Johnny, quite apart from the eventual official record. A matter of goodwill, you might say."

"Would you? What sort of expenses would this goodwill engender, may I ask?"

He detailed them. They were not bad, not bad at all for a branch of the DTI. I looked out of the window at the grey prospect. Any minute now it was going to rain.

"OK," I answered.

The speed of my response took him aback.

"OK? OK? You mean you'll do it?"

"I do. In return for the expenses, of course."

His tone changed. "That's excellent. Excellent. I am most grateful. It will be much appreciated, I do assure you. If it can coincide with some other, er, business which you are conducting, so much the better. The more diversity the merrier. Can we arrange to meet fairly soon? It will need a personal briefing, you realise."

"Of course."

We settled a date and a time at a coffee house just off Northumberland Avenue. I put the phone down and went muttering into the back room, the one I use as an office, to check the business answerphone.

And there was Mario's message.

"Johnny?" His voice sounded thick and excited, not at all his usual cool. "I've got a wonderful cup of coffee for you. With cream and sugar. Give me a call."

That was the only message on the tape that day. There was nothing else at all. I wasn't worried about that; my Swiss accounts had grown enough to engender respect from my bankers when I visited Zurich. A lull in business would not harm me but Mario rarely disappointed; there would be gains to be made from his call.

Suddenly, things were picking up.

I left the machine and went into my little kitchen to make a cup of tea, thinking carefully about Edwards' evident desire for some sort of cover to smokescreen my trip. I wondered why. And Mario: it wouldn't be Italian coffee Mario was talking about.

I took my tea outside to enjoy the breezy view. In front of me, across the road and the heaped shingle, the English Channel was in mid-tide, slapping itself rhythmically against staked breakwaters. To my right, the congested coast sloped away to distant Beachy Head. To my left a closed pier still tottered out over prancing water, creamy domes guarding planked entrances to teetering delights above rusted stanchions. Nearer by, a man and his dog stood dubiously looking over the promenade railings at the stony shore, wondering perhaps whether to go down there and risk a fine if the dog decided to crap on the beach.

In the distance a tanker plodded along the horizon towards Rotterdam or maybe Antwerp. France was out of sight. The sky was grey and the water likewise. No palms or soft trees broke this hard, working sea passage. There were no white-sailed yachts about, nor even a dogged fishing boat, trudging back to Hastings. It looked as though almost everyone had gone somewhere.

Was Mario's coffee Colombian, I wondered, or Brazilian?

Or both?

5

"I've never quite decided," Betty Butler said, later that afternoon, "what it is, precisely, that you do. Apart from this, of course."

I smiled down at her. Outside, the threatened rain had developed into a steady downpour and the faint drumming noise it produced was soothing, giving an extra, warm sense of security to our intimate embrace under light covers in her large double bed. An odd time to be asking, I thought, but then curiosity crosses strange frontiers.

"I am a businessman," I answered.

She snorted, mildly, causing a certain, rather pleasant, muscular contraction. "That can mean anything," she retorted. "From big-time crook to ice cream vendor."

"Oh dear. Does the word businessman bring no other images to mind?"

"Not right now. Not unless you elaborate."

"Isn't Maurice a businessman?"

This reference to her husband caused a frown to furrow the fair brow under blonde locks. "Of course he is. But I know what he does. He's a commodity dealer."

"That's what he tells you."

"Oh, Johnny, really. Don't try to invest Maurice with mystery." She shifted her smooth limbs slightly to get more comfortable and, reaching backwards with a right hand removed from my shoulder, pushed a pillow under the back of her head for better support, so that she could look into my face. Which required a certain supple-ness of form. Then she put the hand back over my shoulder to make sure I stayed the way I was. Which was unnecessary; I had no desire to change my condition.

Her eyes squinted slightly as she looked at me from close to. Her breath was warm on my cheek as she spoke again. "He is only too plainly a commodity dealer, spending all his time in a stuffy City office, peering at a monitor screen through his expensive Armani spectacles. Or talking incessantly about prices on his mobile."

I raised my eyebrows. I am capable of coincidental muscular movements. "So that defines, precisely, what he does?"

"More or less. Oh, I know what you mean. He buys things and he sells things."

"Such as?"

"Commodities."

"Which can mean anything."

"All right, so it can. But usually it's agricultural commodities with Maurice. I do know that. Which is all very hick, you may say, despite all the hype about world prices. But then you may be very hick too, for all I know."

I relaxed the eyebrows whilst remaining firm elsewhere. "Indeed I might. But I don't think so. Nor, I bet, does Maurice. Think he's hick, that is. He sees himself as a wheeler dealer."

"Oh, stop prevaricating. Leave Maurice out of it. All I'm saying is that we've been meeting, no, to put it bluntly you've been knocking me off for over a month now, and I still know practically nothing about you."

"Your mysterious lover. Doesn't that add spice to the stew?"

"Oh, I'm not complaining. I'm not saying it's unpleasant." She moved the hand to the back of my neck and caressed gently, causing me to move equally sensually elsewhere. "I think it's unlikely you're hick, actually. And since Maurice only comes home midweek and weekends, it's been great to have you. Especially since I'm certain he has lots of totty while he's up in Town."

"But it would be disappointing if I turned out to be another commodity dealer?"

"It would be devastating. Absolutely fatal to further fucking, as the chorus girl said to the corpse."

"In that case, I'm happy to confirm that I am not a commodity dealer."

"Well you would, now, wouldn't you?"

"Listen, Miss Mandy Rice-Davis the second, I'm not lying. I am an international businessman with no City office and no commodities to trade. My skills are, it is true, technical and financial, which is boring to ladies. If I played the guitar or painted, no matter how badly, provided I talked about it a lot I'm sure that greater glandular secretions would be excited than business interests can arouse."

"You find my glandular secretions inadequate?"

"Far from it. You're a wonderfully juicy piece. Especially right now."

"Don't be coarse. Most of that, right now, is yours. It took, evidently, no guitar nor oil paint for me to secrete for you. I never thought for a moment that you could be a commodity dealer."

"Why not?"

She smiled. From so near, the movement of her face almost disturbed the air between us, so that I was conscious of the broad, swollen features radiating a positive kindness up to me. "You're too quiet. Almost withdrawn, no, not withdrawn because you can talk well. I liked you as soon as I saw you. You're not aggressive like Maurice's lot, you don't boast about deals." She cocked her head curiously. "Do you really do deals? I mean, if you're a businessman?"

"I do deals. Also, I help people who are doing deals."

"Help? How?"

"I help them with their tax situation."

Her smile faded. "Now that sounds really boring. That could turn me right off."

"I'm afraid that the way in which I help can be very risky. Which is why I don't boast."

"Ah! That's better. More exciting, I mean. It hit me when I first met you at Maurice's conference. I thought you might be shady in some way."

"I didn't say I was shady. I said that there are risks in what I do."

"What sort of risks?"

"From people. Never from my clients. From other people. Usually very boring people, tax men and bankers and others, who like to spoil life's little cheerful occasions."

"Is that what I am? A little cheerful occasion?"

"You are much more than a cheerful occasion. You are one of life's great, beautiful, generous gifts. You have altered my existence. You are, as Psmith once said, a blessing, a boon and, I might add, a benediction."

39

"Who's Smith?"

"A fictional character."

"He certainly had the gift of the gab." She stopped looking into my face and let her head loll back on the pillow. The hand on the back of my neck tightened. "It's shaming, but flattery doesn't half turn me on. The way you talk sometimes gets me all afire. Could you get going again?"

"What a silly question. Of course. Try stopping me."

"Not likely. Ooh, aah, my Cantona; no, no, please don't stop that, don't stop, please don't stop. That."

I kept going, as requested. Soon I would be far away, in South America. *Carpe diem*, as I've said before. Something that Lawrence Edwards remembered, like all those Latin tags he was so fond of. Or, as he would put it, in his precise, pedantic manner which never ended a sentence in a preposition, of which he was so fond.

6

Coffee (which makes the politician wise
And see through all things with his half-shut eyes)

Alexander Pope

"What do you know," he demanded, waving an empty cup at me almost as soon as I sat down, "about coffee?"

The question took me flat aback. A chill of nervous apprehension shot down my spine. All of a sudden everything was about coffee. It brought Mario straight to the front of my brain. One of the semi-humorous codes he and I use for concealment has coffee as its basis: with sugar or without, with cream or without, just beans or fully ground, cappuccino for fringe benefits, espresso if strong, American if dilute, Colombian, Brazilian, Kenyan, South African, Ethiopian, mountain, green, roasted, even Arabica and Robusta. Put into the context of Mario's fax and e-mail exchanges and the code-slang we use, coffee-words can mean many things.

Surely Lawrence Edwards didn't know that? Why should Lawrence Edwards know Mario existed?

"Coffee? I just drink it," I replied, looking down at the flakes of chocolate fringing the foam of my newly-arrived cappuccino and playing for time. "But not for breakfast. Tea is my breakfast tipple."

We were sitting in a café at the start of Northumberland Avenue, close by Trafalgar Square, convenient for Lawrence because his office was not far off and for me because Charing Cross Station was just round the corner. If necessary I could make a slow getaway back to St.Leonards, Warrior Square. It was a sunny spring day and the passers-by crossing the windows seemed to swing breezily down the pavement with a little more brio than I normally associate with London pedestrians. London life seemed good. I wondered if I had been a bit hasty about agreeing to travel.

"You don't," Lawrence persisted, "bother much about its growth, preparation, origins? What it might do to you? Your health?"

I stared at him. He was dressed, as always, in a subfusc worsted suit that seemed neither striped, patterned nor plain, an uneven white shirt and a tired Paisley tie that had been knotted much too often. A nondescript, civil-servant sort of get-up doubtless approved by departments in Whitehall. He must have downed one coffee quite rapidly and was awaiting another. There were bags under his eyes. His skin was pale and grainy. I thought he had been up late.

"It gives me a jolt, Lawrence. Perks me up. What else is it supposed to do? You referring to cholesterol or something? I mean, I don't drink it Mediterranean fashion, with a slug of grappa—Italian *caffè correto*—or brandy, like the Spanish, first thing in the morning. Not very keen on Irish coffee after dinner either. I do like a *caffezinho* as in Brazil, pure dynamite in hot weather, black, piping, plenty of sugar, on the hour every hour as in Turkey, but Turkish is so full of grounds, inevitably clogs your throat. Won't drink sloppy, boiled-milk instant as in Britain, think most American is dishwater, French good but a bit harsh, Italian excellent, Swedish strong and clean, Dutch great with cream, Colombian super for flavour, Brazilian for strength. Never tried Russian; made from burnt turnips or potatoes probably, is it? I believe that Ethiopian, which is the original Arabica, is very highly thought of. Why do you ask?"

Lawrence Edwards paused as another cup was put in front of him and nodded approvingly at its surface. "Quite an interesting round-up, Johnny." His lips flicked at the corners in the shade of a smile. "My, but you do get about, don't you?"

That was the infuriating thing about Edwards. Always on the probe, always the personal observation. Clocking up the little bits of data that probably got punched into some file somewhere, put on the database next to the passport criminal-photo and the fingerprints. A life lived vicariously, a life of stumbling blocks strewn for travellers to trip on. I shook my head.

"Not necessarily. You can get all sorts in my local supermarket."

"Not in your case." His voice was dry. "I think not. I think you've sampled all of those *in situ*, as it were."

"Oh?" Relief, as Mario's codes faded from my guilty mind, made me unguardedly flippant. "As with women, so with coffee, you think?"

He frowned disapprovingly. His was the kind of Victorian moral tone that must separate business from pleasure, life from art, surface from depth. One not allowing compartments to combine into a blend. Blends are murky and obscure the spectrum. Separation was essential. Lawrence Edwards' life, despite its deep underground burrowings, put a premium on surface colour, the appearance of things, the public set of face, the cast of appropriate countenance, on presentation. Since most of life is lived at superficial level, since there is so little time to know events or people in depth, Lawrence Edwards did very well in his chosen profession. To slip into a depth at coffee-time would upset him terribly.

"Come, come, Johnny. A gentleman does not boast of his incontinences. I do not recall attributing such experience to you in that other, um, that other field."

Incontinences; how dated that sounded. I was reminded of one of Somerset Maugham's essays, on the bachelor Augustus Hare of Herstmonceux. He was not, Maugham wrote, a passionate man, having confided to the budding novelist that he had not experienced sexual relations until he was thirty-five years old. From then he said he indulged only once every three months, marking the occasion in his diary. Since, Maugham wrote, most men boast about such matters, it was likely that to impress his confidant, Hare 'exaggerated the frequency of his incontinence'.

"I was joking. But you have by implication attributed so many moral transgressions to me that perhaps it was natural to assume you have had a go at incontinences, too."

Maugham also wrote – in *Cakes and Ale* it was – that it is very hard to be both a gentleman and a writer. Substitute businessman for writer and I am sure that Lawrence Edwards would have agreed; a gentlemanly ethos was one to which Lawrence, despite his profession and the need for contact with people like me, somehow aspired. Poor fellow.

He frowned. "I have not, to my knowledge, done that. On the other hand, you are such a widely-travelled man –"

He let his voice trail off suggestively. Rashly again, perhaps swung by the heady bustle of people passing by, I allowed myself another indulgence.

"Ah. Travel. Always suspicious, eh Lawrence? It was Oscar Wilde who said, when urged to go abroad to escape prosecution, that he had just been abroad. One can't keep on going abroad, he said, unless you are a missionary or, what comes to the same thing, a commercial traveller."

I smiled as I delivered the epigrammatic punch line, then swore silently to myself. Edwards's reaction was just what I didn't want. Instead of riposting or reacting, he went silent. His eyelids lowered a millimetre, into hoods over a gaze that went right through me. I'd dropped my guard, made a mistake. To give people like Lawrence Edwards personal insights, any kind of insights, is disastrous; they are bound to convert them into weapons. You cannot let your guard down with people like that. I made a mental note that I must be careful not to relax when in professional company.

Fortunately, at that moment, a shadow fell across our table. A big man, almost portly, stood beside us, looking down rather gravely at Lawrence. He too was dressed in a rather crumpled suit, the same kind of soft shirt with well-worn tie not quite holding an undone collar together at the neck. His florid face bore the bagginess of little sleep and perhaps much indulgence.

"William." Lawrence spoke approvingly upwards at the new-comer and nodded to a spare chair. "Good. Come and join us. This is Johnny Barber, of whom I have already spoken. Johnny, meet William Pulford, a colleague of mine."

We shook hands across the table. Pulford's hand was clammy but strong, like that of a fit man who has let himself go. His eyes rested on mine speculatively for a fleeting moment, then turned to Lawrence Edwards expectantly.

"I have asked William to join us," Lawrence Edwards nodded as Pulford leant back to gesture at a waiter for coffee, "because he is involved with me, on a somewhat *ultra vires* basis, in what I am about to tell you. He has, as it were, more than an outside interest in our little collaboration, so I felt that he should participate today. I will ask you to excuse me from further explanation. For the moment, anyway."

"If you wish." There were times when Lawrence's tedious hints of important offstage skulduggery deserved suitable reaction, but I said nothing.

"Thank you. Now: I was asking you about coffee. Have you ever heard of ACM?"

"Eh?"

"ACM. Evidently you have not. I'm not surprised. It is an abbreviation for the technical, or rather the chemical, name for a little-known but dangerous form of toxin caused by a fungus, similar to, say, ergotism in flour, which attacks the coffee bean."

"Oh dear, oh dear. A fungus, eh? On beans."

"Your feigned boredom is understandable but inappropriate. The toxin is considered highly dangerous if, in certain circumstances, it is ingested by the human being. The problem is known to exist in other cereal products like grain and so on, which have not been properly processed. Properly dried and stored, in fact."

"Really?"

"Really. The WHO – World Health Organisation – is becoming extremely concerned."

"Well they would, wouldn't they? They have to find something to do, I suppose. Coffee bean fungus could keep them busy forever, could it? Now that smallpox has been stamped out and the Millennium bug proved to be an expensive hoax? Those tax-free salaries and inflation-proof pensions can't be put at risk, can they?" I scowled at him irritably, feeling Pulford's gaze, over his recently-arrived cup of plain coffee, resting on me speculatively yet again. "Surely nearly all cereal processing companies have been alert to such toxins for ages?"

"They have. But in this case we are talking of a new toxin. Dangerous to health. As bad as e-coli."

"For God's sake, Lawrence. Who has been dying from drinking a cup of coffee? Without potassium cyanide in it?"

"It is not a matter of instant death. This is not an Agatha Christie story. The effect, as with e-coli, is to attack the kidneys. Steadily and irreversibly. Before you express any further scepticism let me tell you that there is a syndrome in medical circles known as Balkan Kidneys, in other words damaged kidneys, caused by improperly treated cereals which, in the Balkans, is quite often the case."

I gaped at him but managed to restrain any flippancy of a Buchanesque or Conan Doyle nature involving a Balkan Question.

"Damaged kidneys, eh? I would have thought that the Balkans have other things to think about, just now, than fungoid kidneys."

"They have. But that is not in our province here, this morning. We are concerned with what could happen to coffee. Which is drunk the world over, by literally billions, and is therefore important. As important as smoking."

I managed to ignore the look of approval which had come into Pulford's face as he listened to Lawrence. "Maybe it is, but your use of the conditional says it all. Could, but not is, or even might. Could happen, not what is happening. Billions are not grabbing towards their kidneys and expiring, Balkan-fashion."

He paused, sipped his latest cup thoughtfully, and shook his head. "Wrong, Johnny. It is happening. Not on a very large scale, probably only in those countries which are, how shall we put it tactfully these days, not as professional as they might be, not as careful as the big players. So a minority is affected, probably even a minority of a minority even though they are increasing their presence. But the fungus is occurring."

"Minority of a minority. Third world countries. Sounds like a really important matter. Like 'small earthquake in Chile; not many killed'."

He ignored me and my old non-headline quote. He moved into what might pass for a soliloquy, all the more effective because his ignoring my flippancy made me listen more intently than I had been doing to date.

"The fungus occurs in what seems like a random fashion. At first it was considered to be like any other form of mould, in other words related to moisture. Damp. Imperfect drying, as with the Balkan crops or indeed any crops, grain and so on, that need carefully controlled circumstances. Why should coffee beans not be the same?

Then it transpired that it is not quite so simple. The formation depends on mould, it is true, but a certain configuration of mould. Mould induced by damp, then dryness perhaps, then damp again, *et hoc genus omne.*" He smiled meaningfully as I pursed my lips at this ornamental substitute for *et cetera.* "After it is cropped, Johnny, coffee is shipped all over the world, goes through heat and damp, changing climatic conditions. Research has become necessary to clarify the exact biological characteristics involved."

"You mean that at present no one quite knows?"

"No." His mouth drew into firm contours. "They don't. They are just starting to find out."

"Bully for the men in white coats. The populace isn't exactly dropping from coffee-cropped kidneys though, is it? Why, after centuries of transportation, has this suddenly reared its expensive head?"

"The problem is," he was ignoring me again, "that it is not whole consignments, whole shiploads, not even whole sacks which are affected. It is just one bean here and there. A single bean, sitting in a mass of healthy beans, can be carrying the fungus. Research has to be able to analyse single beans. There is, right at this moment, a programme of scientific analysis which involves measuring single beans, the moisture of them that is, and establishing without doubt that the fungus creating the toxin is related to moisture and the conditions in which it most easily develops. Once these facts are established, the control of the problem will become easier."

"Oh, good. Another lethal cappuccino?"

"Yes, thank you."

"William?"

"I wouldn't mind another coffee. Plain coffee, that is." Pulford's voice was deep, unsurprisingly for such a big man, and without accent.

Lawrence Edwards was unperturbed. "Easier is a relative word, Johnny. A single coffee bean delivered to Europe from abroad weighs less than half a gramme and normally contains about eight percent moisture. A minuscule quantity. To analyse the exact amount of moisture present it is necessary, right now, to use gravimetric methods."

He stared at me with greater penetration as he put significance into the words 'gravimetric methods'. I smiled my most condescending smile. "That means you weigh a bean, dry it in an oven, then weigh it again. The difference tells you the amount of water present."

"Bravo, Johnny. So you know what is meant by gravimetric methods."

"They are not necessarily very accurate."

He had been about to take another sip of coffee but his head moved up sharply from his cup when I said this. His expression became alert, expectant. Never a good sign. Pulford's gaze changed, too; he looked at me with more interest.

"What I mean, Lawrence, is that gravimetric methods, despite what the laboratory men in white coats may claim, tend to have at least a percent or more of human error. If you and I, in a lab, each measured the same thing by exactly the same routine, our results would be different. By anything up to as much as three percent depending on how careful, how well trained we might be. Your mould, or toxin, whatever, formation might be significantly different within this error scale. The coffee bean, you say, has a minuscule amount of moisture in it. One would have to be very painstaking about procedures because a small difference might be the cause or non-cause of formation of the toxin. One's kidneys, let alone the fungus, could hang by such threads, yes?"

They were both watching me intently. For the first time since I'd known him, an expression almost like approval had come over Lawrence's worn, dyspeptic face.

"Quite so, Johnny. Quite so. I'm glad that you've grasped the essentials. It is not, however, solely with accuracy that we are concerned, although that is important. Time is of the essence. And gravimetric methods, especially with the types and quantities of bean of which we are speaking, are very slow and cumbersome. Painstaking, as you say."

"But surely the ICO here in London have extensive facilities with which to do all this?"

I can do it, too, you see: spout initials at anyone.

"The International Coffee Organisation," his dry expression hardly flickered, "is indeed very concerned. We have had constructive meetings with them, both at Berners Street and at our offices. But it is not quite their remit, not quite the way they are set up. They have formed the necessary consultative technical committee and put a research programme into action but there are no facilities on site there. They have had to set the programme up elsewhere. At the laboratory of one of their distinguished members, to be precise."

"Oh? Where?"

"In Switzerland. No, not the famous company you have almost certainly thought of immediately. A small, specialised research outfit dealing in high quality coffee only."

I swallowed the remains of my first cappuccino very thoughtfully while the second I had signalled for arrived. Coffee and, by association with Mario Chiari, Switzerland, were just a bit too close to home for comfort at that moment. Lawrence appeared not to notice.

"This need not concern us, however," he said, grabbing his third cup with relish. "What does concern us is something else."

"What's that?"

He turned and gestured at William Pulford, whose deep voice took up on cue.

"Some time ago the DTI awarded a grant to a chap down in Sussex who invented a new, high frequency microwave moisture sensor. Very accurate. The DTI and local Business Link people were very chuffed with themselves." He paused, stirred his coffee, and looked at me directly. "Lawrence and I get the lists of that sort of thing on a regular basis. The grant was to help this inventor develop the unit into a commercially viable piece of kit. Moisture is important to many process industries and this had all sorts of advantages. I won't bore you with the technicalities."

"Thanks."

"When this coffee bean thing came up, Lawrence and I remembered the sensor freak and put him in touch with the Swiss coffee pundits who were starting to carry out the research. I must say he did his stuff. He said he could build them an instrument which would electronically measure individual coffee beans to a high degree of accuracy on an instantaneous basis. Pop in a bean and up comes the exact amount of moisture in it, probably in flashing lights on a silver screen. It would save months of laborious gravimetric analysis. There were some initial trials on his existing kit to prove the principle would work, and the Swiss were delighted. It was not an expensive item. They ordered one from him pronto."

"A British moisture beanometer no less? Bravo."

Pulford smiled faintly. "Exactly. You may laugh, but it was something of a small triumph. We are very modest these post-industrial days. It showed how keen we are to assist world health research, especially where international commodities mendaciously traded by the City of London are concerned. Produced a bit of kudos for British technology, inventor nerd's grant justified, senior minister at the DTI happened to be at a reception at the ICO and could modestly boast, plaudits from the technical committee, all that sort of thing."

I leant forward to fix him with my own stare. "Success story all round. Was the senior minister that blowhard old crook, Tony Barnwell?"

"Mr Barnwell was the minister involved, yes."

"He wouldn't miss a PR trick. Must have been right up his flagpole. So your department, modestly, would doubtless receive a trickle of the plauditory gush."

"Until last week." Lawrence Edwards's voice chimed in sharply, a bitter edge to its tone.

"Last week?"

"Last week," his face set into an angry expression, "someone broke into the inventor's premises and stole the bloody thing."

I burst out laughing. I couldn't help it.

"What's so funny?" he demanded, savagely.

"Oh come on, Lawrence. This must be the most unsuccessful thief in Sussex. In England. He breaks into a moisture sensor works and pinches a beanometer which must be about the most unsaleable gubbins in the kingdom. Queendom, rather. What possible use could it be to anyone else?"

That was when I stopped. As I've said, people were hurrying briskly by outside. My second cup was empty and so were the cups of the other two men. There are times when I am slow to draw deductions from my own world into simple activities like making moisture beanometers for Swiss coffee companies. Suddenly, however, I found that my mouth was going dry.

"The police," I said. "This is a matter for the police."

He nodded emphatically. "The police are investigating. I have no doubt that they will be as thorough as they always are."

"Which means they'll never catch the thief."

"Of course they won't."

"Or recover the instrument."

"Not a hope."

"You said on the phone that this was not a dangerous matter. I'm not talking about toxins and my kidneys or anyone else's kidneys right now. Or coffee drinking. Specifically. I am concerned with danger in an entirely different sense."

"It is not a dangerous matter. I do not want you to interfere with police procedures. You are not to be involved in any way with the investigation of theft. We merely wish you to make a few enquiries for us, of a commercial and marketing nature. In South America."

"I'm not sure – I am willing to go there as it happens – but – you can tell me in absolute confidence, Lawrence – who has been killed?"

He bridled. "No one!"

"Who is likely to get killed? Me?"

"Of course not! There will be no danger," he snapped, as though anger would drive it away. "The inventor is building another unit as quickly as possible. But he needs marketing assistance with his invention. He's not even very far away from you."

"He may not buy my services."

"Oh, you will be presented as a co-opted DTI business specialist. For free."

I baulked at that.

"You mean I'm to present myself as a gash Department of Trade and Industry consultant? Good God!"

"Your opinion of our consultants must be temporarily stifled. I hope you can manage such a suppression in this case. In view of the fees we are offering?"

I looked him in the eye.

"Let me get this quite clear. I'm to do a pure market research job for his sensors? Contact the right sort of industrial prospects? For the fees we agreed by phone?"

"Yes."

"Amongst the sensors is this beanometer?"

"Of course."

"What do you want me to find out about it?"

"Whether there is a wider market for it and, more important, who is interested."

"And there is nothing about it worth killing for?"

"Of course not! Don't be so melodramatic! It is a simple scientific instrument with a specialised use."

"You have no idea why it should have been stolen?"

"None. Pure speculation, I imagine, by an ignorant felon."

I absorbed this obvious untruth for a moment before looking hard at William Pulford. "And you? What do you think?"

He shook his head. "No idea. As it happens, I will be officially on holiday in the next day or so. Caravanning. But I'll be following up a few lines of enquiry quite separately. Lawrence is your contact, not me."

Lawrence Edwards smiled thinly. "William is a devoted caravanner. I'm afraid I'm too fond of my comforts for that sort of thing."

"Caravan parks," Pulford rumbled, "are marvellous places from which to observe humanity. You'd be surprised. And so, often, are they."

I looked at them both cautiously. "Where, specifically, will you wish me to make these enquiries?"

Edwards pursed his thin lips. "Where do you think, Johnny?"

My mind was already racing with ideas and meetings with people whose identity I'd never confide in Lawrence Edwards or this new, large, William Pulford. Euripides Arochena, up in Belo Horizonte, was among them. Mario would have a visit he'd want me to make, probably with some urgency. And then there was Carlos, I thought, for anything to do with coffee, of course: Carlos Guimares, in São Paulo.

To reach Carlos, Katie.

Katie: a flush began to spread across my loins. I had not seen Katie Gonzalez for nearly eighteen months. Her telephone calls were as wry, humorous and stimulating as ever. Katie would be pleased to meet me anywhere romantic, anywhere that would provide change, glamour and pleasure in the most flattering sense.

Visions of a familiar, unclothed Katie coiling herself around me like an Amazonian anaconda began to disturb my pavement-café consciousness.

I should have known, of course; I should have known at that moment just how fishy the whole affair smelt. I should have asked more pertinent questions about why an outsider, and specifically my sort of outsider, was being used. But I was bored; a bored man is one at his most vulnerable. Betty was good, provided the weekends and midweek when Maurice was home were avoided, but experience said that Betty would soon need a break if the spice were to be maintained. Betty was generous but I had to avoid becoming predictable. She was getting curious, too. I needed to get away for a bit. I needed a diversion.

The prospect of diversions warps the judgement of the idle. Nothing much happens to those who sit by the seaside, waiting. Nothing much except death.

Who said those things? I did.

Edwards was observant, head cocked. Pulford was staring into his cup as though looking for clues to something.

I think I managed to sound casual, even if the answer was obvious. "Colombia, perhaps? Brazil?"

"So very perceptive of you." The dry tone was not complimentary. "Let me now describe the arrangements. The inventor is called Richard Keane. He is expecting you to telephone him tomorrow…"

7

Machinery: machines, work of a machine, mechanism; contrivances, esp. supernatural persons and incidents used in literary work.

Concise Oxford Dictionary

The moment he saw old Duvivier's machine, Mario told me he was delighted. He said that his heart jumped. Just the outline of that long, familiar tangle of sad, deserted equipment made his pulse go stumble-thump. He quickly added that he thought of me immediately but you know how Italians are; charm before truth, even in Mario's case. What he meant was that he thought of himself more than anything but he might, he just might, have thought of me a fraction of a second later as his mind scoured itself for lucrative placings. There would be much money involved in that thought. Mario Chiari's working acquaintanceships, even friendships, sit on the slippery quicksands of mutually beneficial finance.

Anyway, there was a lot of potential. This would be ideal for South America, he just knew it.

He froze his distinguished Tuscan face into a disdainful sneer. To show any excitement in front of a sharp-eyed French receiver would be a bad mistake. Mario of the immaculate hound's-tooth jackets and flattering grey worsteds never revealed enthusiasm to a salesman. He was far too good a salesman himself.

The French receiver was a weaselly little chancer smoking an old-fashioned, greasy yellow cigarette that dropped fine grey flakes onto his stained blue suit. He must have been relieved to see his visitor though he, too, hid his pleasure well. An Italian engineer from the Milan area, involved in the business already, was bound to be a good prospect for a clearance sale. God only knew what scams he supposed the Italians could use a machine like this for once it was tarted up. There were so many frauds going on down in the Mezzogiorno that the receiver didn't like to enquire. He'd probably heard of things being sold twice, even three times, in those development zone scandals funded by the EEC. But there weren't many takers for such a huge contraption just now, especially one mucked about the way old Duvivier had done.

The late owner was typical of tinkering technicians. The obstinate idiots can never leave well alone. They never seem to have heard of the old American expression: if it ain't broke, don't fix it. If Duvivier could have rejigged the coffin handles for his own funeral he would have rejigged until the very last moment. They'd never have got him down to ashes on time.

The two men walked the length of the line together, with Mario pulling a glum face and sucking his teeth noisily at the glue-gunge, pulp dust and litter accumulated all over the place. The building was a country mill of some sort, with original grey stone walls whose rough surfaces held every type of grime you could think of. No one starts up in a building like that any more.

The big frame was a Yankee job, as solid as those Milwaukee Germans ever made them. The heavy castings would take all the attachments they demanded nowadays. There were far too many chain drives at the back but that was the usual problem; Mario had seen it before and so had his mechanics. It was the way they used to build those diaper lines, sometimes right into the mid-eighties. No one does that these days. He could get the chains and sprockets stripped out when the new transmission was built – shafts and timing belts with proper differentials – without too much expense. Mechanical things are not nearly as costly as electronics.

Every step he took made Mario feel better.

The Frog receiver made a lot of stupid remarks about how good a machine it was even though you couldn't use the original maker's name – it had been altered too much for that – but some of the changes added to its value. He said it was still in good running order even though, of course, he couldn't demonstrate it just now because since the bankruptcy they'd had to stop payments to all the raw material suppliers who were owed money. One of them had broken in at night, sent in an ugly gang of thugs with pickaxe handles and a forklift, and taken roll stock back. So there wasn't anything to run it on, and the crew were laid off, naturally.

Naturally, Mario thought, naturally; I bet the poor bastards are still waiting for their wages from you, you mean little buzzard, and wait they will until you and the bloody bank have had all the flesh off these bones and then tell them there's nothing left.

Mario detested receivers; he'd dealt with so many before. Vultures, the lot of them. Yet as soon as he heard that Duvivier had shot himself, Mario contacted the weasel's office. It seemed too easy, really; not even all that far away. One of those so-called development zones that someone else has paid for with yet somebody else's money via a bank that has already charged its fat fees twice all round. Over the border from San Remo, along the Riviera, up into Provence. As though it was meant for him. His guardian angel must be in a good mood; the next morning Mario hopped into his Alfa and was past Genoa, on and over the border before most Frogs were slurping up their croissants and milky coffee. Mario never wasted time.

"Christ," he said to the Frenchman once they'd walked the line. "Old Duvivier really did know how to bugger a machine up, didn't he? Terrible, isn't it? No wonder he went bust. I'd have blown my brains out, too. You couldn't possibly compete in today's disposable diaper market with this thing as it is."

"You can see the production figures," the receiver blustered defensively. "Good output, they got, from this line."

"Oh yeah? Then what went wrong?"

The receiver's yellow cigarette sagged marginally. "Er, a marketing problem, I believe. Nothing to do with production."

"You mean the products coming off this old *cachila* wouldn't sell." Mario has lived in Buenos Aires, like me. A jalopy is always a *cachila* to any *porteño*. "Not to anyone. I'm not at all surprised." He kicked idly at a stack of plastic packages, dislodging a slide of dust. "It must be down to nothing in the books. Come on, what's the price being asked?"

With serious expression, the receiver told him. Mario burst into a roar of laughter and put his arm joyfully round the Frenchman's stained shoulders. "That's rich! That's a good one. I like a joke! A bank must have thought that one up; no one else could be that stupid, could they? No one in business, anyway. You and I are going to get on well, I can tell that."

He grinned fondly down at the irritated face, using the beaming mask he'd developed for business concealment. At least the little stoat wasn't trying to hold a Dutch auction and ask for bids in sealed envelopes; even he knew he wouldn't get a bite that way. Scrap value, that would be about all he'd get unless he could deal with Mario Chiari. Scrap value; even the glue tanks looked clapped out.

Who'd have a go at this, apart from him?

"I've got other enquiries," the receiver said defensively, as though reading his brain. "The Far East are interested."

Mario chuckled. "The Far East? Where in the Far East? The Japs wouldn't look at junk like this; they've got much better junk of their own. The Chinese haven't even got a sprout, let alone a bean. As for the rest of them, Malaysia and those, don't you read the papers? Their money has halved in value. You can forget the Far East."

The receiver glared at him resentfully. "Eastern Europe's been on the phone, too, you know."

Mario's smile widened. "Eastern Europe? They'll buy if you'll lend them the money, sure. When they're not killing each other. Our Mafia's got nothing on theirs; no one'll start up a business using this in Russia." He paused knowingly and gave the receiver a hard stare. "I expect you've heard from that investment crowd in Georgia who claim to have Shevarnadze's ear, haven't you? They've been on to everyone in this game. Well, someone just tried to blow Shevardnadze to pieces – again – so you can forget them, too."

The receiver looked uncomfortable, letting Mario know he'd hit the mark. His face softened. "Come on." He put on his most sympathetic expression. "I think you and I better go for a drink together, out of this awful rat-hole. The dust in here's getting up my hooter."

A week the following Thursday the line was more or less in place in Mario's workshops. It looked a lot better cleaned down and there was a pleasant surprise when he opened the boxes of spares that went with it; there was more there than he'd bargained for. Mind you, the receiver couldn't help but throw the lot in once they'd agreed a price. The receiver would only get paid a slice of what he negotiated for the assets and Mario's persuasive wad of cash – Swiss francs of course, none of those sliding Euros – brandished with great and meaningful aplomb, had made the Frenchman's face lighten at last.

"How about some raw materials?" he asked hopefully as he pocketed a full envelope. "Wouldn't like to buy some good stuff would you? Excellent prices."

Mario shook his head decisively. "Not me. I'm an engineer, not a converter. Try some of the private label boys. And by the way, I thought you said you couldn't run the line because you hadn't got any?"

The receiver had the decency to blush. Not that it mattered; raw materials were for the birds. Mario could get as much as he wanted for test, free of charge, fresh from the producers. The stuff stored in that rat-hole was almost bound to be damaged.

On Friday evening he stood looking down at the line from the platform outside his office and nodded happily to himself at the busy scene in the workshop. There was a lot of potential there. A lot of potential. He could visualise the line running, hear in his imagination the screech of the hammer mill biting into a roll of pulp above the roar and rattle of motors, shafts, spindles and cutters, the flutter of reels unwinding into the web. He'd sent off faxes to the right quarters already. To be back in the market with the sort of potential he and Johnny Barber could realise would pay a lot of bills. A lot of bills. He felt stimulated, excited. A deal like this always put him into a racy mood. He said later that it reminded him of the time he and I did that badge job by sending an Italian machine up to Sweden for relabelling and resale as something entirely different.

Mario and I made real money on that one.

He picked up the phone and in his delight left his coffee talk on my receiver. He had no idea what a weapon he was about to put into my hands.

Or that I would need it.

8

The beanometer geek was a big chap. Nothing like what I had imagined at all. I imagined something spectacled and greyish even though relatively young, with long hair, loose clothes and diffident diction. Richard Keane's dark hair was cropped short, his brown eyes were sharp and his big feet splayed outwards as his gaze challenged mine. He hadn't dressed for my visit. He was wearing a yellow and black quartered rugby shirt with long sleeves and rather shabby charcoal trousers above a pair of spongy boots. His wrist sported a marine waterproof watch with complicated dials on it.

"How are you?" he asked. "All right?"

The accent was part Yorkshire – picked up presumably during his degree time at Sheffield – part Nottingham, North Midlands anyway, unmodified by Sussex life. He held out a broad hand and I shook it.

"Fine," I said.

The hand was strong. I put him at mid-thirties somewhere, a bit heavy but fit. Almost certainly the shirt was for genuine use. His office had been a village shop and had two long display windows going down to the floor, letting in lots of light. For furniture there were two desks, one with a PC and monitor on it, the other with a laptop open and glowing. Nearby was a chipped Formica-topped table with a kettle, dirty cups and bits of electronic gear littered about its surface. Against one wall there was some Dexion racking stacked with instruments, control boxes, circuit boards, wiring, panels and assorted unidentifiable electrical gubbins. A year-planner chart was pinned to the opposite wall next to a poster advertising Jaguar cars. Outside, a pale sun shone on a straggly village street with the usual traffic punctuated occasionally by vast container lorries heading for the coast one way and inland the other. They made the shop shake.

"You're from the DTI, then?" he queried.

"Part of it."

His eyes steadied on mine. "Not Business Link?"

"No, not Business Link. I expect you know the local Sussex lads quite well, do you?"

"One or two of them. They helped get me an innovation grant to get started up, you see."

I waved a folder at him. "So I gather," I said, pretending I'd read all of it. "Seems to have been put to good use in this case."

He grinned. "Some of the money gets wasted, does it?"

"Bread on the water."

"Sorry?"

"Call it opportunity cost. We try to assess every grant as best we can. It's always a gamble. Some win, some lose."

I was finding the tolerant, not-my-money, civil-servant role easy to fall into. I thought.

There was a nod. "Would you like a coffee?"

"Thanks. I expect you've got a massive supply of fresh beans, have you?"

He smiled as he shook his head sadly. "All green. They only want to know about green beans."

"Have to find out how to roast them, eh?"

"If only there were time."

He made some instant coffee, dolloping cold milk onto the brown powder before pouring on boiling water. Lawrence Edwards would have shuddered. I asked for sugar but he hadn't got any.

"You work here all alone?"

He nodded. "Mostly. There's a firm over in Hastings I get to populate the boards and an electronics guy in Bexhill, a pal of mine, who does assemblies."

"Otherwise it's just you?"

"Just me. And my wife. She has a day job with a firm near Crowborough four days a week. We'd be bloody stuffed without it."

There was a brief silence. I thought of asking him why he'd given up a secure, well-paid job with a big company – that's what it said in the folder – to spend his time alone in a shabby dump like this, dependent on his wife's income and hag-ridden by his bank, but knew better. His surroundings would not be important. His mind wouldn't be on other things. And he didn't give a stuff about his bank. According to the folder he was not just inventive but practical as well as good on theory, resourceful, blunt, a bit bellicose in the northern fashion. One or two DTI men had found him difficult; his sense of humour was Yorkshire-ironic, which means sarcastic. He didn't suffer fools at all, let alone gladly.

"I hear someone pinched your bean machine," I said.

"Yes. Bastards." He took a slurp at his coffee. "Can't think what for. Bloody useless to anyone else."

"How did it happen?"

"Someone just broke in—back door there, smashed the lock—and took it."

"Just it? Nothing else?"

"It was standing on the bench over there. Looked good, though I say it myself."

"They didn't take your PC or anything like that?"

"Nope."

"What do the police say?"

He shrugged. "Not much. They think there wasn't much to pinch so the thief took it on spec. Might have been a pikey, they said. Lots of pikeys and diddicoys round here. They usually nick 4-wheelers and garden equipment, tools, and things like that. Whoever it was left my Bosch drill over there. Bit odd, isn't it?"

The question was put in the same challenging fashion with which he'd greeted me. I didn't answer. Just shrugged.

"Don't reckon the police'll find it. They're not very interested anyway." He frowned. "Burglary has a 'low priority' with the local police, and that's official. They're too busy turning out parking fines or waving their little radar guns at hard-working motorists to deal with real criminals."

"How long before you can make another?"

"That was a special. It'll take me three, maybe four weeks."

"Are you insured for theft?"

His eyes dropped again. "The premiums are too high, on a place like this."

I looked about me, slowly. "This instrument, or rather these sensors of yours. Are they used in other applications?"

"Could be. Not that one, though."

"What sort of thing? The others, I mean."

He stare turned a shade pitying. "Anything. Moisture is important in so many industrial processes. Anything that has to be dried. Timber, board, food, chemicals, you name it."

"So you're selling all over?"

The stare became less challenging. "A bit, yes."

"Who through?"

"No one."

"You mean you do all the selling yourself?"

"Mostly."

"How? I mean do you go out and beat on doors, what?"

"Phone calls. Then visits, if they're interested. Word of mouth." He smiled mock-diffidently. "I've even got some leaflets, you know."

"As I understand it, you've got something brand new here, leading edge technology. Shouldn't process manufacturers be snapping these things up like hot cakes?"

His gaze went back to pitying. "You tried any of this country's process manufacturers lately, with anything new?"

I shook my head. My business, for very good reasons, was mainly abroad. "No. I'm an export man."

"Lucky old you. The resistance to new technology in this country beggars description, I'm telling you. If you can get your foot in a door, which isn't easy. Everyone's gone onto automatic phone answering so they don't have to speak to you. 'Just a leave a message.' Which is never answered. And when you do finally get to them, they have dozens of reasons, from technical to budgetary, why they can't buy anything new." He put his cup down. He was watchful, somehow. "Travel a lot, do you?"

"Yes. Yes, that's why I'm here. Maybe we can get a quicker, more positive response abroad."

"Like some more coffee?"

"No, thanks."

"That bad, is it?"

I grinned. "Hoped I hadn't made it too obvious."

He grinned back. "Are you really from the DTI?"

"That's what I said. Why do you ask?"

"Don't know. Forgive me, but you don't seem like one of theirs, not from my experience."

I chuckled. I was starting to like him. "It takes all sorts, Richard. Mind if I call you Richard? I'm Johnny."

"Sure, Johnny."

I pushed my cup of coffee away unfinished. "Let's just say I'm a sort of consultant. On temporary secondment." I stood up and looked around me. "Are you going to tell me all about this microwave technology of yours?"

"Over here," he said.

And he went through it all, water molecules rotating about their dipoles, signal attenuation, frequency bands, why infra-red or radio frequency wasn't as good, pages of charts and graphs with downward spikes on them, wood and cement and food and coffee beans and grain and glue laminations and packaging and God knew what else.

After a while, I stared at him until he stopped in mid-flow.

"Tell me," I demanded, "how much are you selling these things for?"

"About four thousand each."

"How many of them have you sold?"

He shrugged. "About five. Got more out on trial, though."

"Plus the bean device?"

"Plus the coffee bean measurement unit, yes. If it hadn't been stolen."

"But you've already started the new one?"

"Over here," he said.

There was a funny box with a sort of dagger protruding from it sitting on the bench near his laptop. Next to it was a perforated brass slide which, as I looked closer, I saw to be perforated not with equal-sized holes like a piece of Meccano, but with different shapes and sizes of holes, about ten of them.

"There's ten different types of bean it has to measure," he said, picking up some tiny little half-beans from a heap nearby. "Most of them are half-beans like this, but each is of a different type. Then there are two whole beans, like almost round, except that they're oval like the halves, but complete. Each of these holes in the slide is individually machined so that the bean or half-bean in question is held in exactly the same geometry each time you present it to the microwave. If you don't you won't get comparability from one reading to the next because the microwave will see a different surface area. They have to present the same area each time. The way I worked it out, if the lab guy doing the work drops the bean into the numbered hole for that type of bean, he'll get the correct presentation each time. The slide can be moved in and out of the microwave wave guide, which focuses its beam through the coffee bean, each time. That way it's quick and easy."

I stared at the slide, taking in the precision and the simple ingenuity of it, the engraved number under each different hole, the socket-slide into which it was to fit. "You say you've sold five units and the coffee beanometer so far," I said. "How long have you been going?"

"Eighteen months," he said. "No, time flies, perhaps nearer two years."

I pressed my hands together, tightly. I had a feeling that my expression might not be as bland as it should have been.

"I think," I said, "that you may be in need of help, Richard."

"I know. That's what you're here for, isn't it?"

I looked around me. Chronic, it was, chronic, like a scrap yard you shake your head at before you realise that somewhere inside it a sculptor is trying to make a work of art out of all that clobber, turning rubbish into gold all on his own. A latter-day alchemist or sorcerer for whom tiny desktop wonders are everyday experiments was whittling away, ignoring the heavy lorries shaking his windows and the light moving the days slowly round the room. All that tangle of bits and pieces, the laptop and the monitor glowing away, spilled powdered coffee amid green beans which presumably had something to do with the instant version's origin, wires and circuit boards and tiny components like glistening jewels on a dusty bench.

Nothing like my production machinery at all and so far removed from the world of Lawrence Edwards that they might have belonged to different species.

Something I couldn't define was plucking at me, demanding, insisting, saying you can't just leave this like this; you can't, you really can't.

"Yes," I said, letting my hands relax back again. "Yes, Richard. That's what I'm here for."

9

If I chance to talk a little wild, forgive me;
I had it from my father.

Shakespeare: *All is True (Henry VIII)*

Sometime again during 1939 my father was in Callao, the port for Lima, standing on the balcony of his firm's agent's office overlooking the harbour. As he and the agent watched, a Liverpool tramp steamer, single smokestack, derricks hitched at odd angles, steam blowing from its rusty pipework, came alongside the wharf and tied up. The captain and first mate, in soiled white shorts and pocketed uniform shirts under grimy white caps, eventually lumbered down the gangplank to meet port officials.

As they watched the ship's captain shaking hands with the customs and harbourmaster's men, the agent turned to my father and shook his head sadly.

"You British," he said, "you're finished, aren't you? Absolutely finished."

My father was a big man of particularly Anglo-Saxon pugnacity. The firm's agent was a South American of Italian extraction; a clever, friendly chap called Guglielmino something. My father both liked him and admired his business tenacity but you didn't say things like that about the British lightly to my father in those days. He pulled his fuming great pipe out of his mouth, blew a cloud of St Bruno Flake smoke upwards with his head cocked back and started tamping down hot tobacco with his calloused yellow thumb, preparatory to a flaming boost from his big metal lighter.

"What," he demanded, "do you mean by that? Exactly?"

Guglielmino held up a mollifying hand.

"Don't take it the wrong way, Andy," he said. "I'm just making an observation, that's all."

"Observation?"

"Sure. Just look at those two. Look at 'em."

My father eyed the two stained cargo officers. "What's wrong with them?"

Guglielmino sighed reminiscently.

"When I was a lad here in Callao, Liverpool tramps like that came in quite often. I used to watch them, the way we're doing now, from this very balcony, with my father. The ship would usually be a grimy old coal-fired job, sometimes a diesel, streaked with rust and unspeakable discharge-outlet stains down the side. It would tie alongside in an impatient, bad-tempered sort of way, blue smoke and clatter coming from the winches. The booted captain and the mate would clump down the gangplank like those two, except that both would be wearing blue donkey jackets and oily dungarees, the skipper with a clay pipe upside down between clenched teeth. Greasy dark blue mate's caps on their heads. Leather straps below the knee to shorten their trousers, like coalmen. Come to think of it, they looked more like coalmen than anything else. The official meeting them would sign some papers and push off, quick. Everyone got the hell out of the way. If anyone got in the way the least they'd get would be a push or a shove. Otherwise it was a punch on the nose.

"Then the crew would come ashore. The police locked themselves into the police station. All the shops put up shutters. I really mean it; all of them. Two bars, maybe three, on the harbour front, those with tiled floors and walls, and strong wooden furniture, nothing else, no comforts other than the booze, stayed open. Everything else closed, except the worst brothel. For two days, after work, the place would be in chaos, just plain bedlam, at night nothing but the sound of shouts, screams, songs, smashing glass and splintering furniture. In the morning there'd be bloodstains and vomit amongst the debris on the quayside. After a couple of days or more they'd have discharged and reloaded, then they'd steam off snarling quietly, with hangovers, wounds, gashes and doses of the clap."

Guglielmino gestured at the scene he and my father were watching. "Look at those two," he said, contemptuously. "Just look at them. White uniforms. God help us, white uniforms, with shorts. *Shorts*. Polite handshakes. Leather shoes, even white shoes, instead of boots. Documents and customs examinations. Smoking cigarettes. *Cigarettes*. Bunch of pansies. They'll probably be sober for most of the visit." He shook his head again. "I tell you Andy, you British, you're finished. Absolutely finished."

When that September's declaration came, my father was classified into a reserved occupation, trying to keep up exports against the effects of war. He wasn't allowed to come back to Britain for over two years. For the length of those two years, the British disproved Guglielmino's judgement. After a slow start they got to be even more violent than they used to be.

The incident rankled with my father, though. Something about it sank deep into his sub-conscious. You could tell that from the way he repeated the story over a pink gin when we were living in South America as a family, much later. He didn't like to think that the nation's main asset was violence; he hated war the way all First War veterans did. He had a deep desire for decency, fair play, hard work, no shirking. He loathed cruelty and dictators. He was something of a Victorian puritan and deplored sexual indiscipline. He was prepared to tolerate a constitutional monarchy, just about, but he disliked the idea of Royalty, heredity, the landowning upper class, people who never made or sold things. He was an old-fashioned Socialist.

When he was working in Birmingham during the Depression, the Prince of Wales made a visit in a big Daimler car. The thick crowds lining the streets waited until the car appeared then turned their backs on it. My father liked that. He liked the idea of the people letting their rulers know what they thought of them. He was in sympathy with old-style Americans; deeply democratic and perhaps republican. He had many of the Anglo-Saxon qualities: cross-grained, robust, truculent, humorous, pugnacious, irreverent. I often thought he would have made an excellent pikeman in Cromwell's New Model Army except that he would have hated the killing.

Despite all that, he was sensitive to signs of weakness and decline. He grudgingly believed that aggression had to be met with aggression and that pugnacity induces respect. In his heart of hearts

I suspect he had a nagging fear that Guglielmino, random and esoteric as his little piece of foreign observation might be, could possibly be right. It came across from the way he'd look at me, speculatively, over his filthy pipe, as he went through the whole thing yet again. Even though I was just a little boy.

He was a difficult act to follow.

10

When I got back from Richard Keane's place it was raining. The clouds scudding in from the Channel were loaded with grey bellies, sagging like old men's paunches over crumpled flannel trousers. Wind swept the rain down in a dense, splattering spray that hissed on the wet concrete balcony. The air seemed full of gusty water and draughts, producing a blowy, scattered atmosphere fit to dissipate any human concentration. Lawrence Edwards might have been lying to me, but the image of that shop-office stuck strongly to my retina. There was nothing suspicious about Richard Keane; his struggles were transparent. Something had to be done, something constructive, even while whatever agenda it was that Edwards and Pulford were following took its tortuous course.

I felt harassed. I went back into the living room and closed the sliding glass doors to shut off the elements outside.

A warm and empty calm enveloped me.

My living room is modern in the 'thirties sense of being modern. It is without concessions to anything vernacular. No fireplace, no mock-beams, tiling, picture rail. Just a big white box. One wall is lined with books, floor to ceiling. Another has an 18th century grandfather clock parked against it: the engraved dial says *Johannes Barber Londini Fecit* but he's no relation. I got the clock for the name-sake amusement, but as it happens it's a good clock.

Who the hell would steal a machine for measuring the moisture in a single coffee bean?

On the non-bookcase walls are a few paintings and prints, all of them contemporary. The furniture is comfortable. There is no dining table and there are no dining chairs because I never entertain at home. I tend to eat in the kitchen or in front of the television. When I am in, I probably spend too much time in the office room, at the computer.

"What happened?" Betty asked me, not long after we met.

"Happened?"

71

"Oh come on, Johnny, you know what I mean. What happened? You were married once. You were almost certainly pretty conventional, settled, a bit of an executive like Maurice, probably a bit more of a suit than he is. Now you're practically xenophobic. Apart from the fun in bed, it's like you live behind smoked glass. What happened?"

"You're doing the perceptive feminine bit, are you? Pretty well, actually, although I suppose it's not too difficult. Sure, I had a wife, a good job and a detached house. I travelled a lot because that's what I do, what I was paid for. She left, the job folded, the detached house automatically detached itself. Disasters come in threes. That's what happened."

Betty grimaced. "It does, Johnny. It – that sort of thing – happens. To lots of people, though, not just you. How long ago?"

"About ten years."

"Ten years? Christ! You mean you still haven't recovered?"

I grinned at her assumptions. "No. And I'm not going to. I mean, I'm not going back to that. No one is going to make a suburban mug out of me again. I've recovered in my own way. And prospered."

"Recovered." She smiled carefully. "We all have our definitions, I suppose. Prospered? You call Marine Court prosperity?"

I took a look slowly round my room as I thought about her and Lawrence and Richard Keane, then Katie Gonzalez and Carlos Guimares. It's getting a bit neglected, I started to think, a bit remote, almost librarian. When I'm not chasing a Betty or two, I have become something like the City of London: international, efficient, mercantile, sophisticated, predatory, apart. There's an old Jewish saying: what you resist, you become. Betty was right: my presence was so insulated that I might be on an island somewhere, a raft, a satellite in space.

Habits form imperceptibly. Then they grip like glue.

Outside, within yards, the crumbling fabric of St Leonards and Hastings sheltered the aged, the desperate and the mad. The apartment building, designed to emulate an ocean liner in concrete, might be moored offshore. There is, apart from my bedroom and the office, a small single bedroom for the occasional visitor but I can't remember when it was last used. My wife Susan remarried, to the man she took up with while I was away on business. She liked gardening – we had the regulation detached house and half a suburban acre when we were married – and often went to a local nursery to buy plants. That's where she met him. He's become a market gardener and now they live near Lincoln, out on the desperate, flat wet countryside of the fens. I suppose he must spend most of his day in waterproof anorak and wellingtons but he's always home.

Always home; I've often wondered if Susan really likes that. If she got what she wanted.

I felt like having a smoke or a whisky. I was agitated. Someone had taken that coffee-bean analysing machine for a reason. That was no random break-in; there was a sinister purpose in the theft. The joke was that we all knew it, Lawrence Edwards, Pulford, Richard Keane and me, but none of us had yet said it out loud. Why? Why were we not saying it? Why was it stolen? It was knowledge to make you pace up and down or go out on a stupid sortie in no particular direction or phone Betty at the wrong time, just for a chat. She wouldn't like that, though; with Betty, too, compartments were important. She was very specific about compartments. There were times to phone and times not to phone, as with all affairs.

Crazy: an electronic device to measure the moisture in a single coffee bean. Like picking a straw out of a haystack and testing it for something that might pollute the whole haystack.

A whole haystack? Which haystack? Colombia, Brazil, Kenya, South Africa, Ethiopia? Where? Who would react to my enquiries?

The telephone rang in the office, making me jump. A familiar Italian voice reassured my ear.

"Johnny! How are you?"

"Fine, fine. I got your message. You bought old Duvivier's machine, I hear. Congratulations. That'll keep you out of mischief. And the coffee? Colombia or Brazil?"

There was a chuckle. "I got one in Colombia. Barranquilla. *Se va el caimán,* eh? What have you got?"

I chuckled back. *Se va el caimán, se va pa' Barranquilla* is an old

73

song, one version having disgracefully erotic wording. "I've got one in Brazil. Belo Horizonte. So I'll go as soon as possible."

"Perfect! We make a good team, Johnny, you and me, eh?"

"The best."

"You want to come and see the machine first?"

"No thanks, Mario, no need. I've seen too many of those to worry about another. Besides, I can trust you to make it run."

"Oh! Thank you! You are too kind!"

"Fax me the specification and your rock bottom price when you send details of the Colombian, er, coffee. OK? We'll follow the usual arrangements."

"Of course. I'll tell them to expect you. You'll come over when the coffee is ready I suppose?"

"As usual."

"I'll look forward to seeing you, Johnny."

"Me too. Please fax me those details pronto."

"Of course. *Ciao*, Johnny."

"*Arrivaderci*, Mario."

I put the phone down. The machine visit was no problem. Then there would be the attendance at Mario's workshops in Milan. No problem, either. Then the nip over the border to Switzerland.

Switzerland. Where they'd ordered the beanometer that was stolen. I couldn't help thinking about Carlos Guimares or maybe someone like him, someone adept at making a corner in a market or profiting by a panic. How soon before a journalist made up a scoop or punted a wild headline over the right crossbar? It's a small world and ecological matters are very topical. How soon?

And Lawrence Edwards; at the centre of which tangled cobweb was he sitting? Why come to me for his enquiries? Why this time?

Coffee: to my knowledge, Betty's wheeler-dealer Maurice prominently included coffee amongst the commodities he dealt in. Should I phone him? Make some confidential enquiries? Or would Betty, suspicious, then start to think that my attentions had been sparked off by ulterior, mendacious motives?

I stared at the phone for a moment before picking it up again. It wasn't really necessary to tell Edwards that I'd seen Richard Keane;

I hate that sort of obliging subordinate-reportage. But it would show willing and be a good excuse to probe the background a bit further. I dialled his contact number in Westminster carefully, using, as an inbuilt precaution, a 141 prefix so as to withhold my number in case the wrong person replied. His phone rang several times without reply or even an answerphone kicking in before, bit of a surprise, it was answered by a woman's voice that sounded breathless, as though she'd snatched up the receiver after a dash to the desk. I'd not heard of a secretary but then Lawrence usually phoned me, not vice versa. He kept his office arrangements opaque.

"Hello?" A slight windiness, almost a surprised tone.

"Lawrence Edwards, please."

"I'm afraid Mr Edwards is unavailable." The female voice went cool, guarded, even though it had an attractive, educated pronunciation. "Who is that?"

"Oh. Pity. Will he be in later?"

"It's not likely. Mr Edwards's calls were being referred to another extension but they've just started to be put through to me. The switchboard should have fixed it by now. Who did you say it was?"

No, I thought, no, I'm not being passed round like a tradesman, a supplicant, handing on messages, becoming a bit of currency, a cog in some dog-eared DTI machinery which included this interrogative woman. If Lawrence was out, Lawrence was out. I wasn't going to explain myself all over his office. Our business was private; Lawrence wouldn't thank me for broadcasting details of my discreet reconnaissance to anyone else on his patch. It could wait.

"Thanks, but don't worry. I'll speak to him tomorrow, maybe. Oh–" the thought suddenly struck me– "perhaps I could talk to William Pulford instead?"

There was a silence. A silence so long that you could almost feel it.

"I'm afraid that's not possible." It was as though she was uncertain what to say.

"Oh? Why?" I made my query very interrogative.

Another hesitation. Then: "This is very distressing, you see. I'm afraid William Pulford met with an accident last night."

A chill hit my spine. "Accident? What kind of accident?"

"In his caravan while on holiday. Something to do with a gas bottle, I believe. Very tragic. These camping things are so often lethal like that."

"Lethal?" I heard my voice rise towards hysteria. "*Lethal*? You mean he's dead?"

"I'm afraid so." The voice held a calm concern. "Apparently, there's not much left of the caravan. Not much at all. It's – it's frightful. I still haven't got your name. Do – I mean did you know him well?"

"No," I heard myself mutter. My mind had gone into an accelerated panic. "Not at all well."

Who is going to get killed? I'd asked. *No one,* came the irritable answer. *Don't be so melodramatic.*

The female voice recovered, became more affirmative, almost assertive. "Can I help you at all? My name is Parks. Frances Parks. I'm authorised to deal with this desk. As I say, Lawrence Edwards is not here. Who are you? What is it you needed him for?"

"Nothing vital." I put the phone down quickly, sharply. A huge unease took my thoughts away. I hate coincidences. Hate them. Now I did want to speak to Lawrence, to check the solidity of his presence and support before winging away into the blue, but it was unlikely he'd be available for days. Whatever it was that he and Pulford had been up to would be kept from me for at least as long as an investigation took place. I could expect no above-board stories from Lawrence right now.

"Just an accident," he'd say, when I might quiz him about it.

Why was that woman Frances Parks – what was it she'd said –'authorised to deal with this desk'? As though the desk had an existence of its own. An odd way of putting things if Lawrence was only away temporarily on some job or another, or investigating Pulford's death, and would soon be back. She had a disconcerting way of speaking, slightly demanding, one that stopped your own flow of thought. I should have asked if he'd been informed about Pulford but her manner stymied my questions. It was too late, now. Although a fair assumption was that Lawrence would have known about the tragedy as quickly as anyone.

I stared at my silent telephone. This is how it comes to you, I thought, this is how life deals it out. On the telephone, no one there, someone else has gone, there's another hole in the ranks but you'll have to keep going, keep your thoughts to yourself, be patient.

I shook panic away with a physical jerk of my head. It was too soon to draw conclusions. Caravan accidents happened, you read about them now and then, usually about people on their own, people disadvantaged or people who'd been out to a pub for a bit too long and got careless when they came home. Pulford looked the type: florid, overindulged. I had no time to hang about. Lawrence would catch up with me soon enough, or rather I'd catch up with him from South America, by telephone again. He'd almost certainly check with Richard Keane about my visit. A visit that had me speculating in all directions. The problem with the DTI, congratulating itself on having done this or that to assist a business, is that it doesn't ask whether you've got anything to eat this evening; it just assumes that you have and that you're as unscrupulous as the next man.

Which might be true in my case but Richard Keane needed a different sort of assistance.

I still stared at the telephone, blankly. Should I call Maurice to chat about coffee or Betty about amorous matters to relieve my tension? Again, I thought not. I'd give Betty a ring at the right time. If I called Maurice, he'd be bound to tell her. Then there'd have to be explanations, protestations about timing and sincerity. Betty was quick to assume ulterior motives.

No, not now; this wasn't the time. I mustn't get Betty involved in this.

Why not?

My thoughts were confused.

There was no point in endless speculation about Pulford. Though I didn't think it through clearly something urged me to leave, to leave now, quickly, putting lots of space between England and myself. I picked up the telephone and started to make bookings, travel bookings, with Katie Gonzalez at the forefront of them. I was looking forward to a plentiful dose of Katie's restorative passion as well as the information I needed; it had been a long, long time since we'd –

Despite a pulsing feeling in my veins, as though the inner pressure had suddenly risen sharply in response to mental anxiety, I began to hum one of the sexually scurrilous verses of *Se va el caimán* to myself as I dialled.

So often, movement replaces thought.

11

Travel: make a journey, esp. one of some length to distant countries;
act as commercial traveller (for firm, in commodity).

Concise Oxford Dictionary

The road from Barranquilla to Cartagena is no more dangerous than any other road in Colombia, nor does it teeter along the coast that it follows. It is a hot inland highway along which buses encumbered with exterior luggage vie with each other for dominance of the grit-strewn surface. I was content to give them precedence as I joined the westward traffic. My dented rental car had brakes which pulled somewhat to the right, presenting the cheerful probability that if I braked too hard without twisting the wheel, the car was more likely to end up in a ditch than splattered across the front of an oncoming lorry.

But this was no time to demand vehicular perfection. This was time to be off.

I settled myself deeper into the lumpy plastic seat, felt the front wheels wobble as the car picked up speed, pressed the accelerator down a bit harder, frowned into the sunlight ahead of me before finding my dark glasses in my pocket, put them on, and smiled.

Lunch swelled powerfully under my belt, like an organic generator pulsing energy into a veined mechanism. Señor Nassim Serfaty, Señor Nassim Serfaty's two brothers and his sycophantic production manager had browbeaten their local restaurant into producing an extensive fish grill followed by huge churrasco steaks as they bombarded me with questions. Iced beer flowed in my direction. My plate was first heaped with the choicer denizens of the Caribbean followed by softer cuts from upland cattle. The Serfatys were assiduous in seeing to my appetite.

Their hospitality was not without motive, however. Such generously proffered consumption, lavish and challenging, was intended to debilitate rather than fortify. This was not to be a lunchtime of light conversation. The desire for concession clouded my consumption. Clearly, the Serfatys felt that they had not impressed me with the importance of their demands. I was responding incorrectly. Enacting the reverse of the usual textbook selling situation did not suit them at all. There is something about me, I suppose – blue-eyed, fairish, a stocky sort of Anglo-Saxon – a gringo, in short – which presents a deep-seated challenge to any Latin. By way of additional abrasion that morning it had been, to South Americans of Middle Eastern extraction, offputting to have to trade with an Englishman over a machine located in Italy.

When Mario Chiari passed on their details to me and I phoned them, the Serfatys were polite but disconcerted. They had to accept my credentials – Mario was amused to receive their fax cross-checking my story – but they were not altogether happy. As far as visiting representatives went, the Serfatys would have been much more at home with an Italian and more particularly with Mario himself. An Italian might look at them with the same comprehension and might even speak Spanish just as colloquially, with a marked River Plate accent, but he would be more alert, more attentive, fellow-Mediterranean, *simpático*. An Italian might also smile the small, irritating smile that I could not resist as they pointed out the benefits that would come to me if I acceded to their demands. Indeed they would expect such treatment from an Italian. From an Englishman it was offputting because it was a smile, however slight, that showed that I had heard all this sort of malarkey before.

In default of Mario, the Serfatys would have preferred someone less experienced, someone younger, much more enthusiastic.

I swerved to avoid a dust cart and began to relax as I got the hang of the car. Once clear of the scraggy sprawl of Barranquilla's dirty suburbs I believed, perhaps optimistically, that the damp hot air would clear as the city receded. The road should be safe enough because even the worst of Colombia's organised criminals understand the need to keep the tourist trade flowing, especially to Cartagena. All the same, the disorganised ones are not so far-sighted. I studiously avoided the garb of a businessman and wore a short-sleeved shirt of blue cotton with dun-coloured washable trousers. I was careful to avoid carrying a sharp black briefcase and used a small fabric holdall with zipped divisions instead. My other case, a plastic-fabric one, was a supermarket thing that spoke of no prosperity. Although Colombia is becoming steadily more dangerous to business travellers it is like much of South America: perfectly negotiable by the experienced voyager and no worse than, say, New York's notorious districts used to be. When I phoned my invitation to Katie and suggested the historically romantic Cartagena she was pleased. There were many other parts of South America which, to Katie, presented greater problems. In Rio, for instance, it has long been dangerous to stop your car at traffic lights after dark. Lamentably her home city of São Paulo is now exactly the same; there, crossroads with traffic lights present a night-time game comparable to Russian roulette.

The Serfatys' food was very enjoyable. It is not often that I indulge quite so much but business etiquette demanded I should not upset them by appearing to stint their hospitality and I was determined not to let it hamper my attention to detail. I also knew that Katie would absorb all the energy I could muster later on. The fish was fresh and the steak excellent. I made appreciative noises as I tucked in with gusto.

The Serfatys were extremely discontented with my proposed disappearance from Barranquilla that afternoon. When a visiting European salesman arrived for such negotiations they wanted to dominate his movements; they did not think he should be canvassing other companies for similar opportunities. This was very specialised, very particular. It would ruin their plans if someone else were contemplating such a large, similar investment.

"Don't worry," I assured them. "There's no one else here interested in this. The engagement I have to go to is a personal matter. Purely personal."

Nassim Serfaty scowled, unconvinced. His dark face crinkled as his mouth drew into a peevish line. "But we must finish our discussions. We must continue this afternoon."

The men across the table all nodded at me expectantly. Their eyes glittered under dark brows. Who could refuse to clinch such a deal?

Why would a salesman want to dissipate this momentum? I shook my head in transparently simulated sadness as their anxiety radiated towards me. "We are far too far away from agreement," I said regretfully, sipping the icy beer. "Your offer is much too low. We both need time to consider. Of course I can make special arrangements to accommodate your financial needs but such arrangements are not inclusive in our price. Extra services inevitably incur extra costs."

That had their lowered brows beetling in unison. They hated it every time I referred to extra costs.

"It is very easy," Serfaty said, his expression tinged slightly puce with anger, like the oxblood-coloured shine on his polished leather shoes. "I have told you. I am willing to sign this afternoon, to give you a cheque, a draft, anything you like, against your delivery guarantee. This deposit of ten percent will be yours."

I forced myself to think, then, of Katie's lower lip, her ripe, elegant body and the fond way it would wrap itself around me later that day in Cartagena. Our overseas meetings, as we thought of anything outside Brazil, tended to be more passionate, more adventurous, more uninhibited than the rare occasions I could get to São Paulo. Katie is a great girl and has been far better to me than I deserve. There was a time in New Orleans, for instance, when I arrived late and she was already in bed, with the sheet drawn up, waiting as the round-eyed bellhop dropped my bag and scurried out with his tip. Katie had thrown the sheet back for me to leap upon her with a cry of joy: things like that were unforgettable. They helped me to ignore Serfaty's disgraceful mendacity, to smile at his insulting attack on price, to evade his desire to stampede me into an agreement too soon.

"Look," I said to him, producing what I hoped was a frank but not unfriendly expression, "I think we should get something quite clear. I am in a unique position to over-invoice by whatever you want. The third party commission can be paid anywhere you like. The Italians cannot possibly do this now, especially with their new fiscal regulations in force. Even in Switzerland there are some very difficult safeguards. A British arrangement is the safest. But the price of this machine is the price I have given you. I can't change that. What I can do is to send any excess you stipulate to anywhere required. Few machinery companies will play this game now. None of the new equipment makers will do it, that's certain; only a trading outfit like mine."

My control was taxing my patience. I could feel a prickling down my spine. If it had not been for Serfaty and his typical, avaricious, demeaning idea of what decent business negotiations were, I might have been with Katie the night before, ignoring her plea for a rest after her journey up from São Paulo.

Serfaty sat back abruptly. Tension etched deep, dark lines into his face. I kept my expression bland, unemotional, thinking of Katie and not him. It was ironic to think of myself using Katie as a distraction, to cool my condition this way. Ten years ago I might have been disconcerted, even upset. Ten years ago I might have jumped at the prospect of clinching the deal, leapt at it, given it all away in my obvious eagerness to lessen the hostility and finalise things, depart with a contract in my bag and a smile upon my face. But I was younger then. I was a company executive. My motivations were different.

Self-employment brings self-knowledge, like no study of psychology or philosophy, no reading of Jung or Freud can ever induce.

Ten years ago, with Katie in prospect I would have been beside myself with lust, unable to concentrate or put two logical thoughts together. Now I was in charge of myself. The Serfatys and their unctuous production manager glared at me as I pondered my detachment. This was not a game for the inexperienced; this was my game, my own fist of cards to be put down, one by one, in careful sequence. This was no corporate policy job, no executive-answering situation. No reports would be written, no business-publicity about contracts won would be trumpeted to trade magazines. No DTI man would post plaudits for export effort. No superiors would get an explanation nor would such superiors get, to please their idle egos, the opportunity to rescind, partly or wholly, what I had agreed or done. My independence made that sort of meddling extinct.

83

Lawrence Edwards would get no reports, either. It had nothing to do with him. This was not about coffee fungus or the theft of an electronic instrument. People like Serfaty needed my intervention for specific reasons, clandestine reasons, and there was no cause to explain or to give ground. As an employee I would not have dared drive so blithely away that afternoon but such executive accountability, such dependence, such sources of guilt, had long since been abandoned.

As I motored further out from Barranquilla the smell of hot country dust and humid air overcame the town aroma of concrete and wet cement. Palm trees with broken leaf-shards on thick pineapple-like tops were rising over the blown litter everywhere, above the papers and advertisements for olive oils and colas, the tin cans and crumpled polyethylene sheeting that gleamed and shimmered in roadside gutters or clung to the rusted carcasses of abandoned vehicles. I settled myself comfortably into the sticky plastic car seat. It was a familiar sight out there, a sight indigenous to South America, the Middle East, India, anywhere hot. I felt almost at home. The crossroads with the sign to Tubará off to the left and Santa Veronica to the right shot past as I rattled on towards Loma Alta. I could have flown from Barranquilla to Cartagena but this was what I preferred, what I had set myself to enjoy. A car provides liberty. Air travel incarcerates. Soon the road would move closer to the coast, the hot, damp, Caribbean coast, with its dark people and lax feelings, the blood pulsing with an expectation of cloudburst or throbbing with the release of precipitation. Gusts of Caribbean air, like those from a fan in a camp kitchen, came to ventilate my clothes with the odorous, greasy exhaustion of a fish and chip shop. I began to feel the first stirrings of desire.

The row about payment terms had been openly bad-tempered. Serfaty had thrown his pen down on the table in contempt. Cash terms? Incredible. A thirty percent deposit followed by a Letter of Credit? An insult. He was not prepared to put down more than ten percent. He would not go to the expense of an irrevocable Letter of Credit confirmed by a first-class bank. How dare I? No one else wanted such things.

"Think about it," I smiled as I ignored his posture. "We'll meet again on Monday, shall we?"

What I would have said, ten years ago, was that of course everyone else wanted such things, even more expensive and permanent things, by way of payment, and that international monetary documentation is well-established the world over. But now I didn't; there was no point in protesting or extending fruitless arguments. We both knew that he was lying. Without a confirmed and irrevocable letter of credit, once the goods were delivered Serfaty would delay payments, prevaricate, renegotiate, possibly even steal the machine outright.

"Monday?" Serfaty actually spluttered. He couldn't believe that I'd keep him waiting until then. Other salesmen probably always cringed to him, Middle East style, but it doesn't always pay to follow the textbooks on selling, especially not the servile ones. People never respect what comes easy.

I managed to leave without further unpleasantness. Either Serfaty suddenly accepted that I wasn't to be rushed or, more likely, he was hoping to short-circuit me in some way. His eyes had taken on a calculating look. He might even call Mario. I wasn't bothered; the effect of the heavy meal in that hot climate had been the opposite of what might be expected. I was brightly alert as I drove off, feeling flushed and slightly swollen, like a prize bull that has been assiduously fed before being released into a herd of expectant cows. I overtook a billowing bus that farted gusts of diesel smoke from under its rubber wheel skirts then a few lesser cars, taking care to let the shiny, expensive ones go past.

After Loma Alta I skirted the sign to Santa Catalina and drove through Bayunca. I felt no apprehension, no alarm. A police car overtook me and its uniformed occupants hardly gave me a glance. To the side of the road, in a bar flanked by scabbily-vined pergolas, a group quarrelled and capered, waving their arms at a black man encumbered with a guitar. Papers littered the dust around a dead dog.

If you make competent executives redundant, destabilise their lives, you move them into the shade. Survival is everything; in the shade there are both luxuriant and etiolated growths. Those moved into the shade can use knowledge of the light for many purposes.

I wasn't going to concede to Señor Serfaty that day, or any other. Exhilaration had begun to possess me. I checked the rear-view mirror carefully. No one was following me. I was sweating, whether from food, lust or climate I wasn't sure. The mere fact of arrival made me sit up and blink in excited anticipation as I took in every detail. The dual carriageway of the Avenida Santander has been driven between the thick fortress walls of the old town of Cartagena and the outward sea which once lapped them. From that side, as the dented rental car sped urgently to its destination, the original looked beached, stranded like a huge stone vessel separated from its element. I watched the walls, massed sloping angles punctuated by pillboxes, sawing past me on my left while my nose sniffed the surf and maritime decay blown from the line of the black sand beach to my right. The wind was full of insects and the smell of crabs. A tinge of grilled crustaceans salted my saliva.

I turned the bend to the Bocagrande district, passing from medieval to modernism, from colonial to the concrete. Layered hotels pointed white and skyward in package-tour tiers of isolated American luxury intended to insulate the visitor from Colombia. Up there, above the ground, Katie would be waiting for me, perhaps ready to repeat her welcome of New Orleans. A tight, pressurised tingling suffused my veins as I drove into the car park of the hotel and locked the unremarkable vehicle. I strode into the foyer and felt my clothes starting to congeal immediately around me, to stiffen frigidly in the air-conditioned dryness.

A porter took my cheap suitcase and, after I had registered – Katie had booked the room in her name so I was now officially Sr. Gonzalez, which made me smile, even in my agitation – the two of us were lifted up to the correct floor.

After a lifetime of fumbling the porter opened the door and I paid him off with a curt tip. Inside me the parrillada of fish seethed below the churrasco steak and iced beer but the room was cool and empty. There were two double beds, both meticulously made. Katie was nowhere in view but I saw her case and some casually discarded clothes strewn over a chair.

The shower was running in the bathroom.

My clothes fell to the floor like easily-shed leaves from an autumn tree, but an autumn tree that is inexplicably damp and hot and feverish. I grasped the handle of the bathroom door and found it locked.

"Katie?" My voice was thick with desire.

The running water stopped.

I twisted the handle again, savagely. "Katie?"

There was a low laugh from within. I heard other sounds: a click, shuffling. Then running water again.

"Katie!" I twisted the handle again, intending to rattle it. The door flew open to the touch.

She was standing, wet and dripping, her back to me, looking at herself in the big mirror as she stooped over the washbasin and half-turned, big-breasted to the reflecting glass. There was a mocking smile on her face.

She didn't even have a towel on.

Her eyes widened.

"Johnny! Look at you! So impatient!"

She stooped a little further over the basin to turn off a tap, then straightened as the smile crumpled to an expression of expectant passion.

I crossed the bathroom in one huge sweaty stride to grasp her. Her mouth met mine and the soft wet envelope of flesh was crushed, vibrant and pliant against me.

12

> Salesmanship: skill in overcoming the opposition or apathy of the
> prospective customer.
>
> *Concise Oxford Dictionary*

Everyone has their own route to the clinch point. Sometimes it's not
the obvious one. Mine was a little devious. The critical bit would be
during the lull after the storm. That's when I needed my father's
good luck.

He had a keen sense of timing but not in the way you might
think. Around 1930 he was Manchester sales representative for the
Renold and Coventry Chain Company, working from Deansgate.
He was a good technical sales rep, cheerful, large, knowledgeable
but respectful, competent and handy with useful suggestions when
visiting textile mills being converted from belt to chain drive. Offices
never had much attraction for him. He liked to get out and about to
see different sorts of people in their factories, chat to foremen and
fitters who liked their own aggression returned, or cast a knowledgeable eye over plans in drawing offices full of waistcoated
draughtsmen with white shirts and sober ties. Things were more
formal then.

Foden Steam Wagons were still in existence even though petrol
and diesel engines had made the cumbersome old haulage engines
obsolete. There was a long chain that was used on the steering system of the Foden involving a horizontal arrangement of sprockets
and ratio reducers. It was thoroughly unsatisfactory, with lots of
backlash, making a Foden Steam Wagon hazardous. The driver
would frantically twirl the small low-geared steering wheel through
revolution after revolution to try and get a bit of turn to the front
wheels as tons of vehicle lumbered along. Fortunately the Steam
Wagon was not exactly fast; a sedate pace was its best. An old
chargehand who supervised me on my first Cincinatti milling
machine claimed to have got up to thirty miles an hour downhill on

the Holmes Chapel to Sandbach road after a riotous pub night but nobody in the tool room believed him. They said a Foden could never get up to that speed.

The long steering chain cost fifty pounds. In the days of bicycle chains costing a few pence, fifty pounds was a major order. My father was on four pounds a week plus commission. If you sold a Foden steering chain, he said, you could go home for the rest of the day.

One rainy morning my father had to go out to a contractor's yard at Warrington where they had some Fodens. It was tippling down. As he walked from the station – reps didn't get cars then – up a long incline to the yard, my father got wetter and wetter. By the time he reached the yard he was soaked through.

In the corner of the yard there was a hut with a corrugated iron roof. A small chimney pipe billowed out a bit of smoke. My father headed for the hut and entered. Closing the door, he stood inside, dripping. The foreman of the yard was sitting in a wooden smoker's bow chair, tipped back, with his booted feet up on a cast iron stove, smoking a pipe. The windows were tight shut and the air in the hut had become a thick fug. The waistcoated, shirtsleeved foreman did not speak; he cocked an eye at my father, grunted and gestured at a chair beside him.

My father took off his sodden trilby then his raincoat and hung them on a rusty hook on the wall. Underneath, his suit sported huge wet patches and his collar was wringing. Below the knee his trousers were soaked through and his shoes squelched as he crossed the dirty wooden floor. He sat down on the indicated chair, briefcase to hand. The foreman continued to smoke his pipe. So far he had not uttered a word.

"For some reason," my father used to relate, "I don't know why, I was irritated by his attitude. That grunt and the nod of the head. In those days people had more manners, even factory hands. I got it into my head that I wouldn't speak until he did. After all, when it comes to it, I can be as stubborn as the next man. So I sat down and said nothing."

The foreman smoked on. After a while, my father got out his own pipe and lit it. The fug in the hut became denser. Rain drummed heavily on the corrugated iron roof. My father's clothes began to dry out. By putting his feet up and moving his shoes carefully on the iron stove, he made sure that they and his socks steamed gently as the heat reduced the moisture in them. He basked in the fuggy warmth and enjoyed the pull of his pipe. Outside, he could hear the splashing of a broken rainwater pipe or gutter. Inside, it was peaceful and dry.

An hour went by. My father still held his silence. Eventually, the foreman slowly took his pipe out of his mouth. He spoke in a deep growl, as might be expected from a tough foreman in a rough haulage contractor's yard.

"You'll be the chap from Renolds, then?" he asked.

"I am," my father answered, shortly.

"Hm," grunted the foreman. "I thought as much. I'll say one thing: at least you haven't tried to talk me head off." He put his feet back on the floor and stood up. "Here, I'll give you an order for two of those steering chains."

And he did.

There isn't, not anywhere, a manual on sales technique that has that gambit in it. Not one. It's a great story, perfectly true, which my father was fond of repeating, as with so many of his favourite stories. But, like many parents' experiences, it's not necessarily transferable.

The problem was that it wouldn't work with Lawrence Edwards. It was totally irrelevant to my approach to Carlos Guimares. The key to Carlos was no bored haulage foreman with a filthy but peaceful pipe to smoke. The modern world doesn't work that way.

As any woman will tell you.

13

Katie and I lay side by side on one of the wide beds, entangled among the rumpled sheeting. Outside, the heat of the marine afternoon in Cartagena had declined to a drowsy evening which produced muffled noises amongst the tropical humidity. We were calm, beached like two pale-skinned mammals on a sighing shore of sated appetites. Conversation, frenetic for a while as it caught up with carefully selected items of the past – Katie, too, has her compartments and so, certainly, have I – had dwindled. Companionship had taken over from passion. Katie had closed her bare legs possessively over one of my thighs yet somehow managed to turn the top half of her body sufficiently to give her room to hold her paperback, *Captain Corelli's Mandolin*, at sighting distance. She had put her glasses on and was reading whilst I was sort of dozing between physical and verbal engagements, to use acting terminology. Our murmured compliments had languished.

If this seems surprising, a bit domestic at such a moment and place of contact, it reflects the long friendship Katie and I had developed. Ten years of romantic encounters bring a lot of knowledge and either great confidence or utter distrust, as much as those two extremes can really exist between lovers. Katie and I were pals as well as performers in the sexual circus of life. I took no offence at her desire to look into the character of Captain Corelli while I still lay, gathering strength again, beside her.

I brought the novel for her from England, reading it myself on the flight over. Now I was wondering if I had been wise. It could stimulate many of the ideas and theories about love, life and its significance with which Katie tended to bombard me during our sojourns together, even while I might frantically be unbuttoning her or bent on more distracting activities. Human significance is a very difficult concept to cope with when more immediate urgencies prevail. But there is a price for everything and for sex the price is usually highest.

In my cheap zip-case I had a copy of *Cuba Libre* by Elmore

Leonard, a boyish return to the culture of the Western after favourites like *Get Shorty* and *Freaky Deaky*. It was great. I thought that Elmore Leonard was much more my sort of author than Louis de Bernieres but Katie would be bound to take me up on any admission of adventurous enjoyments, get me into a cultural argument, wrangle over my superficial view of life.

Was it something Lawrence Edwards and I had in common, this desire to avoid falling into depths? The thought perturbed me as I shot a quick glance at my companion, immersed in the literary exploration of complex human relationships on wartime Greek islands. Was I falling into the same trap? Had the man decided to use what he saw as a gadfly, rather than the astute, observant resources at his disposal? Could the surface of life be forever skimmed, its deeper incumbencies avoided?

Katie's intent expression as she turned a page reproached me for past concentration only on the now exposed, golden-brown delights that had stirred my imagination in Northumberland Avenue. Her absorptive stillness was evidence of a side from which I usually flinched, causing remonstrance and unnecessary distances. She had often told me that I wasn't at peace with myself, hadn't come to terms with my quintessential nature, things that suggested profundities I had affected to ignore. She sometimes pressed bits of nodal quartz from Minas Gerais into my pockets or luggage on the grounds that I needed relief at nerve centres. Chakras, she called them. Even now she might demand to put one on my chest, somewhere above the solar plexus. A small, red, grey-veined rock obelisk adorned my desk in St.Leonard's, serving as a temporary but suggestive paperweight. These things were important to Katie who read about them constantly and I hadn't the heart to tell her I didn't use the obelisk for physical or metaphysical purposes. My problem wasn't my quintessential nature. It was the upheaval and destruction, ten years ago, of everything I had depended on.

But this Cartagena reunion, I suddenly realised, meant much more to me than the fleeting pleasures we had just enjoyed. Katie was almost a constant, a contradictory permanence, through the temporal existence I had deliberately chosen. Like a genie, she allowed herself to be conjured up whenever I wanted, and her concerns, like those of the true genie of Arabian Nights, went beyond my immediate requests. A slight shiver, despite the climate, wrinkled my spinal cord at the disturbing notion that this ready availability might become evanescent. I would hate that. I needed her solicitude, no matter how flippantly I appeared to treat it.

During a pause in one glorious session a few years back in her country cottage at Atibaia – that's a place a couple of hours into the countryside outside São Paulo – she said quite commandingly that I should read Jung. She said that Jung was the great sage and master physician of the soul and that, philosophically and psychiatrically, reading Jung would calm me down and sort me out. By sort me out I think she meant it might fill a vacuum she had perceived somewhere in my psyche, a vacuum in the sense of a lack of spiritual or metaphysical curiosity. At the time I did not want to agree that I was so incurious because it would have meant an admission of a philistine, engineer's dismissal of such fantasies – or what I perceived to be fantasies – and there would have been yet another spat to interrupt what to me were more important satisfactions. When she said that Jung would bring perspective into my life, possibly even a touch of understanding of the beyond, I cravenly agreed to look into the matter and renewed my activities of a more venal nature with greater enthusiasm.

When I got back home I happened to come across a paperback of Jung's in the discount store Olio Books in Robertson Street and snapped it up, cheap. Actually it was an autobiography entitled *Memories, Dreams, Reflections* which Jung, according to his own introduction, had started reluctantly at the behest of a lady assistant but soon found, as often seems the case with much autumnal reminiscence, that it became an abiding daily obsession.

Which was hardly a calming start.

Being more interested in biography than philosophical theory, innocently considering it then to be real life rather than fantasy, and undeterred by an introduction that should have been a warning to me, I continued to read the book. In most recollections childhood far outstrips adulthood for fascination but it was not far into the early, self-conscious meanderings that I came across the three-year-old Jung having, according to his detailed account, certainly before the age of four, a lurid repetitive nightmare about a huge phallus situated in a stone-vaulted but red-carpeted crypt in the meadow behind Laufen Castle. His mother's voice interrupted the nightmare as the fifteen-foot phallus, made of skin and flesh, erect on a red cushion on a king's golden throne, stared upwards to the heavens with a single eye set in its top.

"Yes, just look at him," Jung's mother called out, in the nightmare according to the adult Jung. "That is the man-eater!"

At this point Dorothy Parker's dictum came to mind. I ignored Jung's interpretation of the significance of this ithyphallic symbolism and hurled with great force rather than putting lightly down, finding that calm was the reverse of the effect the book was having. What the very young Jung evidently needed, if the story were true, was a lot of cold baths.

"Jung," I said to Katie on the telephone a day or two later, "has not helped very much. Quite the opposite. I am not calm," and told her the problem.

Katie was by then immersed in arrangements for the establishment of a sort of ashram at her Atibaia cottage. She was concerned to put theory into practice and had the funds to make a modest start. My pugnacious vibrations threatened to disturb the meditative contemplation for which she was preparing herself ready for that weekend, when an assorted group of acolytes was to assemble with her.

"You are hopeless," she retorted. "Even Jung can not impinge on your earthy, technical, engineering philistinism. When we hold our evening transcendental meditation on Saturday, I shall have trouble cleansing the garden temple of the memories which I associate with you."

"I certainly hope you will. Considering what we did in what was then called the summer house rather than the garden temple. Particularly on that swing." I chuckled. My mood was improving already. "What a transcendental motion that was; you'd better not meditate too much upon that, otherwise one of the male contemplees will have his work cut out afterwards."

"God! You are so dreadfully Anglo-Saxon. Appalling. You cannot help being coarse. I have to ring off now."

I remember chuckling as I put down the phone. The only way I could cope with Katie's metaphysical pressures had been with flippancy, something which she always said distinguished me from Carlos Guimares. His response to theosophy was positive. In beliefs and superstitions he was rather like the late Sir Jimmy Goldsmith. This susceptibility was a source of much of Katie's influence on him, in addition to the obvious. It occurred to me, now, thinking of my assessment of Lawrence and its uncomfortable corollary, how deliberately blind an eye I had turned to qualities which might have drawn Katie closer to me.

The rustle of a turning page in the murmuring quiet of the Cartagena hotel room disturbed my reverie on these matters. A little guilty at my own dozy silence, I moved towards Katie and slid a hand across her bare stomach, squeezing the rippled waistline, where discernible, with affection.

"It seems to me," I murmured, almost into her ear, "that psychology, for adults, is dogged by psychologists' excessive interest in children and animals, even in experimentation with them, behaviourally of course. One of the reasons why women are so interested in psychology and its offshoots is because of the children thing— physical biology, behavioural matters which are simple but fascinating to observe at first hand, and so on. It's partly sort of chemical, I suppose. Tubular, even."

She shut *Captain Corelli* with a snap, leaving that female-appreciating, woman-deferential, musical, unassertive hero clamped tight between pages until she had dealt with me and could release him later, allowing his character to fructify yet again on the open sheets.

"What," she demanded, "are you saying? Actually?"

"Well, for instance, if you have a Jaguar car and it goes wrong it is no good someone talking to you about the workings of a Baby Austin or, say, the problems of casting bronze, timing valve openings and stringing electrical wiring in explanation. You need a much simpler fault-finder which is, however, based on complex knowledge. Ironically, because the Jaguar is far too developed, too sophisticated, merely to describe the elementary principles of the combustion engine or of leaf spring suspension is not much help. And yet, I suppose, it is arguable that without that basic knowledge you cannot progress to understanding the Jaguar. It is also rather like, say, defusing a complicated bomb set off by an alarm clock. You may not understand the bomb but if you do not know how an alarm clock works you can not even begin to deal with the menace."

Her expression betrayed impatience. "You are spouting truisms and your metaphors are getting mixed."

"Oh, I'm no good at being metaphorical. I leave that to you. I was simply trying to draw simple comparisons in order to assist my rudimentary, unsophisticated engineer's brain to cope with a field you know so well. Amongst other things."

Her eyes, so close now to mine, narrowed. She took off her reading glasses. Her breath, hot but fragrant, steamed my cheek.

"What is it you want?" she demanded.

I opened the hand that squeezed her in the waist region and, on bare flesh, traced lines with my finger that I knew made karmic vibrations tingle in transcendental zones. The effect was not what I intended. She rolled over abruptly, put her legs to the ground, rose, wrapped a flowered cotton wrap right round her body, moved a chair sharply about to face the bed, sat on it and stared at me. She was upright and interrogatory. Her expression reminded me of a kindergarten teacher I once had. Not one I remember with affection.

"There is something you are not telling me. I know how you feel about psychology already. Don't condescend to me. Since we met I sense that there is another agenda. Why are you here? Apart from the obvious. What are you up to?"

Noting that concealment was now evidently in order, I moved the sheets discreetly to hide what Shakespeare might have referred to as naked frailties, plumped up a pillow, sat up and supported my neck with it as I moved more upright against the bedhead. I looked back at her without flinching.

"I am here," I said, "because Mario Chiari has got an excellent baby diaper production line he is reconditioning. There is more than a sporting chance that the Serfaty outfit, mendacious though they may be, will buy it. I had to come to Colombia to effect the transaction. No, the possible transaction; let me not count chickens before they are hatched. In order to sweeten what is a distasteful business necessity I suggested that we might meet here. I have never been to Cartagena. I have always wanted to go. There are people – I think, from what you have said to me in the past, that even you rank amongst their number – who would say that my ill-planned life has plumbed such depths that I, and only I, am desperate enough to undertake dodgy business excursions into what is regarded as a lethally dangerous territory. Most machinery salesmen would avoid Colombia like the plague. I do not see things that way. Quixotic if you like, but I do not. I have always wanted to come here. I needed an adventure and my historical enthusiasm – a typically overdeveloped British obsession with the past, you will also say – urged me on. So here I am. And here, providentially, are you. I could not think of anyone I would rather be with here than you. I have not seen you for ages. I phoned to suggest this wonderful opportunity be grasped with both hands – to coin a perhaps suggestive phrase – and when you said yes, my happiness was complete."

"Liar," she said. But not with absolute conviction. "Stop prevaricating. Get on with it."

"Katie, I have told you may times, much as you detest it as an English cop-out for real emotion, that I am very fond of you as well as having more obvious interests. I am. We are great in bed together and life makes such delights all too rare. We are both old enough to know that. In addition, time is on no one's side. We may have all sorts of other entanglements; as you have also often said, we have never fooled each other. But it hasn't only been just a powerful physical attraction, has it? There's much more: there is a part of my heart which Katie Gonzalez will always occupy. Always. In other circumstances, with other timings, things might have been very different. I know; we've been through this before. I'm only repeating what you already know."

She still frowned during this but her expression modified a little. She had ever hated the English expression 'fond of' in relation to human passion, regarding it as a milksop piece of matinée romantic dilution unworthy of Latin consideration. My acknowledgement of her feeling was not just for appeasement. She was absolutely right, despite a long and confusing peroration I once had from her on the difference between a lover, a lover-friend and a friend-lover, all too complicated for me to grasp.

She opened her mouth but I held up my hand to restrain her.

"There's more. As you, with your intuitive antennae, have somehow guessed. Now that the initial fervour and thunderstorms with which we always meet has calmed a little, you are full of questions. I shall conceal nothing from you. I admit that there is something else. You see, almost as soon as I had phoned you and made the necessary arrangements, an example of serendipity so extraordinary, so coincidental as to be astounding, occurred."

Her eyes widened even though suspicion still lurked in them.

"Serendipity? Coincidence? Serendipity is an invention of Horace Walpole's, you told me once. The faculty of making happy and unexpected discoveries by accident. I have been well instructed by you, haven't I? In certain things. I have made contributions in others. Coincidence, I remember, when you had had a lot to drink once down at Guarujá, you used in an argument to demolish religious belief. Which is nonsense. Which strikes at everything in which I believe. As well you know."

Her chin tilted upwards in challenge. Things were going even better than expected.

"Did I? I don't remember that. Well, well. You know how it is, sometimes, with a jolt or two under one's belt. Things slip out. Anyway, the fact is that, as I say, almost as soon as I had made the arrangements with you, two things happened. Quite amazing seeing that I had only just arranged to meet you, the day before."

"What two things?"

"Firstly I received a fax enquiry from Brazil for my machine."

"Who from?" she demanded.

"A company called Texteis Arochena up in Belo Horizonte. Why?"

A look passed over her face, fleeting but significant. "Nothing," she said.

I sensed I had entered a compartment of hers, one which might be important. "Do you know them?"

She shrugged. "I know *of* them. They are quite a big firm. That's all. You know what I think of your machinery business." Her expression returned to the interrogatory teacher-mode, closing down any further pursuit of the subject.

I decided to put Texteis Arochena to one side. "After I had made my plans, I was called up to London and asked to carry out a piece of consultancy whilst in South America. Into the possibilities for a certain electronic invention. Straightforward consultancy, market research no more, but it was extraordinary. Quite amazing."

"Was it?" Her face became less taut, more curious. "Why?"

"It meant that within a day of fixing to see you, I found I would have to come to Sao Paulo in addition to Belo Horizonte. To see you officially. You see, the invention has to do, amongst other things, with the detection of toxic fungus in coffee."

"Coffee?" The expression, which had opened in surprise at my use of the word officially, clouded again.

I cleared my throat. "Yes. Coffee. Beans, to be precise. Green beans. Apparently under certain circumstances a fungus which may lead to toxins can occur."

She said nothing. Her eyes had narrowed.

"I have been asked to look into this matter. Quite independently. The instrument is used to detect significant levels of moisture. I really couldn't believe it. It means that in addition to our meeting here, after I finish with the Serfatys I have to go up to Bogotá to conduct some interviews. Then I shall follow you down to Brazil. Where as it happens I have the other potential customer, Texteis Arochena, for the machine as well as my research project to pursue."

Silence.

I cleared my throat again. "Tell me," I asked, "has Carlos really kept all his coffee interests? I thought he was going to sell them."

Then I waited. Outside, the murmuring sounds had gone silent, or seemed to have, in the suspense.

After a few seconds the answer came.

"I sense you know he has." Her voice was soft. "You've checked, haven't you?"

"Well yes, I have. At least, I wasn't sure. The International Coffee Organisation in London – I visited them before I left – were very co-operative. They gave me a list of people and organisations I might visit. In Colombia and Brazil. None of Carlos's companies was on it. Then I remembered that he had a part-share, you told me once, in a coffee plantation. In Minas Gerais somewhere. I did do a bit of checking. There's a nominee company of his which effectively controls another one. Which in turn has quite powerful coffee interests."

"You may not meet Carlos, Johnny. I will not allow it."

"But he is still as powerful in that field as he is in others? The food and grain and all those?"

"We agreed not to discuss Carlos once. We agreed. You have brought him up twice now."

"I'm sorry."

"You do not need Carlos in order to do your research into this – this device."

"Well. Perhaps not. But without Carlos I do need you. With you on my side, he is quite unnecessary. Oh, I shall make the necessary enquiries with the recommended list I've got, and so on and so on, but everyone knows how powerful Carlos Guimares is and everyone will be giving me anodyne answers anyway. You are the keeper of his gate. The chatelaine of his office. His head of administration. If I have you on my side I have everything I need. If you are on my side?"

She didn't answer. She was still watchful, assessing.

"Carlos probably wouldn't meet me anyway. Wouldn't acknowledge his involvement. He'd refer me to someone else, a technician or a coffee technologist or maybe a manager. He has always, from what you used to tell me, worked in the most low-profile way possible. That's his technique. Rather mirrors his private life. Doesn't it?"

Her eyelids were now lowered over the narrowing. "I think maybe you are very jealous of him."

"Me? Jealous? Why should I be? I rather believe the boot might be on the other foot."

"Ha! Don't flatter yourself!"

"Why not? Carlos knows of my existence, doesn't he?"

"Yes he does."

"Does he know you're up here to meet me, now?"

Her chin tilted again, with pride. "Maybe. Maybe not."

Had she really been brave enough to taunt him with me? I was sure there was some revenge element in her ready acceptance of my invitation. Katie was always pleased to see me and liked to have her independence but usually there were discreet limits. Carlos was probably misbehaving himself again.

"What did he say when you told him?"

She shrugged expressively.

"Let me guess. If you did. He said, Go on: enjoy yourself. Get it out of your system. We're grown-ups. See if I care. Your Englishman will soon scuttle off back to his wet island like a defeated pirate. Didn't he? He knows you'll be back to him whatever break you may have. It will be business as usual. And when he's finished with his current amour you'll still be there."

Because you'll have to be, I thought, but didn't say it. Running Carlos's administration provided Katie with power, real power, in a country where such situations are hard to achieve, especially for a woman. Through him came so much to Katie: money, security, respect from underlings, decision-making, chauffeurs for special occasions, her own secretary, control, gifts from those who knew that quite often the only way to Carlos was through Katie. Courtiers, some of them became, to achieve their ends. Katie could take her pick of such obliging gentlemen. And sometimes did.

Food for thought.

"The thing is," I went on – I was treading on thin ice now –"what you and I have is quite independent of the pressures to which we both have to bow. It's apart from all that. You don't owe me anything. Quite the opposite, in fact. It's because we like each other, as well as the sex. Which is great. We are friends, usually. Across two

103

sides of the earth. Over the last – my, time flies – ten years. Am I right?"

She nodded slowly. "Yes. But that is something that worries me."

"Why?"

A slight frown of concentration came to her brow. "It is not that it is not flattering to find that old lovers still think of one. It is nice, and I am flattered. Even if the motive may be venal. Although I am prepared to give you the benefit of the doubt: I mean it is still venal but also for friendship. Yet you worry me because I think by now you should have come into a firmer relationship. Not just for sex; I do not believe you are short of that. A relationship should have come to you that is more significant. You haven't found one. You are atavistic. You have historic interests in places like Cartagena because the English always have them; they think the past is somehow better or at least more exciting than today or the future."

"Now you are contradicting yourself. My distinguishing feature is a mental avoidance of the past."

"The immediate past, maybe. But not the longer term. I am speaking of your private life; you are somehow repeating yourself. Not only in your business, which is a disgraceful monotony for an intelligent man. Even with me, here, this is a repeat. It is nice to have long-term lovers but people should develop. I do not see that you have developed."

I paused before replying. In these circumstances there is a grave danger of saying the wrong thing. A careless word with someone like Katie, but with almost any woman, and you're into self-analysis like slipping on a bar of soap. Something to be avoided at all costs.

"Katie," I said, "I can't answer for myself. All I know is that an opportunity to see you came up and I jumped at it. There may not be another for years. In my own shallow way I thought you might want to jump at it, too. After all, we both live lives bounded by business circumstances. Is it so reprehensible, so atavistic as you call it, to want to seize the passing moment? I thought: Katie has greater ties than I have. She might want a break with an old friend. To show that she's not yet haltered by her daily responsibilities. Or can be taken for granted. Is that so unusual?"

She shook her head. "Of course not."

"And wasn't my timing fortunate?"

"As it happens it was. You see, you have omitted one thing," she said.

"What's that?"

She smiled wryly. "The frisson of the forbidden element. And the independence you mentioned. I need my independence. My breaks from that business." She stood up and let the wrap drop to the ground. "Carlos doesn't know I'm here. He thinks I'm in Atibaia, at what you call my ashram, with a bunch of gloomy meditators, while he's taken his latest down to Punta del Este." She made a small grimace. "He is a gambler and belongs to several exclusive clubs. One of them is at Punta del Este and he pretends he needs to get away to gamble. But I know who he has taken with him because it is my business to know. Every time. As usual it is someone else's wife. He gets bored just by the idea of contemplation, of an ashram like mine."

Something Carlos and I have in common, I thought. But said nothing.

She got on the bed and crouched over me, naked, her face close to mine. "You will not meet Carlos. I forbid it. But I will help you, Johnny, even though you don't deserve it, with the introductions you will need. I can even give you some Colombian coffee contacts in Bogotá. And maybe some information, provided it does not compromise Carlos."

I opened my mouth but she put a careful finger on my upper lip to prevent me from speaking. "I am glad that you have acknowledged serendipity. Or maybe there was something even more significant at work in this extraordinary coincidence? Something important for both our lives." Her smile became a cunning one as she began to unwind the sheet I'd put over myself. "Just for once you will have to do as I tell you, won't you? I will be the leader, will I not? Before we change and go down for a drink and the very best dinner Cartagena can offer?"

14

The cool calm of the hotel room, isolating me from Cartagena, had a tranquillising effect as I dialled Lawrence Edwards's office. It was time to pick up the threads of what had happened to Pulford. Katie was downstairs, engaged in the complicated morning treatments of a beauty salon in the foyer arcade. I had a break in which to get back to reality. Five hours difference; Lawrence should be there, he must be there. The connection was fine; I heard the unmistakable British ringing tone, reassuring, completely unchanged, burring away in what would be the dull, damp atmosphere of Victoria Street.

It wasn't Lawrence who answered, nor the breathless, educated lady called Frances Parks. It was a man's voice, calm, deliberate, not relaxed. This was someone prepared, alert.

"Robinson," the voice said. No more.

"Lawrence Edwards, please."

"Who is that?"

"This is Lawrence's number, isn't it?" I was starting to get hot, despite the soothing air conditioning.

"Who is that?" The repeat had a tone that wasn't sharp or condescending. It was factual, like a lawyer at a hearing.

I gritted my teeth. Bugger these cool, Victoria Street mandarins. "I wish to speak to Lawrence Edwards," I said, making each word deliberate, as though he couldn't hear properly.

"Who is that?"

"What do you mean, who is that? Who are you? Is that Lawrence's number or isn't it?"

The voice remained calm, educated, balanced. "I'm afraid Mr Edwards is no longer available. My name is Robinson. All Mr Edwards's calls are being referred to me. Can I assist you?"

I managed to stifle a cry of rage and distress. "Look here, I'm calling from Colombia. My name is Barber. Johnny Barber. Where is Lawrence?"

There was a fractional hesitation then the voice came back, just as cool as before. "Mr Barber." There was no recognition in the way my name was pronounced. Just sort of 'Mr Barber', with an emphasis on securing the name, like you do a name you haven't heard before. "I'm sorry, but I've got bad news. Lawrence Edwards is no longer with us, I'm afraid. He met with an accident a few days ago. I am Graham Robinson. I have taken over his operations desk; can I help?"

A sudden tightness across my chest must have affected my voice. "Accident? What sort of accident?"

"A car. Knocked him down. While he was out walking his dog."

Dog? Dog? My mind wobbled. I had no idea Lawrence Edwards really had a dog.

"How – how is he?"

"I'm afraid he's dead, Mr Barber."

"*Dead*?"

"I'm afraid so. I'm very sorry to be the bearer of bad news. I have been going through his papers and will do my best to catch up. There's quite a lot to absorb, quite apart from my own work. I'm sorry if it's a bit of a shock. Did you know Lawrence well?"

If he'd been through my 'papers' as he called them, he knew the answer. It explained his lack of sentiment.

If there were any such papers.

"No," I whispered. "Not well. The car that knocked him down: did they –?"

"I'm afraid not. Hit and run, it was. The police are searching, of course."

"Of course."

Catch them? I could hear Lawrence saying. *Of course they won't.*

It occurred to me, belatedly, that this conversation was almost certainly being recorded. Hence the careful pronunciation of my name.

"Is there anything I can do to help, Mr Barber?" The distant Robinson's voice was still calm, disembodied. There was a minimalist aspect to the way he spoke, a sparing of content that set my nerves on edge.

Killed, I'd asked, who has been or is going to get killed? And he'd pushed the idea aside with irritation in his voice.

Should I mention William Pulford to this Robinson man? Should I elaborate at all? Explain myself? No; my inner caution screamed no, say nothing, say absolutely nothing! "No thanks," I answered, then thought quickly. "I just phoned to tell him everything is going to schedule."

"To schedule." The repetition confirmed my belief that recording was going on, recording based on what? Ignorance or knowledge?

"Yes. I promised him I'd call, just to confirm, when I was over here."

"Confirm. I see."

"It's a terrible shock, Mr Robinson. The news, I mean."

Especially coming straight on top of Pulford's 'accident' I thought, it wasn't just a terrible shock for the normal reasons. They must have happened within a day, possibly even hours, of each other.

Where did that place me?

"I'm sure. Very sudden." Robinson was still unemotional. "Some of us here at the office still haven't quite taken it in. I expect it will come home at the funeral in a few days' time."

"Yes. I'll—I'll be in touch again. Fairly soon. When I get back."

"Very good. But if I can help in any way in the meantime, do give me a ring, won't you?"

"Thank you. Yes, I will."

"Is there a contact number where we can reach you? I'd like to note that down just in case."

"No," I said. "No, there isn't. I'll be travelling. I'll see you when I get back."

"I look forward to that. But could you leave a –"

"Goodbye."

I put the phone down, quickly. What a bastard, I thought, what a cold, Victoria Street, noncommittal bastard. A great drop of sweat splashed onto my hand. I went into the bathroom and washed my face, breathing deeply and trying to lower what felt like the pressure from a cross-compound engine thumping up my blood.

Now, in addition to William Pulford, Lawrence Edwards was dead and the man who'd taken over his desk showed no signs of recognition, none at all, of my name or purpose.

15

"Richard? Are you all right?"

"I'm fine. Johnny? Where are you calling from?"

"Colombia. You're sure?"

A deep chuckle. "I'm sure. My legs and arms are still working. Don't know about the brain, of course. What's up? You sound very tense."

"How are you getting on with the new beanometer?"

"It's coming on fine. Another week or so and I'll be sending it off. What's eating you?"

"Richard, can that bean machine be used for anything else? Anything else at all?"

"No, not really. You've seen it – it's not set up to be used for other things. Why would anyone want a bean slide for ten different types of coffee bean on a moisture meter, if they weren't measuring beans?"

"But moisture. That's all it measures? All it can do?"

"That's it. Come on, Johnny, what's got into you? I don't make bombs or rockets or mines or something. The power's only eight milliwatts. Eight thousandths of a watt. Fractional. You couldn't make a cup of tea or fry your eggs with it. It wouldn't even warm your socks on an autumn morning."

"Did you know Lawrence Edwards?"

"Who?"

"Lawrence Edwards. A DTI man. It was he who put me on to you. Did you meet him?"

"Never heard of him. It was one of the locals who – oh, wait a minute, I believe the local Business Link man did mention a Mr Edwards when he told me you'd be calling. Bigwig up in Victoria Street, he said. Never met him though. Why?"

"He's dead."

"What?"

"Dead. A car knocked him down while he was out walking his dog."

"Oh dear. Poor bloke. Did you know him well?"

"Not well. Oh, well enough. In a business sense."

"Nothing suspicious, is there? Did they get the driver of the car?"

"No they didn't. And I don't believe they will. I hate coincidences, Richard. Hate them. Tell me: did you meet Tony Barnwell at the ICO?"

"The what?"

"The International Coffee Organisation. Barnwell's a junior minister at the DTI."

"Never been to the ICO. I've only dealt with the Swiss guy from the coffee company. Isn't Barnwell that bloke the Opposition tried to land with an investment scandal last year? He was cleared but the papers reckoned he was a bit near the wind, wasn't he?"

"That's him. Lawrence Edwards said he trumpeted about your invention at an ICO reception. I thought you'd have been there."

"Me? I'm just the poor bugger who makes these things. People don't invite me to receptions."

"You've never met Barnwell or Lawrence Edwards?"

"Nope."

I asked him, I thought, I asked Lawrence Edwards who was likely to get killed and he snapped at me. No one, he said irritably, remember, no one's likely to get killed. *Don't be so melodramatic.*

Fat lot he knew.

What did he know?

"Johnny? Are you still there?"

"Sorry, Richard. Lawrence's death has upset me. I thought maybe someone was after another beanometer or something."

"What on earth for?"

"I don't know. Look, take care, Richard. I'll keep in touch."

"Any prospects yet?"

"I've just got here, Richard. It's a bit too soon to be saying."

"I could do with the business."

"I know. I'll do my best. But you take care, you hear?"

"OK. You too, Johnny."

I put the phone down. Then I heard the sound of Katie's key inserting itself into the hotel door lock.

16

Katie was cheerful and chattered away happily. She'd bought a cotton jacket and some baggy beach trousers. She said things were cheap. She came into the room in a bustle of glossy activity, opening her suitcase, holding things up to herself while gazing into a full-length mirror, talking to me over her shoulder. She looked good enough to eat.

"On my way through Barranquilla I saw quite a lot of coffee heading for the docks," she said, in the middle of something else but still paying attention to thoughts about me. "There must be opportunities for you to do a lot of research there."

"I shall. After you've gone."

"Will you see Señor Serfaty again?"

"Of course," I answered, as cheerfully as possible. "He'll have to come over to Milan to see the machine running."

"Good. Will that please you?"

"It's as good as one can get. No one buys without seeing the machine. If Texteis Arochena do the same, there's a fair chance the machine'll go. I look forward to being in Brazil for many reasons."

She shook her head in mock sadness and put on a knowing look. "What a business, Johnny. Why do you persist with it?"

I walked over behind her so she couldn't see my face and took her shoulders in my hands. "Don't let's start that all over again."

"But you must plan for the future. It's important. This business of yours is so transitory, so pedestrian. Each time is a one-off, no continuity. You could do something more long-lasting, more creative."

For a moment I was tempted to respond that my persistence with my business followed the same reasoning as her relationship with Carlos Guimares, to whom she would soon return, like Proserpine going back to Pluto, but that would have invited trouble. So I kissed the back of her neck whilst thinking up a suitable reply. In the mirror my face looked pale and drawn. If I wasn't careful, she'd notice.

Whatever Lawrence Edwards knew had almost certainly gone

with him. He might not even have made any notes about me. There might be no 'papers' to go through.

What on earth had he found out?

I breathed, muffled, into the back of Katie's neck. "H.G.Wells said that the life of the average commercial traveller was far more exciting than any author or writer's. He was right. The same could apply to many other so-called creative activities."

"Now you are being defensive," she said, smugly. "It seems that you do not believe that your occupation is creative." Then her expression changed. "What are you doing?"

My hands had moved off her shoulders, sliding round to the front of her. I wanted at all costs to avoid too much talk or for her to look at me directly.

"What do you think?"

She pouted into the mirror. "I've just had some very expensive treatment. And my hair is in perfect shape."

"That's why you're completely irresistible."

"I knew you'd be up to trying this," she said. "I'm not sure that I should let you."

"No? You may think that my machinery business is transitory but consider what a creative artist would do. In these circumstances?"

She chuckled.

"In these circumstances," she said, "just as in most others, artistic people tend to be egocentric. They talk interminably about their work and themselves, instead of – of progressing." She smiled at me in the mirror and slid a hand round to my thigh. "I much prefer the average commercial traveller."

I managed to smile back at her in the mirror as she lowered her newly-treated eyelashes alluringly.

Sometimes, an average compliment is enough.

17

For the record, I met Katie at the reception for a trade exhibition, which I had been ordered to attend in São Paulo. She was standing on the edge of a circle surrounding Carlos Guimares, seeming bored as the great man held forth to some group, his back to her. Even when he had his back to her his possessive radiance encompassed her like a magnetic field, so that it was certain she belonged to him, as did anyone who worked for him. But she looked delicious; mature and shapely, stylishly but not ostentatiously dressed, enough makeup to highlight her fine points but not enough to look painted. Her judgement of appearance for business purposes was dead accurate. A Brazilian friend with engineering interests introduced us and was suddenly buttonholed by an important client who bore him off to another group. Katie and I found ourselves face to face, alone.

"You're English?" she queried. "From England?"

"That's me."

"But I heard you speak to someone just now in Spanish. With an Argentine accent."

"An accident of youth. One has no control over where one's parents choose to live, however temporarily."

She smiled and I felt her eyes go over me appraisingly. Afterwards, she said that she was furious with Carlos over a new conquest he was almost deliberately parading, so she made up her mind that moment. However, she had to give the impression that the initiative was in my hands. I was allowed to fetch her a drink. As we talked, we moved away from Carlos's circle, sliding out from that possessive radiation. She sensed, as a woman will, the lack of other commitments in me without probing into the separation I knew to be imminent back home. It was cleverly done, all of it. Almost professional, premeditated. We even ended up using one of Carlos's spare downtown apartments, to which of course she had the key. For the rest of that visit to São Paulo my business attention was minimal. It was the start of a long, intimate and flattering friendship, not without its turbulence, that added restorative dimensions to a life that had threatened to turn in on itself. We needed each other, or the use of each other, for quite different purposes: Katie for separation, me for company. She was right about my not being short of sexual opportunities after my divorce. Katie provided something entirely different and I had every reason to be grateful to her. Without Katie my life might have become impossible.

Another exhibition provided me with the second turning point of my life. Mario and I met in Geneva, at one of those once-every-three-year things in Palexpo, a vast hall where the big companies take up great blatant blocks in the centre and little ones cringe in booths round the edges. I got there in time to be told it was all over. I could finish after the exhibition, take my cheque and go, please not to make a fuss. The company had been sold. I was part of the fall-out.

"You've done a great job, Johnny," the new managing director said, slurping some plastic-cupped lager from a fridge on the stand, "all over the place they say so. But we're retrenching. Downsizing. Call it what you will. We don't want that machinery any more. It's only the core business from now on."

The day after the axe fell I was standing at the edge of my dismisser's booth with my hands in my pockets, thinking this was utterly pointless when along the aisle, threading through the desultory visitors, came a man I vaguely recognised. He was smartly dressed in sports coat and dark grey flannels, looking urbane, relaxed, but bright-eyed. An Italian, with dark smooth hair, very clean-shaven, slim build. One who clearly took good care of himself.

He saw me looking at him and smiled as he came over. "I know you," he said. His voice was friendly, with only a slight accent. "You're Johnny Barber, aren't you?"

"Yes. And I recognise you, but I can't quite – "

"Mario Chiari." He was unruffled. "I met you briefly in the Sheraton in Buenos Aires when Jorge Tchinnosian was getting people to quote him for machinery from all over. We were in competition for the plant down in San Luis. You're a kind of *porteño*, aren't you? Me too."

Memory flooded back. I reached out to shake hands with him. "Of course. I remember now. You're the reconditioner from Milan," I said. "Yes, I was brought up in BA when I was small. You haven't been going all that long but you've got quite a reputation."

He bowed modestly. "Thank you. So have you."

"Neither of us won that one of Jorge's. But you pipped me to the post in Valparaiso last year."

"And you beat me in Miami."

Despite the numbness I was feeling, we grinned at each other in professional amity. Then he gestured at our stand, with its photos of machines, bits of kit, a video with a big screen trundling out the action on some carefully contrived line. "How's it going?" he asked.

I shook my head. "It's all over. For me, anyway."

He nodded sympathetically. "I heard some rumours. These things always get around. Corporate stupidity is everywhere. What are you going to do?"

"I haven't decided yet." Next, the defensive lie came easily. "One or two offers to follow up."

His face was serious, watchful. "Have you time for a coffee?"

"All the time there is."

We went off to a coffee area and sat at a table. Around us men in suits with big labels pinned to their pockets talked loudly about materials and company politics. A shadow passed over Mario's face as he observed them.

"A suggestion," he said.

"What?"

"Don't go and get another job. Don't work for any of these idiots."

"No?"

"No. I have a much better suggestion. You should be an independent. A broker."

"Me?"

"Sure," he said. "Johnny Barber would be much more use to many customers as an independent. Abroad. On an offshore island with no exchange controls, no Euros, no Brussels-bastards. Have an arrangement in Switzerland, a trading account, a branch, which I for instance dare not have because of our own controls and the tax inspector. So you would be able to arrange some of my sales internationally."

"Why couldn't you?"

"I could, of course. However, more and more sales in third-world countries – and some not so third world – depend on third party commissions. You know? Especially in the development or assisted zones. But the regulations about third party commissions in Italy nowadays are absurd. An independent abroad, offshore, can circumvent them."

I stroked my jaw thoughtfully. "Third party commissions," I repeated.

"Sure. You must have been asked many times?"

"I have."

"But you couldn't do that, eh?"

"No. At least, only in a very small way."

"A small way? There is no point in small third party commissions. As an independent you could accommodate any requirement. Which is what counts. You know how it's done, don't you?"

"I've a good idea."

"All you need is the right contacts. In this country." He looked around the great exhibition hall to remind me that we were in Switzerland. "I have to be at arm's length, you know?"

"I know."

"There are many deals I could do which I can't do now. I have heard a lot about you. Everyone trusts you. That is the biggest asset you have. Don't throw it away."

"Let me get this straight. You're suggesting I become your agent and distributor outside Italy, right?"

He smiled carefully. "In a way. But not exclusively. And nothing on paper. There will be business I need to keep for myself. There will be other business for which I'll need you. You can also do as many other kinds of business as you want, providing we do not clash. It's a gentleman's agreement, Johnny. That way we're both independent. There's no limiting each other. Nothing written down. I would not hamper your own development nor you mine. But we would co-operate closely."

I must have hesitated because he leant forward anxiously over the table. "The British dimension is one you can use to great advantage. Don't take another job, Johnny. You can do much better. You must remember many opportunities you couldn't follow whilst working for those dumb clucks." He jerked a head in the direction of the people round us and of the stand. "Companies like that are so musclebound they can't move. A bunch of stupid executives, playing stupid executive games in return for a company car and a comfortable seat in a plane. They care nothing for you, who have travelled the world for them. Nor will the next crowd, if you go to work for them. Besides, their power is nearly finished. I'm driving back to Milan tomorrow. Come with me. I'll show you the workshops. We can talk a lot more. You can make a decision then. How about it?"

I learnt afterwards that was Mario all over. Quick, decisive, prone to snap judgements, although in this case it turned out he'd been watching me for nearly two years.

But not from a balcony in Callao.

"OK," I said. "I'll come with you tomorrow."

We shook hands.

From that moment I have never looked back. Betty might scoff at Marine Court but it provides a cover for prosperity carefully concealed.

On the other hand when Katie would reproach me, in one of her semi-mystic, semi-psychic modes, with not being in control of my life, not coming to terms with commitments or quintessences, she had a point. Except to my meetings with her, I've never looked forward, either.

Now, forward or backward philosophies apart, I needed her. I wouldn't be able to do the next bit on my own.

18

In Colombia, the coffee bean research went OK. It went like most of that kind of research does. Most of them said the whole thing was a storm in a teacup, like I did when Lawrence Edwards first talked to me about it over his cappuccino in the café off Northumberland Avenue. Consumerism and bureaucracy gone crazy, they said. No danger at all. The incidence of the fungus-toxin problem was fractional throughout the world. Who's died of coffee? Besides, this was Colombia. Colombia: you know? The place where the best coffee in the world comes from. Where 'we' have all these quality controls and safeguards and 'we' make sure that standards of processing and drying are the most modern, the most advanced, the most thoroughly and rigorously enforced quality control standards there are. Our laboratories are the cynosure of all quality control eyes.

So why steal a coffee bean moisture sensor? I didn't ask them that.

Maybe, they said, maybe the Brazilians might have a problem. Or the Kenyans or, more likely, the Ethiopians or the Indians. Anyway, the ICO would deal with the matter; a technical programme was in hand; assurances could be given. Of course they supported the research sponsored by the ICO. Naturally. That is what the ICO is there for. They referred all enquiries about this fractional problem to Berners Street as a matter of routine, to where suitable responses and suitable reassurances could be given by properly trained, indeed legally trained, people used to dealing with the press and so on. What was the precise nature of my enquiry? A coffee bean moisture meter? They smiled politely, showing courteous interest. The technology could also be used on-line, to check drying processes? More polite, headquarters, suited executive smiles. There were technicians, laboratory technicians, who might be interested in the application of this sort of technology in the field. A professor or two at suitable universities would be glad to have details.

But he wouldn't steal it.

This was interesting, they said, futuristic, but clearly a matter for individual coffee enterprises, of assessment commercially at the end of the day.

By people whose laboratory jobs would be threatened by the replacement of gravimetric testing by modern, on-line technology? Pull the other one, matey, I muttered to myself. An assessing lab man can find a million shades of technical doubt about a new measurement device that threatens him, any amount of precision-related, abstruse queries to keep him in work. If a gadget will revolutionise an industry, solve a process problem it's had for decades, before you plunge your money always remember Machiavelli:

'There is nothing more difficult to plan, more doubtful of success, nor more dangerous to manage than the creation of a new system. For the initiator has the enmity of all who would profit by the preservation of the old institutions and merely lukewarm defenders in those who should gain by the new ones.'

Which was not something I was ready to say to Richard Keane, not yet, although doubtless he had already been finding out the same thing in his own way.

The problem with thinking Machiavelli was that his *dicta* made it less likely that someone would steal the bloody thing, not more. Let alone kill for it.

I did my work in Barranqilla and Bogotá after Katie and I had done the sights of Cartagena, those forts where Drake won and Vernon and Wentworth lost, leaving South America clear of British conquest. There was no further contact of any kind with Victoria Street. After a memorable weekend I put Katie on her flight back to São Paulo with fond and genuine farewell regrets but I was not too upset. I said I knew I'd see her again soon. She smiled enigmatically, a smile that said don't take too much for granted, my lad. She liked to do that, to keep the frisson alive.

In Barranquilla, Serfaty went through another caper about my attitude but since I wasn't budging he agreed to come to Milan to see the machine. Which was what he intended all along. My visit had been part of a softening-up process, no more. Business, other people think, is boring because of its set rituals and lack of intellectual stimulus. I think it's like serving at the start of a game of tennis: you can't win if the ball doesn't go obediently into the opposite quarter of the court, but you can never be certain how it will come back.

After a day or so I phoned Katie at her flat in São Paulo to see if she was safely home. There was no reply. I left a message on her machine. Her absence made me feel uneasy. The next day I tried again, visualising Katie, fragrant and well-dressed, back in her executive role. There was still no reply, at a time when she should have been home. This increased my anxiety. All too soon, normal life closes back in again. Foreign adventures, foreign affairs, rapidly lose their exhilaration once work and familiar routines take back their grip. Katie had responsibilities, a place, a position to maintain. She had Carlos to deal with. Her English pirate was a peripheral being. Was she regretting my proposed reappearance? Did she not realise I needed her now, urgently?

I tried to clarify the terrible thoughts that were gathering in my head. When I got back to my hotel room after my various inter- views and enquiries each day, I sat thinking about Pulford and Lawrence Edwards. He'd never asked me to do this kind of thing before. He used to tap my brains, pose hypothetical questions, pos- tulate situations full of innuendo. We had an odd set of conversa- tions now that I thought about it. I kept in with him for the reasons I've already stated: it's better to know where the sharks are than to have to quit the ocean. I think he liked to have me to bounce ideas off, make enquiries that very often had to do with documentary credit frauds – they are, after all, the most successful way to steal money these days – seen from someone at the operating end. Conversely, Lawrence's lines of questioning gave me insights into the way that his kind operates.

He'd never introduced me to a colleague before. William Pulford was a first-off. Had Lawrence had some kind of premonition of danger, some deep reservation that just this once led him to spread the risk in case something happened? He must have thought that William Pulford was substantial, someone who could look after himself; why else bring him into our conversation?

I began to wonder if Lawrence was just lonely. Maybe he thought of himself as a kind of policeman with an informant, a grass, a snout, which was a galling thought. He never got any specific case knowledge out of me in previous conversations, except for a particular case over the fraudulent shipment to South Africa, on which I'd helped him. Usually, we were too much at arm's length for specifics, confining ourselves to theory, matters of mercantile law and observed practice. So why, now, this particular enquiry, this particular subject? What extra dimension, one that his regular enquirers weren't right for, did it have?

Had he recorded my engagement? What on earth had he been doing? He must have cleared the expenses somehow, informed a boss of some sort? I was sure that Graham Robinson was only a squeaker. Much more senior men lurked behind him. What did they know of me?

And that woman, Frances Parks: who was she? Where had she gone?

The clandestine aspect nagged like a sore tooth. Lawrence could have had a slush fund, accountable only at certain regular intervals. Suppose he had decided to keep this enquiry under his hat until the very end, made no record? So no one knew about me? The Robinson man almost certainly didn't, not from what he'd said. Yet telephone conversations could have been recorded, my name must be down somewhere in Lawrence's list of contacts, a list that Robinson would now be combing through. It was, however, possible that so far no record of what I was actually doing was down on paper anywhere in Lawrence's department. I could be alone. I might have been entirely private to him.

Oddly enough, as long as I was in Colombia I felt quite safe; Bogotá is no problem for the experienced traveller these days; Cali is the place to avoid, along with up-country villages. Crazy though, wasn't it? A drug peddler, a mugger, might have a go at me any time but not for things inspired by Victoria Street and stolen coffee beanometers and worse. Why? I wasn't a threat to anyone in Colombia, that's how I rationalised it. And Victoria Street wouldn't be keen to follow me there; people who work in Victoria Street aren't hot on risking themselves, personally.

Colombia has become like so many places: somewhere where you don't put an arm with a watch on it out of a car window, somewhere you always take precautions, have locks and grills all over your house, don't walk alone at night. Somewhere that you get nervous at the traffic lights if anyone looks like coming up to the car, where women don't wear even the cheapest jewellery to go downtown shopping if they ever go downtown shopping. It is a place where your car is worth killing you for, where people break in and torture you before killing you, where you get so you don't leave your hotel if you start thinking too much. I once saw a German walk out of a hotel in Baltimore carrying a camera and a gent's natty shoulder bag with his money, passport and credit cards in it slung over his shoulder. They sliced the lot off him, roughly, so that flesh got sliced too, within sixty yards of the hotel entrance. So maybe Colombia's just like everywhere else now, only more so.

I did the rounds but I didn't seem to be getting anywhere. No one showed any real interest in me or the coffee bean analyser.

If I had been a threat to anyone in Colombia I wouldn't have got out of Barranquilla alive. Or been able to operate in Bogotá.

I decided I was wasting my time in Colombia. If I was safe, I wasn't getting anywhere. I must be a long way from that moisture sensor.

Where was Katie? Why had she gone so completely off screen?

In a bit of a temper at the way she'd vanished, I called Betty for a soothing chat about something, anything, other than the things that were bugging me.

She didn't answer either.

I caught an early flight to Belo Horizonte.

19

"Nassim called me," Mario said. "He says he and his brother will be here in Milan at the end of next week."

"Good."

"How are things with Texteis Arochena?"

"Going to plan."

"First come, first served, eh? The first to put his money down gets the machine."

"As always."

I was in Belo Horizonte, among the mountains of Minas Gerais. From outside, Brazilian sounds and smells came through the open hotel window: Latin calls and cries, a distant throb of samba, wafts of coffee and frying of food. I had been served with the regulation papaya for breakfast but hadn't eaten it. I find it sickly at that time of the morning.

The line between me and Mario in Milan was as clear as could be but down in São Paulo Katie still didn't answer her home telephone.

She wasn't at Atibaia, either. I was worried about where the hell she had got to.

"The machine is coming on nicely, Johnny. We've run it up to three hundred already. But it's costing. Everything is so expensive these days."

"Sure."

"I'm glad you didn't yield on price."

"Of course not."

"Nassim Serfaty sounded just a little piqued about you. A little strange, he seemed. Well, maybe not piqued so much as disappointed. A bit distant, detached. He said you were a serious man, which is good, but not very co-operative."

"That's what I'm there for. If he wants the usual commission arrangements, Mario, he can't argue."

There was a chuckle. Financial shenanigans always appeal to Italians. "You'll use the usual company?"

"Most likely. Or perhaps another this time. Spread things about a bit. It's important not to be too visible."

"*Eco*. You're a boy, Johnny, really you are. How are you? Trip going OK? The Colombian girls obliging?"

"Fine, Mario. Just fine."

"Take care. See you soon."

"*Ciao*, Mario."

"*Ciao*, Johnny."

I put the phone down, thought for a minute, picked it up and called Katie's office number. We had an agreement that I didn't often do this; she didn't like pleasure to interfere with her work image, but sometimes it was necessary. Like when I was anxious.

Eventually, I was put through to her extension.

"Alloa?" That's how it sounds in Brazil.

"That must be Gladys," I said cheerfully. "It's Johnny Barber here."

"Senhor Johnny!" The very feminine voice of Katie's frilly secretary turned a tone richer, deeper, yet even more feminine at the same time. Boss's lovers were, according to Katie, an enduring source of employee speculation, scandal, gossip, amusement and prestige. Probably in that order. "How are you?"

"Fine, Gladys. You?"

"Oh yes." She drew out the positive just a shade over the respectable. "I am very well."

"Is Katie available?"

"No, I am sorry Senhor Johnny, she is not here just now."

"Oh. Will she be back soon?"

"Actually, I do not know. I think she is travelling, doing a special project for Senhor Carlos."

"I see. Do you know how long for?"

"I'm sorry?"

"I mean, do you know how long she will be away? Is she in contact with you? When are you expecting her back?"

"Senhor Johnny, I don't know. Maybe she will call in soon. Do you want me to give her a message?"

"No, that's OK. Just tell her I called and I'll call again in a day or two. When I'm in São Paulo."

"Very good! You are coming to São Paulo?"

"Yes I am."

Gladys's voice turned a shade richer still. "Senhora Katie will be very pleased, I am sure."

"I'm glad to hear it."

"But of course! I will tell her."

"OK. *Obrigado*, Gladys."

"It's always a pleasure, Senhor Johnny."

Oh is it, I nearly muttered as I put the phone down again, oh is it Gladys my girl, I wouldn't be too sure if I were you. Katie hadn't mentioned any special project while we were in Colombia. She said she was looking forward to seeing me soon. Was this departure due to a sudden change, a freezing of affection, or some iffy scheme of Carlos Guimares'? Something to keep her away for a while? If so, why? He'd never bothered much about my visits before.

My phone rang. Still half-muttering, I picked it up.

"Senhor Johnny? Johnny Barber?"

I recognised the voice of Euripides Arochena, the head of Texteis Arochena. I had already spent a couple of hours in negotiation with him and his managers. Arochena, like Gonzalez, is originally a Spanish surname, northern Spain actually, but this Arochena was as Brazilian as they all are, even to the extent of being christened with one of those Greek Tragic or similarly semi-Classical first names so beloved of the country. In this case a playwright, hey?

"Senhor Euripides? Yes it's Johnny here."

"We must talk. I am coming to pick you up. Please leave your hotel and go to the corner. By the kiosk. About twenty minutes?"

"OK."

I put down the phone and looked out of my hotel window with a slight smile. Our negotiations, so far, had been as much dramatic fiction as the works of the original Euripides. In this case the company's managers provided the theatre audience.

I did not have to wait by the kiosk for very long before Arochena's vehicle rolled into view. He was wearing dark glasses. I got in from the pavement at his quick, guilty gesture from behind the wheel. He was small, plump, middle-aged, quizzical, driving a large Japanese car far too powerful for a driver as cautious as he was, nervously flicking his gaze from side to side to watch the prolific, abandoned traffic for which Brazil is famous as we pulled out from the kerb.

Or maybe he was looking for something else.

"We will go out of town a little," he announced. "There is a small park where we can stop and talk without disturbance."

"As you wish Senhor Euripides."

"Please. Call me Euri."

"OK, Euri. I'm Johnny."

"Your hotel is comfortable?"

"Fine."

He nodded almost absently, flinching at a truck whose rattling mudguards menaced close by. Conversation languished for some fifteen minutes until, after traversing a suburban boulevard lined with dark trees, the car pulled into a formal park rather like those in most provincial cities the world over. There was a bandstand, a children's section with swings, flower beds and well-worn grass. There were notices forbidding the practice of football. He got out of the car, still in dark glasses, and I followed, noticing how his lightweight suit threads glistened where the sun caught its creases, just as scalp glistened through the threads of his hair.

"How about an ice cream?" he queried, heading enthusiastically towards a white, windowed vehicle adorned with parodies of Mickey Mouse and Donald Duck before I had time to answer.

"Coffee flavour," I said, as he turned in front of a picture card at the counter to ask which type I wanted. Appropriate, I thought.

He grinned vaguely, ordered a coffee ice cream and a pistachio and turned to scan the area from behind his shades. Seemingly satisfied, he took delivery of the ice creams, paid for them and gestured towards a bench under nearby trees.

"Let us sit."

We strolled across, licking the ices.

"You have been to Belo Horizonte before?"

"No, never. Nice place. Developing fast, eh?"

"But Brazil?"

"Many times."

He nodded, satisfied. "You know, then, how difficult things have been for us recently?"

"Indeed. It must be very hard to keep ahead in business."

"Just so." He sat, and I sat next to him. "I have been grateful for your patience, Johnny. It is most appreciated. Many Europeans, and especially Americans, do not understand our problems. The debt repayments –" he sighed, as all Brazilians do when mentioning this topic – "are crippling. I believe that the American bankers should wipe the slate clean. Think of the money they have put in as an investment. Liquidate it completely and start again."

For a moment I hesitated, pedantically ready to ask him how he defined the word investment and whether a return of some sort was what was might be expected, but decided not to. I just nodded sagely. At least, it was what I consider to be my sage mode of nod.

"You are sympathetic, I see that. And you have been very professional in your quotation and discussions so far. I am grateful to you for your discretion. My managers now, they are a different question." He took out a handkerchief and wiped a fleck of ice cream from the corner of his mouth. "They do not see the business the way we do."

"No?"

"No. For them it is simply a question of the pay cheque at the end of the month, security, their families of course, and recreation. I do not say that they do not do their jobs, they would not be allowed to continue if they didn't, but they do not have the perspective of an owner."

"Indeed not."

"We have had a very difficult time. I have to consider my long-term security. You understand?"

"Of course." I nodded approvingly. Well I would, wouldn't I? The very root of my existence was about to come to light.

Arochena put on a serious expression. "I am committed to Brazil, as committed as anyone, as much as these politicians we have who destroy our economy, devalue our currency and line their own pockets with funds in foreign countries. Bribed by Americans, Japanese, Germans and others."

"Ah."

"You are a man of the world, Johnny. You know what I mean?"

"Indeed I do." Another approving nod. "What can I do to help?"

"To the point, eh? You really are an Englishman. Always to the point. You must realise that I have to safeguard my interests. There are other people quoting for this contract, for this machine. The Americans in particular are very keen. And there is a big Japanese company, too. They are pressing very hard, with very good credit terms. One or two of my managers are quite enthusiastic about their equipment."

"Their prices must be much higher than mine."

"Exactly. I do not say you are not competitive, although theirs are new machines. Even though we do not really need a new machine, here in Belo Horizonte, people do not always see things that way. Especially not the authorities. But tell me: you did provide some margin of – of negotiation?"

"I did, as you asked when you originally phoned me."

"But not enough, Johnny. The margin I mentioned is not going to be enough. Things have changed a lot here in the last few weeks. One could say that they have changed dramatically. It is important that you provide more."

"I've already quoted. Your managers have copies. It would be difficult to alter the figures now."

"You have only one machine? You couldn't quote for say a higher specification, an enhanced production line? A faster machine? At higher price?"

Well, well, I thought, Johnny my boy, you are in demand these days. He wants more jam put away for him. In Switzerland. But Mario's machine is the only one on my books just now.

"Euri, I could arrange for a quote to come from one of my other companies. Without my signature. A quote that would look quite different even though it would be the same machine. When you come over to Europe to see it running, you could fly to Switzerland. I'd drive you over the border to Milan. To all intents and purposes you'd be buying a machine in Switzerland from a Swiss operation. My name would not appear on any documents. My – my Swiss partner, who is a lawyer, would do the necessary. That way an extra margin could be accommodated without problems. I am assuming it is a question of extra margin we are dealing with here? To be put away in an account of your choosing as originally envisaged?" I put on an earnest expression. "This is quite normal, you understand."

He licked his lips. Just across from where we were sitting a pair of women strolled across the grass, calling out at a gaggle of brown children who ran shrieking behind them.

I kept my expression earnest as we watched them walk by. "It is important, as you say, Euri, to consider the future."

He nodded, letting his eyes run upwards into the surrounding tree tops as though there might be microphones in them, listening.

"Very important," he whispered. "And you can arrange this, Johnny?"

"With ease. Have done so many times. You can trust me because it is my business, the business in which I stay."

He nodded again.

"What sort of margin are you looking for, Euri?"

A thick tongue flecked with cream came out to lick his lips.

"Half a million," he whispered. "Dollars, of course."

"That's no problem. I'll send a new quote, from a new company, for a machine for one point six million. That way we'll get what we want and so will you. With a little to spare for negotiation and expenses."

He nodded again, wiped his lips again. "You will forgive me for asking this: what safeguards can you offer? About the half million, I mean. If we pay in full, how do I know you'll transfer the money?"

Half of them ask this, half of them don't. They know they're vulnerable about the excess payment, dependent on my good faith to transmit the 'third party commission' after the principal is paid. Although there are separate documents that can be drawn up to cover such arrangements, notarised letters and things like that, I've not heard of them coming out in court anywhere.

I shrugged. "We can get a sworn affidavit at a public notary, if you want. That's the normal safeguard. But I'm not aiming to retire, Euri. My reputation is my business capital; I've never welshed on anyone."

He patted my arm. "I'm sure, I'm sure. Forgive me for asking but you know how the world is nowadays…"

His voice trailed off.

"I understand," I said. "I'll get a letter drawn up and have it notarised when I get back. The best way is to pay the commission in stages. Probably four or five. Half a million might raise eyebrows."

It occurred to me then that he hadn't said what they all usually say: that the money isn't for them personally, it's for the business, for their financial partners, for reinvestment, for keeping the voracious banks at bay, for any reason except personal greed.

"It's your money, after all, Euri," I said. "Why should governments tell you what to do with it?"

He nodded again. "Things have changed so much," he said. A sad note had come into his voice. "To ensure that my company survives I have had to do drastic things. Accept a refinancing. These people are very demanding, they always are. They do not see the business the way an owner sees it. With them it is all just money, not decades of family involvement, effort, employees. Just money. Cash flows and fantasies on paper. They attach such significance to these paper fantasies. If life were like that, there would be no need for any of us, but they use these papers to criticise, to indict, simply because things in reality never turn out like they do on paper."

"Banks are voracious, Euri."

"Not only banks. Financial groups, industrial groups. Here in Brazil they are remorseless. I have to secure my future."

I frowned. "You mean you've taken out loans? Or had to dilute your equity?"

His mouth drew into a bitter line as he finally let out the painful truth. "Dilute? If it were only dilute it would not be so serious. But I have had to reduce my equity to a minority. It was the only thing they would accept. The only way I could ensure the survival of my company."

The brown children had drawn off into the distance. I stared after

131

them, feeling a coldness overcome the warm afternoon air. What Arochena was telling me was that he'd been taken over, bought out, downgraded. His days were almost certainly numbered. Once he'd seen through this new machine project and passed on all his knowledge, they'd heave him out of the door like an old sack. No wonder he wanted his half million safely stashed abroad.

"Who are they?" I demanded. "The new owners?"

"A financial-industrial group. Kellerman, they're called. They have textile and many other interests."

My gaze went out beyond the park towards the hills around the city.

"Including coffee?" I asked.

"Yes. They are quite big in coffee. And animal feeds." A look of alarm was on his face. "You know them?"

"I've heard of them. I've no connection. Have no fear. My discretion is assured."

His expression relaxed in relief. "They are quite big. It's not surprising that you know of them, though they normally work in a rather quiet way. Come, I will drop you off back near your hotel. You can arrange to send the new quotation soon?"

"Oh yes. It'll be very quick."

"Excellent. I much appreciate your efficiency, Johnny."

He stood up. Ice cream time was over. But I hadn't finished yet.

"This group financing you," I asked. "Who's their chief executive?"

He turned full on to me as I stood up as well, close to him. "I have not met him personally. Just his executives, far down his organisation. He is an influential man here in Brazil. Kellerman is only one of his many interests. My company is not nearly important enough for his attention. Why do you ask?"

"Just curious."

My voice was hoarse. Why had my throat gone dry?

Arochena's expression was still bitter. "Guimares. His name is Carlos Guimares. I do not think we need to worry about him." He smiled apologetically, revealing a fleck of pistachio on one of his front teeth. "We are far too small fry for him."

I managed to smile back, trusting that coffee ice cream was absent from my own front choppers. "I'm sure we are," I responded.

I hate coincidences.

Where the hell, I started to wonder frenetically, is Katie?

20

São Paulo was the same as I always remembered it. A vast Latin New York, sprawling in and out of control under hot clouds, spawning new skyscrapered centres designed by unrestrained architects, spreading over old derelict suburbs, always driving, dynamic, industrial. Rio you can keep; Rio is a rip-off for tourists, never the same since I first saw it from the deck of a Royal Mail steamer, the *Alcantara*, in the magic mist of morning when life was an opening bud not a tired old blossom. Rio is for the travel magazines bent on wearing pretty paths down to hard core; São Paulo is for real.

I used, in my abundant executive days, to stay at the hotel Gran Ca D'Oro or the first Hilton, at the top of the Avenida de la Republica. I could stroll down the barking pavements to buy a paper at a kiosk or drink a tiny piping hot *caffezinho* – almost as much sugar as thick black coffee, a pure blood pressure pump – at a stand or sidewalk café. I could speculate whether the newspaper kiosk was the same one my father used to mention when he trumpeted that on the Republica there was a newspaper vendor who could speak five languages fluently – pause for effect – and had nothing to say in any of them.

Once, at Katie's behest, I took an all-in apartment for a week, which turned out to be no more expensive than the small, good hotels I normally use. When we started off and were more reckless I stayed at Katie's – it was a bit of sexual scalp-waving on her part – but then she decided her image had to avoid that sort of thing. Her position in the company was getting more responsible, more serious. Or maybe she got frightened of Carlos, despite her mystic influence. There had to be limits to her impudence.

So where the hell was she?

I went round to her apartment block, surveyed the area for menaces, then chatted up the doorkeeper/porter, the *sereno*, who guarded the lobby from intruders and watched the underground garage on CCTV. Bandits in São Paulo have been known to wait until a woman drives her car through automatic doors into the garage, nip in behind the vehicle and grab her when she parks in the convenient, sound-insulated gloom. One woman of my acquaintance was held up at knifepoint in a lift in a big office building. The intruder took her handbag and shopping, made her strip down to her knickers, took her clothes and then ran for it without pausing for any brief sexual gratification. She thought she was lucky. That's big city life for you these days.

The *sereno* in the porter's lodge was a new guy and didn't know me from Adam. He was genial all the same. Senhora Katie had left a few days ago, the company car came for her, she had a bag, not a big one, like say overnight. That didn't mean anything. Katie had clothes in different places. No, there'd been no one else to visit, just the maid to clean up as usual. Was I a very old friend of Senhora Katie's? How was life in England, what a disaster the last World Cup was in France, all Brazil was still shaken up by it but Tokyo will be fine. Were Manchester United still top of the Premier Division, fantastic finish to the Bayern Munich match wasn't it, but they had a lousy visit here, behaved arrogantly, didn't take it seriously at all.

We parted on excellent terms.

Still no Katie. Katie had without doubt known all about Texteis Arochena and said nothing. Now she'd disappeared, just when Euripedes Arochena was at the mercy of Carlos Guimares.

I went downtown, the old downtown I knew so well, the Republica near the square, drank a *caffezinho*, bought a paper, leafed idly through it as I sat at a table on the pavement, thinking. The business news didn't say anything about coffee in particular, just things about demand and prices and international speculation. There was mention of the hi-jacking of containers en route to Santos now and then. Nothing new, it said, to that. I leafed over another page, preparing to discard the newspaper, and stopped.

Images are like a game of pelmanism; memory holds the key.

There, in a side-column about economics and visitors, was a face I knew. A blurred shot of a suited man at the airport with other suited men beside him took up nearly half a page. Minister Anthony Barnwell, it said in the caption, arriving from the United Kingdom, for talks on unilateral agreements for the development of Brazil-UK trade. I recognised him right away: that blowhard Tony Barnwell, Secretary of State for some ramification of the DTI, well out of the mainstream but full of bull nevertheless, the man I'd last thought of when talking to Lawrence Edwards in a café off Northumberland Avenue. The man who'd made the best publicity possible out of Richard Keane's coffee bean moisture analyser. Who'd been at a reception at the ICO, according to Edwards.

So what? Coincidence, that was probably what.

I hate coincidence; as you get older, you hate it more and more.

A Secretary of State must surely have a thousand items on his agenda? I looked again. A paragraph below the photograph said that Barnwell would be talking to relevant Government officials now that stability was returning to the currency and there was much positive action to take on both sides. He'd be meeting business leaders as well. In a prepared statement he said he welcomed the joint ventures between British companies and Brazilian ones in interior development of an ecologically approved nature. The world worried about the rain forest but he understood Brazil's needs. He was sympathetic to the current situation in the coffee markets because coffee, after oil, is the world's most traded commodity and Britain, as an oil producer, knew only too well the problems and stresses incurred by surpluses in commodities so essential to certain markets.

I lowered the paper, thinking: the current situation in coffee markets?

I'd done quite a bit of work up in Belo Horizonte, from the coffee angle as well as Euripides Arochena's. There were all sorts of problems everyone wanted to talk about. Brazilian coffee is known for strength because a lot of it is from the Robusta variety, often dry cured – Colombian is mainly Arabica, wet cured – but not always – which puts many of the Brazilians at the cheap end of the market, in competition with Africa. They do grow Arabica in Brazil, recognising that this is the most widely cultivated coffee in the world, with a richer, more aromatic flavour, but it is easy for an outsider to oversimplify things. All sorts of people have intervened, bought up plantations, brought other methods, a bit like Australians producing claret in Bordeaux. It can be very emotional to the locals. Then there are factors of climate, altitude, yields, soil, picking cycles, mechanisation. Growing was not the only problem. Crime came into it.

Crime?

Between the plantations and the coast, en route to Santos for export, containers of coffee beans were being hi-jacked by bandits who didn't seem to have heard of quotas, price regulation and international agreements or, if you are unkind, cartels. These containers disappeared quite regularly, so much so that the paper I had in my hand right then regarded the crime as pretty routine.

You think fungus is a problem? You want to sell an electronic device to measure infinitesimal amounts of moisture? There are more pressing things to worry about, they said to me, on my rounds. We're not neglecting any aspect of processing but there are priorities just a little more trying on the nerves than how an occasional bean isn't quite the right dryness and decides to develop an esoteric toxin. That no one drinking his Mocha Java or Jamaican Blue Mountain is going to notice.

They said they didn't need a sensor.

We wish, some of them said, we had the time to sit and think about things like that. It would be nice to do research instead of checking washed beans spread out on mats in the sunshine for three weeks, having to rake them several times a day to ensure even drying before they're milled to get the dried hulk parchment and silver skin off, as they do in Brazil. Before they're bagged and sent off as green beans.

Then they get stolen.

But Tony Barnwell was here in Brazil, right now, just at the time the beanometer was missing and someone had knocked both Lawrence Edwards and William Pulford into the middle of the next world.

I hate coincidences.

The newspaper said that the British Minister was holding a reception this evening at an international trade institute at which Anglo-Brazilian traders and businessmen would be present to meet him. They would put forward informal views on the direction in which mutual co-operation between these two friendly countries might progress with particular reference to the EEC's attitude to the world's developing economies, especially such aspects as debt servicing and access to EEC markets.

At the table next to me a muscular brown girl with a bare midriff crossed her legs to let a mini skirt ride right up her thigh. She leant forward to take a cigarette from her companion, a silver-haired man in a check shirt, black trousers and black leather basketwork shoes no gentleman would dream of wearing. The man smiled as the girl's eyes smouldered at his, pulled a lighter out of his shirt pocket, clicked it with a practised thumb and let the girl hold his hand as she steadied the lighter flame to the end of her cigarette. Her hand slid down his wrist in a caress as she blew a puff of smoke sideways, then she settled back in her chair to show even more brown, firm, smooth thigh almost as good as Katie's.

The lighter was a modern, gas-fired, automatic, mass-produced, unadjustable thing. No metal case with hinged sprung lid, petrol filler cap, knurled striker knob, flint adjustment, flame length adjustment, perforated wind guard, maybe even a knitted wick. None of that. No advert for the Caterpillar Tractor Company. Not much scope for engineering skills or too many picaresque uses in hotels down in Rio Grande do Sul.

Richard Keane had given me a pack of his business cards to use in case of really specific, genuine enquiries. The pack was still intact. It was no good sitting about hoping for messes to be cleared up by someone else or for Katie to reappear by magic. Nothing happens to those who do nothing.

I got up and headed back to my hotel to change, feeling a tingle of irreverent anticipation.

I hadn't been to an official trade reception for ages. It was at a trade reception that I'd met Katie, caught my first sight of Carlos. Fate had made trade receptions symbolic.

It was time to apply my lighter to a pile of soiled tissue paper.

21

"There is," his secretary apparently said to Mario Chiari that afternoon, "someone watching this factory."

Mario was looking at the installation drawing for a Fife edge guide he was about to fit to the non-woven feed roll on the machine and was preoccupied.

"What?" he demanded.

The girl, who was called Chica, gesticulated at the outer window. The wide office straddled both outer and inner walls so that the windows on one side looked over the car park towards the main road from Milan to Sesto San Giovanni or Monza. The other side looked over the workshops. Chica's desk was by the outer window. When she was typing at her PC she could relax occasionally by looking out at the weather and thinking that working here was not like working in central Milan, there were no nice shops to look at at lunchtime but at least the boss didn't seem to think he had the right to bend you over his desk for his pleasure. Or screw you in his car on the way home. He was obsessed by his machines but otherwise he was a nice man, considerate, and rebuked those two apprentices when they said coarse things to her down in the workshop. Not that Chica couldn't look after herself and give them back the rough edge of her tongue, so that one of them, Piero, the gentler one with the curly hair, blushed in shame.

"That Fiat Uno," she said. "The red one parked just off the main road near the bus stop. It's been there every morning this week. There's a man in it with a mobile phone and a pair of binoculars. When that last delivery truck came in with the steel bar we ordered, he made notes and then used his phone."

Mario put down the drawing and went to the window, frowning. Part of him disapproved of Chica's window gazing, part wanted to praise her. The area had, like all of Milan, a chronic parking problem. There were cars scattered all along the side road to the factory, on the verges beside it and, where possible, in the aisle down the centre. Most were small Fiats of mass production, anonymous, ubiquitous, unremarkable. The red one Chica was talking about was no different, dulled by mud, at least four or five years old. She must have very sharp eyes, he thought, young eyes, because I can just make out that there is someone in it, at the wheel, but it's hard to see what he's doing.

"You're sure?" he demanded. "It looks like any other Fiat Uno to me."

"Every day this week," Chica said, straightening her back so that her bosom stood out prominently for a brief moment. "I didn't pay much attention because there are always reps stopping on the side road here and that's what I thought he was until I noticed the binoculars. They all have mobile phones these days but binoculars—what does a rep want with binoculars? There's no scope for a Peeping Tom here."

Mario deepened his frown, trying to make out the car interior with more clarity. He compressed his lips, then drew back from the window. If it really was a prowler, an investigator, who the hell was he working for? The tax man? No; Mario's relationship with the local tax people, corporate, personal and VAT, was sometimes fractious but certainly not so terminal as to be in any way requiring this sort of observation.

On the other hand, his Swiss funds might have been leaked in some way, but he didn't think so. Mario was an expert in disguising Swiss funds.

Was it the competition, maybe? What competition? The new machine builders were too grand to bother much with him but one or two of the rebuilders like himself might be mounting a jealous watch. What good would that do them? They all knew how these machines were rebuilt, it wasn't rocket science for God's sake, most of the applicators and the guides and the electrics and electronics came from the same companies.

So who? And why?

"Go to the workshop," he said to Chica, "and tell old Guiseppe, who has eyes like a hawk, to go up on the roof behind the water tank

140

and get the licence number. You show him which car but don't let the driver see that he's caught our attention."

Mario had a pal in the right administrative office, one to do with parking fines and traffic offences, who owed him a favour. Once he had the number he phoned up his contact, who said it would take a little time. True to his word and his obligation he phoned back an hour later. The car didn't belong to any administrative office, tax or otherwise. It was registered to a private individual called Bernasconi. No particular private individual as far as the contact knew; never heard of him. The address was suburban Milanese.

Mario thanked his contact and said the favours were back to him now. He went to the window, pretending to give Chica some work and scowled out at the Fiat. A snoop; whose snoop? Why? A sudden mad idea that his wife might have put a snoop on him crossed his mind but he banished it quickly; he wasn't giving her any reason for such suspicions. At that moment he said he then thought of me, Johnny Barber, but you know how Italians are; always out to flatter. It could very likely be that, he thought: something to do with Switzerland, or Johnny, or the two of us together. I'll have to warn Johnny next time he calls.

22

Government trade services were not popular with my father. He had an instinctive dislike for officialdom and lumped the Board of Trade, as it was before it became the DTI, together with the morass of technically ignorant, bureaucratic interference he resented. He thought that the Government simply hampered good business. Lawrence Edwards must have perceived a residue of this in my attitude and hoped, in his own dyspeptic fashion, either to catch me out or to get me to admit some sort of respect. I felt sorry about that but it was too late to apologise for my remarks about DTI consultants. The whole thing started early on, with a blunder by some ex-colonel in Lima my father often recounted, another good story I'll save for a more suitable occasion.

I once told him that things had changed quite a bit since his day but he wasn't convinced.

"They're all cocktail parties and games of tennis," he growled. "Useless. Parasites. We don't need ambassadors any more, not with modern communications, and businessmen should run the trade offices. Until 1914 Britain had just nine ambassadors abroad. We were powerful then. There are dozens of the pompous little beggars everywhere now. Parkinson's Law."

I got to Tony Barnwell's cocktail party in São Paulo at what I thought to be a well-judged moment. That was well after it had time to get going. Never arrive too early if you don't want to be the subject of unwanted attention. The venue was at a Centro Empresarial of the modern sort, built away from the old city centre in a rapidly developing location but isolated in corporate grandeur from downtown, like say Canary Wharf is from London. It still smelled vaguely of cement and freshly-cut marble, like an hotel on the Costa Brava.

There were three grey suits blocking the doorway to the reception suite; one a worn forty-odd in suede shoes, with long untidy hair and an old narrow trouser style. The other two had short back and sides in the Essex manner, with lower halves in baggy strides above crinkled black leather feet. One of them was Brazilian. I gave long-hair, narrow trousers my borrowed card and caught a glance of approval as he looked at my own suit, one of Tunbridge Wells' finest I'd pressed myself with a travelling iron. Inside, beyond these three, I could hear a hubbub of voices. A waiter went past with a tray of glistening drinks.

"Mr Richard Keane?" Long-hair consulted a sheaf of papers. "Keane Electronics? I don't think I've got your name on this list."

"Just got to São Paulo," I brayed genially. "Lawrence Edwards and Graham Robinson at the DTI in Victoria Street said to be sure to come to this. We've just been given a Smart award. Electronic development, you know? They said they'd e-mail you to make sure. Mustn't miss it, they said."

"Oh gawd," the English one of the short back and sides Essex boys groaned, "it wasn't a UK Trade e-mail was it?"

I grinned. "That's it. Bit hard to download, those things, I find, actually. My Internet browser always makes a hash of them. Either says my printer hasn't got enough memory, which is rubbish of course, or that there is a fault. It's the Not-So-Smart award now, is it?"

"Hash?" he grumbled. "Mine crashes the PC nine times out of ten. Especially if there's a .tif attachment. Freezes it bloody solid."

"It's called technology," I said cheerfully. "In the old days they used to post things to you. Then there were telexes. Why they can't use the fax is a mystery to me."

Long-hair was still looking at my card. "Sussex," he said, getting things back under control. "You're in Sussex are you?"

"East Sussex, yes."

"Not too far from Bexhill that, isn't it?" He was still squinting at the card; you'd never guess we were in São Paulo.

"About seven miles inland."

"Nice country round there."

"We think so. Sheep, hops, electronics. All the rural industries."

He managed to smile. "Look, there's obviously been a slip-up somewhere, Mr Keane. The Minister's very keen – oh, forgive me, no pun intended – to make sure as many British businessmen come to this as possible. Good for the image and all that. Please go ahead. Help yourself to a drink. I'll keep your card for the record if that's OK with you."

"Of course."

"I can't give you a lapel badge because we've not been advised you were coming. I can do a hand-written one if you–"

"Forget it," I said. "I hate lapel badges. Need my glasses to read 'em."

I gave the Essex e-mail boy another grin and sailed past up a short flight of marble stairs into a reception hall. The hubbub was a bit misleading because the place wasn't all that full, sort of medium full, but voices bounced around the new hall's acoustics. A waiter hove alongside and I took a glass of white wine off him, Chilean it was, but I suppose you don't get Lamberhurst or Sedlescombe much around São Paulo, not even at an official British reception.

A rather flustered guy in a lightweight suit that was far too pale in colour for an oversize constitution bustled out from the throng and said, "Welcome, Mr – ?"

"Keane," I responded obediently. "Richard Keane. Keane Electronics."

It's funny what the word electronics does. If I'd said Keane Machinery or, say, Keane Paper or Keane Bog Roll Processing or Keane Activated Sludge, which probably all make much more money and employ many thousands, he'd have flinched, made some excuse and gone barking off back into the crowd. As it was he blinked, beamed and said electronics eh, that's the ticket, I must meet the Minister, he'd be delighted to see me.

"Bully for him," I said.

We threaded through a mainly masculine mob punctuated by occasional overdressed ladies, some secretarial, some wifely but some obviously executive, flashing their peepers at all and sundry surrounding them until we came to a brief clearing, a respectful pause, as it were, in the elbowing jungle. A tall, pinstriped, horn-rimmed Tony Barnwell stood talking to a group of businessmen who seemed to be hanging on his every word. As we approached the whole group leaned backwards in an exaggerated laugh posture and then righted itself again. The Minister must have cracked a joke, following which he smoothed down his distinguished, flowing white hair and took a tiny sip from a wine glass full of orange juice.

"May I introduce?" The light-suited Larry took advantage of the pause that followed. "Mr Keane, Minister. Keane Electronics."

"Ah." Barnwell turned a rather intense stare on me as others fell slightly back and we shook hands. "Electronics, eh? One of our key development projects. Instrumentation, is it?"

His face had a worn but prepared sort of look, the skin leathery but perhaps dressed with something, like an actor about to go on stage. I wondered whether he used a foundation cream, shook the thought off, smiled at him.

"Yes," I said, wondering if that meant he'd remembered his posturing at the ICO about Richard's analyser. "That sort of thing."

"What kind?"

"High frequency microwave. For moisture sensing."

"Really?" Still no overt sign of recognition but, was it just my imagination, a slightly tense look to the corners of the crinkled eyes, a caution in the set of the dressed face. "Are you doing business in Brazil?"

"Not yet," I answered, easily. "My first visit, actually. Coffee's the thing for us."

"Ah." He actually flinched, then put his face back to normal, if what I was coming to think of more and more as a mask could be normal. "Excellent. Coffee, eh? Excellent. You're in the right place, then. Nothing like prospecting the market yourself."

No, it wasn't tension; following the flinch, it was puzzlement. Something had thrown him; I was wrong. I wasn't what he'd expected. Yet Richard Keane had never been to the ICO himself, had dealt with the Swiss almost at arm's length except for a visit by a technical nerd from their laboratories who'd done all the assessment and approval before the order had been issued. So what had Barnwell expected?

Someone younger, perhaps.

Or no one at all? Was someone watching Richard?

"I hope our chaps from the DTI have been helpful?" he queried, official hat suddenly coming on, formal response taking over like an automatic programme on an officious computer.

"Very good. Most informative. I just wondered–"

"Minister?" Light-suited Larry was back again, hopping on one foot. "The Chamber of Commerce delegation have arrived." He turned to me. "Sorry. Have to wrench the Minister away."

"Ah." Barnwell's expression exuded relief. "Please excuse me, Mr, er–"

"Keane. Richard Keane."

"Yes. Of course." He almost peered into my face, as though to memorise it. "Excuse me. Duty calls." His eyes, which I now noticed were brown, held mine intensely. "I hope your trip goes well. Perhaps we can catch up with each other later."

"I hope so."

"Good luck, then."

"You too, Minister."

He looked a bit startled at this, grinned vaguely, nodded, and plunged off in the wake of the light suit. A dour-looking man in a charcoal jacket smiled wryly at me.

"Short and sweet, eh? Had your pep talk from Our Leader?"

"Oh yes."

'Government on your side and all that?"

"Never."

He chuckled. "Nor mine, neither. Never heard of a level playing field, that lot. Bloody third world concessions to every crook in existence."

I didn't answer. Barnwell had stopped in front of four well-dressed men, all Brazilian presumably. Lightweight Larry was doing some introducing. I didn't know three of them but the fourth sent a paralysing chill down my spine. He'd got a shade heavier and his hair was greyer. He'd probably say the same of me if he remembered what I looked like from a younger photo of me on holiday in Bariloche I knew Katie used to have somewhere on display in her flat.

She had one of him too. We were like trophies.

It was Carlos Guimares.

He looked as fine-tuned as ever. As though he'd just come out of the barber's and been fitted, as he emerged, with a brand-new suit from the finest tailor in town. His skin was without blemish, his brown eyes wide and compelling, his smile knowing, intelligent, receptive yet assessing, the expression not revealing the snap judgements made every time he looked at a man or, usually with more interest, a woman. Impeccable. Distinguished. Rich, unmistakably rich, and powerful, used to getting his way every time.

There was a good deal of handshaking, talking, elbow gripping, general meeting and greeting going on between Barnwell and the group, including Guimares. Other sleek-looking directorial types started to join them. The dour man continued to spout into my ear about government ignorance on manufacturing industry. I let him, grunting monosyllabic answers of assent to encourage him to keep ranting.

After a while, the group started to divide into lesser units. Guimares and Barnwell seemed to stay naturally together, as two of the most important people present except for a couple of Brazilian high-up trade ministers, might well do. They stood face to face, too far away for me to hear what they were talking about. Barnwell, casually, turned as he was talking to let his gaze sweep the room. It stopped on me for just a little longer than I liked. He turned back to listen to something Guimares was saying then answered, speaking quickly. Guimares paused; just as casually, his gaze came round to look at me. A still moment kept him gazing, the stare going fixed. Almost with an effort he broke the stare and turned through a hundred and eighty degrees to speak to someone. A man in a dark suit appeared beside him, listening. Then he glanced quickly in my direction and nodded.

I was fixed.

" – there isn't one of them that's ever made or sold anything," the ranter was saying. "Lawyers, teachers, social workers, lecturers. Professional politicians. No idea. No idea at all. Haven't got a clue. Wouldn't pay 'em in washers."

"Excuse me," I said, walking round him and away through the

crowd to reach the other side of the room, putting my glass of wine down on a table by the wall where there was a clear passage to the door. Moving off as fast as I could without actually knocking anyone over.

I'd seen too much. I knew, without rationalising or explaining or hoping against hope to myself, that I was in dire straits.

I'd just seen much too much.

23

They came for me after dinner. There were two of them. I realised I'd noticed them together, lounging on the street corner when I went out to eat. Now they were following me, one ranging ahead of the other in seemingly aimless crosses of the road, both getting closer.

They were shorter than me but harder, much harder, certainly slimmer and far more muscular. One had light canvas trousers, one dark blue. They wore jackets, loose jackets, one reddish, one brown, over white T-shirts. One was balding, one dark-haired. They had a much more purposeful walk than any casual pedestrian, a brisk, short-stepped, ball-of-the-foot motion. It was only a matter of where an intersection took place, not when. It didn't matter how competent they might turn out to be. I'm not capable of much by way of serious self-defence, not these days, and I'm never armed.

I suppose I should have stayed in. I could have done without dinner that night. But the hotel, although clean and modern, only had breakfast facilities. When I got back from the reception I was agitated, pacing up and down, trying to work things out, things like Carlos Guimares and Tony Barnwell, Tony Barnwell and Carlos Guimares, and then Katie and me and me and Katie and Katie and Carlos and a missing thing for measuring bean moisture electronically. It didn't work; nothing worked. Steadily I got not so much hungry as needing to go out, to find some displacement activity like eating; eating always helps the mind as well as the body. Where the hell was Katie? Why didn't she tell me about Texteis Arochena?

Katie's loyalties were too complex for my fevered mind at that moment. I left my room and walked a few blocks to where there was a local restaurant that served most things but the best usually based on Italian cooking.

In the old days I used to eat things like *feijoada*, the heavy kidney-bean and meat stew that kept farmers and slaves in energy, because it was traditionally Brazilian and unusual for me, until Katie steered me off it as too fattening. I like eating local specialities. If in greater company, I'd go for a business-executive sort of meal, maybe a *churrascaría*, the equivalent of an Argentine *parillada*, where the meat grill goes on and on for ever and you just keep eating the skewered steaks, roasts, chops and sausages they bring sizzling to your table and drinking iced *Chopp* lager until you're stuffed, can't take any more. I've always been lucky enough to have a healthy appetite; in Buenos Aires I make a point of going to the *El Mundo*, an old traditional restaurant on *Maipú*, between *Lavalle* and *Tucumán*, that does the best *bife de churrasco* for a very reasonable price, or maybe a *bife a caballo*, with a fried egg on top.

Anyway, I ate a light meal of fish and rice, something quite safe and digestible, with a glass of white wine, taking my time and having a *caffezinho* afterwards despite the lateness of the hour. I was feeling much better, quite bright from the coffee, my mind clearing and asking me the right questions, starting to believe I'd panicked, over-reacted at the reception. I strolled out of the restaurant thinking I must get back and make some notes before a certain line of mental enquiry faded.

And then I saw them again. I was sure I'd seen them before, near the hotel. After taking one or two turns, slowing and speeding my walk, they were still there. I wasn't mistaken.

The area was mixed residential, with shops and some offices. The pavement surfaces had those grey latticed tiles or slabs you get in cities all over South America, a bit uneven, running up close to the trees that punctuated the edges like a row of leafy sentinels. There were cars along each side of the road. The lighting was variable; there were houses and small apartment blocks, shops containing furniture or small groceries still lit up, maybe lit up for the night, the occasional bar, a *tintorería* or two for the clothes-conscious, a big *ferretería* – ironmongers – on a corner, a bright takeaway serving the equivalent of Kentucky Fried Chicken. Cars and even a bus roared past. From somewhere there came a smell of bread baking. It was getting late and lights were going out. I was heading away from my hotel, towards a more seedy central area with more bars, nearer to the old part of town. I wondered whether to break out into a run, changed my mind, went into a bar, sat down, ordered a beer. I needed time.

The bar was quiet but at least there were people in it, two or three regulars hanging onto the counter, odd couples at a table, three old men immobile over thin glasses of something sticky and sweet. The tabletops were marble, old-fashioned, and I put my hot palms down to cool off before using the frosty beer glass as a chiller. One of the followers passed by outside, pulling a mobile phone from his pocket. The other wasn't visible. I hadn't got forever; they might just nip in and do me then and there if the instructions said so; it was only a question of time.

If they had been going to shoot me, I reasoned, they'd have done it by now. This was to be a mugging job. If fatal, it would look like a mugging gone too far. Street thievery, nothing with sinister over-tones. An uncertain end, like a gas bottle accident in a caravan or getting knocked down by a car whilst out walking your dog.

Poor old Lawrence Edwards; precise, pedantic, principled, left like a broken sack of bones in the gutter.

What had he done to deserve that?

I found it hard to lay the deaths at the door of Carlos Guimares. Would Carlos really send someone all that way just to do William Pulford and Lawrence in? I had no doubt that the two prowlers out-side were locals; Tony Barnwell could command few such facilities here. My flight from the reception had been instinctive, Carlos-inspired, and evidently prudent. But why? Why me, now? Just for being here, for seeing Carlos and Barnwell together? Or for using Richard Keane's card? Had there been some fateful message from the DTI to Barnwell now that Robinson knew of my existence?

On the other hand, I had been trying very hard to contact Katie. Carlos would almost certainly know that; his intelligence system would embrace Gladys and those around her. So was this just jeal-ousy?

An image of the immaculate Carlos came to me. Katie said that he was proud, deep, complex as well as promiscuous. Promiscuous men practice many deceptions. It becomes a habit. According to Katie, Carlos was highly educated, urbane and well read as well as a legendary tycoon. As a young man he had been quite academic, a classical scholar, before deserting to Mammon. Even now he was prone to quoting parallels from ancient history, parallels which included the savage rapine and swift terminations of Greek and Roman myth. He might be a modern business entrepreneur but his judgements were terrifyingly timeless, predatory, opportunistic within careful, expansionary plans. Carlos saw most people as did the ancient Gods: amusing pawns to be used for power, amusement, gain and pleasure. Yet Katie swore he accepted many of her Jungian, semi-religious, philosophical credos.

Carlos was a paradox: dangerous, proud, experimental, yet oddly mortal. I held the cold glass tighter, feeling a shiver down my spine. I was apprehensive, hot, feverish but strangely elated. Does a fox on the run feel such fearful animation?

I finished the beer in about ten minutes, paid for it and left, looking both ways as I reached the pavement. Neither man was in sight. I began to walk slowly down the street, reluctant to leave lighted areas, watching. To my right and left the intersecting streets led away from the corners into darker regions; I prayed that the visibility on my current, busier road wouldn't start to peter out. I began to hope the pair were just shadowing me, not intent on incapacitating or worse. My instinct told me not to indulge in wishful thinking. I still hadn't worked out how to get back to the safety of my hotel.

Then I saw one of the men coming towards me.

It staggered me that he'd got ahead, pre-empted my direction. He was about three-quarters of a block away, half-lingering at a shop front, half-moving in my direction. I whirled round. The other one was an equivalent distance behind me, doing the same. These were professionals. In artillery terms, I was bracketed.

It was getting near the end. I remembered discussing Donald Campbell's death with a pal once, watching that terrible filmed moment when Bluebird lifted off the water at Coniston to whirl over and over, end over end in the air at high speed. You could hear Donald Campbell's voice on the recording, saying she's over, she's gone right over, and I wondered what the hell the last thought to go through his mind was before the terrible smash into the unyielding incompressible lake water, the impact that left nothing of him but wreckage and his boots.

My pal was a jet pilot, one who'd had a few dodgy moments himself when flying with a display team. Thoughts, my pal said, he wouldn't have had time for any thoughts, he'd be much too busy. The moments before impact, you're in a frenzy, doing things. Anyway, Donald Campbell was obsessed by his father, Sir Malcolm, all his life. Trying to keep up with his dad's reputation and speed records, bursting himself to better them like something out of Oedipus Rex. Do I mean Oedipus Rex? Death wish, mate. Wouldn't give up, would he? Couldn't quit. It was inevitable he'd come to a sticky end.

The next intersection, ten yards away, revealed a side street with more bars, red flashing signs in female outlines, the unmistakable lure of regions dedicated to venality. Between two parked cars, off the pavement, stood a sturdy black girl with bare stomach, low-slung knitted top clinging hardly to cover enormous knockers, low-slung mini skirt demonstrating every indentation and protuberance essential to the stimulation of lusting man. Her broad mouth widened into a toothy grin as she saw me staring frantically at her, mind racing.

"*Alloa mi amor,*" she called throatily. "Are you coming, or what?"

I nipped down the pavement to stand beside her in a flash. "Where?" I demanded.

She stuck two fingers in her mouth and emitted a piercing whistle. From nowhere a clapped-out Volkswagen Beetle taxi came bellowing down the road, one of Brazil's unsilenced classics, only two doors, no seat beside the driver, you just nip past him into the back and he pulls the passenger door shut with a cord. The car stopped in front of us with a badly adjusted squeal. The door swung open. At the intersection the two men came round from opposite pavements and came at us in a steady, menacing strut.

A knife gleamed in the leading man's hand.

"*Cuidado!*" I yelled getting my Spanish mixed with Portuguese as I pointed at them. I couldn't think of the word for muggers. "*Cangancheiros!*"

The black girl stuck her fingers back in her mouth and emitted piercing whistles in a sort of anapaestic pentameter. The biggest, blackest bloke I have ever seen in a check shirt came sailing out of a doorway on our side of the road and met the first of my two pursuers with an outstretched arm. The pursuer whirled as his shoulder was grabbed and pivoted. There was a sort of choking slap and his whole frame jerked. A knife and a mobile phone clattered onto the tarmac. The girl stepped forward and drove a stiletto heel into the mobile with satisfying cracking of plastic before she kicked the knife off into a gutter-grill. Another choking smack and clatter as the pursuer bounced against a parked car and thumped down onto the roadway. The second man paused, wisely, holding up his empty hands, palms flat in a mollifying gesture. The big black pimp shook a fist at him and snapped something in colloquial Portuguese. The second man moved away to stoop over his colleague. The big black bloke beamed widely, held the taxi door open and jerked an imperious thumb at me.

This was no time to prevaricate; I went in like a ferret, followed by the girl.

"Have a nice time," the big man said, grinning, and slammed the door.

The taxi moved off, clearly under prearranged instructions, with a rattle of air-cooled engine. A sense of hilarious elation began to possess me, waves of liberating emotion, a buzzing of ridiculous, nonsensical, semi-hysterical relief.

With One Bound, Johnny Was Free.

The girl pushed herself against me lasciviously. I peered at the generous breasts, now surging nakedly out of the clinging top. She was a girl, all right; none of that transvestite nastiness. Her hand began to caress my flies. The driver, peering into his mirrors, chuckled approvingly. My blood buzzed with fear, excitement and liberation.

"What happens now?" I could have asked.

But that would have been stupid.

And ungrateful.

24

When my father started flying round South America in 1938 it was a more dangerous business than it is now. He used to relate that when the KLM three-engined Fokker took off from Curaçao to Bogotá, it was so loaded with passengers, cargo and extra fuel that it seemed hardly able to get off the ground. The pilot would halt the plane at the very start of the runway, jam the brakes on, run the engines up till they screamed on full power and the whole plane shuddered, let the brakes off sharply, lurch away down the tarmac and watch the sea come trundling and bumping up towards them as the speed gradually increased. At the very last moment, as the roaring air seemed reluctantly to push up under the wings, the flight engineer would wind the wheels up to give that final, extra bit of lift and the heavy-bellied plane would stagger upwards lumpily, climbing slowly out over the waves. My father understood all this much too well. Propeller planes had no mysteries for him.

Contrary to romantic historical conception, my father was a dedicated two-seater man. When I used to twit him about Von Richtofen and all those Jadgstaffels or whatever they were called, single-seat Albatrosses and those, shooting down lots of slow British two-seaters over the trenches, he would shake his head.

"It might have been like that for the first two or even three years of the war," he rumbled, "but when we got up in the air in 1917 the Jerries used to clear off. Soon as they saw us. None of them would hang about for a Bristol Fighter."

He thought the Bristol was terrific. Fast – about a hundred and thirty miles an hour in a dive – and heavily armed, with two Maxims firing through the propeller and a Lewis gun aft for the observer. A deadly machine.

When I doubted what my father said about aerial combat in those days I read all the books I could find: *The Wind in the Wires* by Grinnell-Milne, and Bishop the Canadian's book, and all the Americans: *One Man's War* by Bert Hall, *Nocturne Militaire* by Elliott

White Springs and *War Birds; the Diary of an Unknown Airman*. Later on, much later on, I read Alan Clark's *Aces High*. The Yanks all said the same thing: a single-seat German wouldn't attack a two-seater on its own. They attacked in pairs or threes, often from underneath. So maybe my father was right; he said you could always turn inside a fast single-seater while your observer hammered it with the Lewis gun, and if you got your Maxims onto it, it was a goner.

All the same, Bristols got shot down.

My father did not think that he had joined the legions of the celebrated, or that there was anything historic in what he'd done. He said that provided you were alert technically the Bristol F2b was an extremely reliable aircraft. Apart from the fighting the life was far preferable to his days as an apprentice in the Metropolitan Cammel and Carriage Works iron foundry, starting at fourteen years old, six in the morning until six at night with the odd early release to go to night school.

He was always a lucky man. His squadron got sent to Egypt to support Allenby's army, chasing the Germans and the Turks out of Palestine. He said that compared with the Western Front, where a pilot's life was short, it was a doddle. The air opposition cleared off once they sighted the Bristols and though there was quite a bit of flak it was nothing like France and Belgium. My father much admired the discipline of the retreating German columns, holding together even when the RFC were strafing them and the Turks, starving and unpaid, were deserting in thousands. The pilots, observers, and the ground crews had to live on a tin of bully beef, hard biscuit and a pint of water a day for weeks on end as they moved up through the desert towards Syria. Despite his belief in robust and regular meals my father said he was never healthier.

One night a long time ago, at my home, the film of Lawrence of Arabia was repeated on television and there they were, RFC biplanes, diving on the German and Turkish columns amongst the splendid desert mountains. I saw my father a day or so later and said I'd seen his lot in the film, hadn't really noticed it before, and had he seen it?

My father was in his little garden shed, potting some tomato plants. He took his pipe half out of his mouth and put on a sour expression.

"T. E. Lawrence? Lawrence of Arabia?"

"That's the one."

My father's lip pushed out below his pipe. "We got a lecture from him when we first arrived in Egypt. Strategic stuff, it was. Political. And the ethnic part, of course. To do with Arabs. Odd fellow. Very odd. Didn't think much of him, I'm afraid. Not the sort of fellow I'd like to share a hut with. Not at all."

When the war was over my father had to wait months in Cairo before he was repatriated. There was a lot of trouble with Egyptian nationalist terrorists and discipline had to be maintained. One night, on patrol with a sergeant and some men in a forbidden quarter of the city, he heard a terrible row coming from the upper storey of a dubious building. Some Australians who had been gypped in a nightclub the night before threw a piano out of a third floor French window. My father was a very musical man – he could play Handel's Largo on the piano and had a shot at an old cello from time to time even though his apprentice-engineering fingers were more suited to the blacksmith work he loved. He was also something of a carpenter-cum-cabinetmaker with a deep respect for well-made furniture. Like anyone who has left school at fourteen, he had a massive admiration for culture and craftsmanship; a fine piano was symbolic to him.

Nevertheless, he said the sound that piano made when it hit the cobbles was the most satisfying noise he ever heard in his life. A loud bang and splintering of bursting cabinet work overlaid with an obbligato of splanging piano wires as they and the metal frame snapped. Unique. Unrepeatable. A zenith in the joy of destructive abandon.

There was a hushed silence as the ringing, once-in-a-lifetime cacophony died away. His men froze in their tracks. The sergeant stood rooted in awe for a few seconds then plucked urgently at my father's sleeve.

My father said that even in the dim street lighting his sergeant's face shone with delight.

"We'd better get along, sir," he whispered. "Otherwise we might have to arrest them."

"Quite right, sergeant. Quite right. On our way. Look sharp over here now, men; this way it is."

They left the scene before anyone saw them.

Skilful retreat can be instinctive.

25

The next morning, after office opening hours, I was onto the phone like a scalded wasp.

"*Alloa?*"

"That must be Gladys. Hello Gladys." My voice was hoarse.

"Senhor Johnny! How are you?"

"Gladys, I want to speak to Katie. She's not at home or at Atibaia. I've already tried several times."

"No, Senhor Johnny, she is still away."

"Away where?"

"Oh, I do not know, Senhor Johnny."

"When will she be back?"

"In some days, I think."

"Some days? Have you spoken to her?"

"I beg your pardon?"

I was back in my hotel. I returned in the early hours and overslept. I was as dry as a bone, hot, feverish, sated. *A gentleman does not boast of his incontinence.* My mind was full of guilt, resentment, elation, suspicion, huge coffee-coloured breasts, fear, bewilderment, buttocks, slippery surfaces, poundings and humpings, oral images and ministrations previously beyond imagination, hot breath and laughter, statistics, research, machinery, violence, coffee beans, Sr Nassim Serfaty, throbbing, the snapping of plastic, Euripides Arochena.

My temperature was off scale.

I clenched my teeth. "Have you actually spoken to her? In person?"

"No, Senhor Johnny, I have not spoken to her. But I have had a message to say that she will be away a few days more."

"Who from?"

"Pardon?"

"The message, Gladys, the message! Who gave you the message?"

Gladys's tone became more formal. Evidently I was pushing my luck. "From the office of Senhor Carlos. I think Senhora Katie is very busy with a special project for Senhor Carlos. As I said before."

"I see. But you don't know when she'll be back? They didn't tell you?"

"No. I am sorry. I don't know."

How the hell, I thought, can you run an office organisation like that? So that no one knows where you are or when you'll be back? But this was Brazil, not Europe or North America; the rules were different here.

Guimares rules.

But Katie? What happened to her?

"And there is no way of contacting her?"

"No, Senhor Johnny. I am sorry you will miss her this time."

Oh will I, Gladys, I muttered to myself, oh will I? You've obviously been told that I will. I'll see about that.

"I'll speak to Senhor Carlos then. Carlos Guimares."

Shocked silence. Then: "Senhor Carlos?" Gladys's voice took on an incredulous tone. The importunate lover demanding communication with he of the *droit de seigneur*, the supremo, the generalissimo? Incredible. Madness. "Senhor Johnny, it is very difficult to speak to Senhor Carlos. He is the President of the company. He is not here, I don't think."

"Let's just try, shall we Gladys? Put me through to him, there's a good girl."

"Senhor Johnny –"

"Just try! Don't be frightened. He's only another man, Gladys, President or not."

"I am not frightened." The tone was first resentful, then dismissive. "OK, for you I will try."

There was a silence, a clicking of mechanisms, the silent coursing of electronic connections. A new voice, a woman's, oldish, said something incomprehensible in Portuguese.

"I'd like to speak to Senhor Guimares please," I said, in English, in my most formal, educated voice.

Educated English came back. "Who is that, may I ask?"

"My name is Barber. Mr Johnny Barber."

"Of which company?" The voice brought to mind a firm iron-grey matron in some vast sterilised ward, making sure a patient didn't get out of bed no matter what the pressing need.

"I'm with the DTI – the Department of Trade and Industry – in England."

"Oh, I see, Mr Barber. Our contact with your organisation has not been through you before, has it?"

"No, it hasn't. I wish to speak to Senhor Guimares about an entirely new matter."

"I'm afraid Senhor Guimares is not available right now. Can I take a message?"

"Sure. You can take a message." There was a pause while she waited. I composed my thoughts. "It's in three parts. Would you be kind enough to write them down?"

"Certainly."

"Are you ready?"

"Yes, of course."

"Then here it goes. One: tell Senhor Guimares that I'm still alive despite the efforts of his assassins last night."

"The efforts of his what?"

"Assassins. As in murderers. Do you want me to spell that for you?"

"Mr Barber –"

"Two: I have no doubt that he is in some way responsible for the disappearance of an important piece of electronic equipment designed to detect coffee bean toxins. He and his accomplice, Mr Barnwell. I'd like to talk to him about that. And three: unless I have a clear communication with Katie Gonzalez, his head of administration, whom I'm sure you know very well personally, within the next three hours – that's either a personal appearance or a phone call – I'm going to the police to report her disappearance, abduction and possible murder."

"Mr Barber –"

"The police. Three hours. Here's my phone number and room number. Tell him not try violence again."

"Mr Barber –"

"Kindly repeat the phone and room number to make sure you've got them right."

She repeated them. Correctly. I put the phone down. I was shaking. I picked it up again and dialled long distance.

The answering voice at the other end had a comforting, relieving, northern edge to it.

"Hello, Richard here."

"Richard? Richard Keane?"

"Yes. Who's that?"

"Johnny Barber."

"Oh, how are you, Johnny, all right?" In the background I heard a rumble and could imagine a big container lorry shaking his village shop-office as it thundered thoughtlessly by.

"I'm all right, Richard. I think. But how about you?"

"Fine, fine. Well, skint actually, but otherwise OK. How's it going?"

"It's a bit fraught, Richard. A bit fraught. Everyone here says that fungus is not a problem. Tell me: have you finished the replacement beanometer yet?"

"Oh yes. Just finished last night. I'll be sending it out by DHL today if my account isn't too far in the red."

"And it works and everything?"

"Of course it does. Do you think you can you sell a few more? Things are getting a bit tight here."

"I think," I said cautiously, "the market for that version is a bit special, Richard. A bit special. But there are lots of other opportunities for the technology. Anyway, your Swiss client will be glad to get the replacement at last."

"I bet they will. Been badgering me nearly every day."

"No other problems or break-ins?"

"No. Dead quiet, it's been. How's your trip going?"

"Interesting. Very interesting. I'll tell you all about it when I get back. Listen, Richard, take good care of yourself, you hear? And that machine. Good care, now."

"I will," he said cheerfully. "Have no fear. I'll hold on to the beanometer until DHL call."

"Good boy."

I put the phone down. I needed a drink, went to the mini-bar, emptied all the little cans of orange juice, four of them, into the bathroom tumbler and drank the lot. Then I drank two cans of mineral water with three aspirins. Some sort of balance began to abate the feverish sensations but most of the liquid still vanished, blotting itself into desert-struck organs drained arid by the night's activities. It would be days, even weeks, before I felt like action again. There is nothing to be said for getting old; as someone said, old age is not for sissies.

I sat down on the bed, leant back on a comforting pillow and began to doze slightly as I thought and waited for Guimares to react. Katie's disappearance was a nagging sore on a raw mind. I shouldn't have asked her up to Cartagena. I shouldn't have involved her at all, not told her about the coffee bean thing or maybe even Texteis Arochena. Knowledge is power but knowledge is dangerous. I should have asked her maybe to meet me in São Luis do Maranhão instead; Cartagena was a resort too far. If she'd gone to São Luis, which is still in Brazil, maybe Carlos's attention wouldn't have been distracted; if I could lure her out of Brazil to Colombia, where else might I lure her? São Luis was still Brazilian territory, Carlos's territory, a place he could control, a pardonable if irritating fling but not an evacuation, not a possible desertion. He'd got more possessive in recent years, she said so, the old trips abroad like New Orleans and Paris couldn't be done so easily now.

I should have made it São Luis. São Luis would have been interesting; I've always wanted to go to São Luis. And Valdivia, in Chile. And Porto Bello, in Panama. All mingled with British history. Why did I have these historic, atavistic interests? Are other Englishmen the same?

The phone didn't ring. No one seems to return calls these days but surely Guimares wouldn't be able to resist that message?

I picked up the receiver and dialled Lawrence Edwards's number.

"Robinson," a male voice said. I felt disappointed. The female one, that Frances Parks, had had more authority than the cautious Robinson.

"Graham Robinson? At the DTI?"

"Yes?" The tone was cautious.

"It's Johnny Barber here. I'm in Brazil."

"Mr Barber!" A relieved, synthetic warmth washed down the line. "This is indeed fortuitous. I was just wondering how to get a message to you."

"Oh?"

"Yes, indeed. There has been a departmental review, you see, following the departure of Lawrence Edwards. My elders and betters felt that a new *coup d'oeuil*, as it were, might be advisable at this juncture. Lawrence was an excellent fellow, excellent, but he had what one might call his little idiosyncrasies."

And I'm one of them, I thought, go on: tell me I'm an idiosyncrasy, one of Lawrence Edwards's little idiosyncrasies, and I'll kill you, you faceless DTI fucker, strangle you with my own bare hands once I get back. If I get back.

"Your boss is out here, you know," I said.

"I beg your pardon?" I'd actually disconcerted him.

"Your boss. Tony Barnwell. Papers are full of his visit."

"Oh I see." There was a relieved chuckle. "He's not my boss. Not our boss either, to be absolutely specific."

"No?"

"Indeed not. One does not report to immediate political masters in this particular branch, not directly anyway, but Mr Barnwell is a Secretary of State for quite a different branch. Entirely elsewhere."

"I see."

"Glad to hear he's flying the flag successfully out there, though. Now: there's been a reappraisal, as I say. We will of course honour any commitments that Lawrence made to you, recorded commitments that is, up to and including this point, in regard to expenses, but I've been instructed to advise you that your enquiry is at an end."

"End?"

"Yes. As of this moment."

So he was recording our conversation. I didn't answer.

"If you have other commitments, business commitments of your own, doubtless I expect you will want to complete those. But from our point of view an immediate cessation is instructed."

"You mean I'm to come back?"

"Oh, we're not demanding your immediate return or anything, just ending our brief to you."

"What about my report?"

"There's no need for that. Once the decision was taken to terminate this line of activity, it was agreed that no further expense should be incurred. You've had a bit of a let-off in that regard."

"What about Richard Keane?"

"Who?"

"The man who's built the beanometer. What about him?"

"I don't think he's involved, is he? Oh, I see what you mean. No, the enquiry into that project has been withdrawn. There clearly isn't the potential there to justify our support. He'll supply the replacement unit to meet his own commercial obligations, I'm sure, but we have no commitments to honour in that direction."

"So he's on his own?"

"He's perfectly at liberty to apply for the usual support grants through the usual channels, for technical development work and so on. I believe there are such regional schemes, assessed by technical experts as to the merits of such support."

"You mean it's all over."

"I think you could say that, yes. It seems that Lawrence was perhaps going a bit beyond his remit in engaging you in this matter but after all it's a very low-key business, isn't it, just a minimum of expense since you were already going to the area anyway."

"Lawrence agreed generous expenses with me, including my air ticket. I am here at his specific request."

"Oh dear. Oh no. There's nothing on file here about that. What we are empowered to pay is daily expenses of one hundred pounds a day up to a maximum of eight days. If you'll send me an invoice, I'll get it authorised for you as soon as possible."

"*What?*"

"Eight hundred pounds. That's the amount we can pay without having to apply for full grade authorisations, you see. Against vouchers, of course. Lawrence hadn't put anything on paper about his agreement with you, so I'm afraid my head of department is unlikely to agree to anything more. Indeed, he feels we are showing goodwill, indeed would like to show our goodwill, to you in view of the sad circumstances, but with regret can't do more."

"Incredible. What about his boss? Your boss's boss, that is?"

The voice became very formal. "You are at liberty to go through an appeal procedure for further compensation but I can tell you it's very lengthy and, in the absence of written evidence, is unlikely to succeed."

"I'll send you an invoice," I said. "But I'll get you for this."

"I beg your pardon? You'll what?"

Timing is everything, as in the theatre. I put the phone down and shouted 'shit' at the window.

The phone promptly rang again. I picked it up.

"Mr Johnny Barber?" The iron-grey matron's voice tinkled like ice in a tin jug.

"Yes?"

"I have Senhor Guimares for you."

A silence, then a voice, foreign but not accented, not the voice of anyone with a British or American education, smooth but clear, speaking in English, low, reasonable, unemotional.

"Hello Mr Johnny Barber."

"Hello Senhor Carlos Guimares. Thank you for calling me back."

The first time we'd ever spoken. The man I'd shared – no, this was no time to be thinking about things like that.

"I felt I better had. I got a most garbled message which was said to be from you."

"Garbled? Your secretary took it down most carefully."

"To me it was garbled. The message of someone not completely coherent. It implied that I made an attempt on your life, which is not true, and that I am involved in theft or deception, which is also not true."

"No?"

"No. You must search your mind for enemies capable of doing

166

such things, Mr Johnny, perhaps as a result of your lifestyle. I am not one of them."

"No?"

"No. Despite what you may think, I am not. And Katie is perfectly well, working for me as she has for so long, after her holiday."

"I want to speak to her."

"I'm afraid she is not available just now."

"Look here –"

"Not available. I can tell you though, with absolute certainty, that when you are back in England you will be able to speak to her. Just send a fax from your office confirming your return."

"I may not return. I have matters to look into in the coffee business just now, here."

"Have you? I do not think so."

"Does Katie agree with your suggestion?"

"Indeed she does. I think that she feels she has had enough excitement for the moment and that it would be inappropriate for you to meet just now since you deceived her as to the real reason for your visit."

"That's rubbish."

"Inappropriate. Her own word. She specifically asked me to convey her regrets to you and to advise you to return. Your business here in Brazil is finished, Mr Johnny Barber."

"Is it? I wonder why you say that? What are you up to with that beanometer you and Barnwell stole?"

"I haven't the faintest idea what you're talking about. I think it would be more cogent to ask you what you are up to, impersonating a much younger man at an official trade reception. And also misrepresenting yourself on the telephone as a DTI man."

"I didn't impersonate anybody, I –"

"Oh yes you did. There are several witnesses to it. You even used a card which can be shown in evidence. In Brazil, as in England, it is an offence, Mr Johnny Barber, to assume false identities. Especially in order to gain access to an official reception."

"That's pretty pathetic. Can't you drum up anything better than that?"

"Several witnesses. If the right complaint is made, you could be detained for quite a long time."

"Rubbish."

"You really are out of your depth here, aren't you? By the time your impersonation was checked and the necessary depositions obtained, weeks, even months, could pass. Our jails are not enjoyable places. The best thing you can do now is to leave."

"What have you done with Katie? I want to speak to her."

"Oh yes, then there's the deception of Katie. You told her that you fixed to meet her in Cartagena before your little piece of research was organised but that's not true, is it? Once you were offered the work you naturally decided to exploit her, and through her, me. It was all false pretences again. She is rather disappointed in you, Johnny. You see, I have not *done*, as you put it, anything with her outside my normal working relationship with my head of administration. She is away, on a project of importance to our group. Unavailable to you. You cannot come butting in here, an outsider racketing about like a tourist, making demands of this sort, especially not to me, after the way you have behaved and the lies you have told. My staff, my executives, are my responsibility; I must protect them from people like you."

Then why, I thought, are you bothering to speak to me? What is it that I know, or have got, that you need to extinguish? How do you know that my coffee research has been terminated, no, not terminated, axed? You must have arranged the termination with Barnwell, despite what that faceless goon Robinson says. And how do you know what the timing of the whole affair was? That it was arranged before I phoned Katie? No one except Lawrence Edwards could know that, surely?

"So I'm to take your word for it? She's just away working, incommunicado for no particular reason and as soon as I get back, if I send a fax, communication will be resumed?"

"Precisely."

"Incredible. You make it sound so natural. Which it is not. How do I know that Katie's not dead?"

"Oh really, Johnny! Mind if I call you Johnny? I feel that we know each other, in an indirect sense. We Brazilians eschew surnames."

"It's OK with me, Carlos."

"Good. Katie is my head of administration, a key member of my staff, my right-hand lady, you might say. Do you really think that I'd allow anything terrible to happen to her? Quite apart from other considerations, things that go back for years between us, she is necessary to my operations. I can not allow her to become unavailable outside agreed timetables."

"We are none of us indispensable, Carlos."

"Oh yes we are! You must not adopt that terrible, nihilist philosophy so prevalent in business, Johnny. It does not suit you and you know how indignantly Katie would reject it. We are all unique, irreplaceable."

"Your faith is heartening. But I can not imagine how you are preventing Katie from communicating with me."

"My dear Johnny, I am not a chauvinist by any means, but violence and flattery are part of a language women understand all too well. Even if they know that neither threat is real, it brings a positive response since such comprehensible language implies concern. Katie and I work closely, we are together nearly every day. What do you think she would understand if I did not behave with territorial emotion? She is safe and working for me. That is how it must be, apart from agreed holidays. She knows, now, that you have behaved badly. If you go shrieking to the police you will achieve nothing except deep embarrassment to Katie and to yourself. Those whom the gods would destroy, they first make mad. Think carefully about your behaviour and its impression before acting even more rashly."

I managed to bite back a natural answer. "I have your word that she is well and agrees with this?"

"You have."

I thought for a moment. This was his territory, not mine. There was nothing more I could do here; the coffee bean research would get nowhere. But Katie had said she would help me. Was I to accept banishment meekly, be sent off like Beckham shown a red card?

Quite clearly, I was not wanted in Brazil, not just by Carlos but by Tony Barnwell, with his rapidly executed DTI authority. My presence, the presence of a pseudo-Richard Keane, had upset something badly.

I did have my weapons, weapons I could use at the right moment, my way, in my time. I could be back, sooner than any of them could possibly imagine. It would have to be a case of *reculer pour mieux sauter*, surely.

My silence had somehow disconcerted Carlos Guimares. His voice sharpened.

"If you wish, Johnny, I will get Katie to fax you, to your number in England, within the next twenty-four hours. In her own writing. It will be waiting for you on your return. Will that be sufficient to reassure you?"

"You guarantee that?"

"I do."

He and a host of people really did want me out of Brazil. Why?

"Very well. I shall leave. Right away."

A surprised silence. Then, "How very wise. I am glad that you have decided to see sense."

"I take it that I won't be attacked on my way to the airport?"

"I can not imagine why you should ask me this question. But I am sure it would be wise to leave directly, before someone offended by your deceptions takes official action."

"Goodbye for now, then, Carlos."

"Goodbye, Johnny."

I put the phone down. I noticed that my hand was shaking. They – he and Barnwell and the jobsworth Robinson – had achieved much more than preventing Katie from embracing me again. They had cut off the coffee bean research, all the information I thought that I'd get through Katie, prevented all further elucidation of Richard Keane's alchemy. Brought it to a full stop. Carlos was even prepared to use Katie, an assurance of her compliant communication, to get me back home, out of this place.

Why?

Fury seethed for a moment. I felt like John Wayne's lot in *El*

Alamo: no one tells me to cut and run, nobody, even if I want to and have good reason.

Or was that *The Magnificent Seven*?

It didn't matter: I was going to be as cold, as Mediterranean-Mafia as the best of them. I was going to get them all for this. All of them. Skilful retreat or strategic withdrawal, I was faced with a long, defeated journey home, missing Katie, bewildered by what was going on, scorned by the DTI. It wasn't going to be a peaceful trip.

And as it happened, Carlos lied.

26

I took a taxi to the airport. I didn't trust Carlos Guimares. I sneaked out of the hotel in casual clothes, with my two bits of casual soft luggage, using a side door. Then I walked a brisk block and waved down a passing taxi, not one that might have been prowling around the hotel front. I chose a fairly modern, more powerful-looking cab than the run of the mill. These seemed suitable precautions to take.

They weren't enough.

I told the taxi driver to take me to the airport. He was a rough-looking fellow in tattered check shirt and khaki trousers but genial, as São Paulo taxi drivers are, honest most of them, honest enough on one occasion to tell me, when I was confused by the devalued decimal currency, that I'd paid with a note ten times too big. Not many European, or London, cabbies do that.

I sat back for a moment as we accelerated away down the busy street, then moved forward and leaned over to stick the equivalent of ten dollars in the top pocket of his check shirt.

"What's this?" he demanded with a grin. "You want to stop for a woman on the way out there?"

"Can you tell if we're being followed?"

He frowned suspiciously, his spine stiffening. "Followed? Why?"

I made my voice confidential. "A lady. Her husband is after me."

He smiled broadly, relaxing his big hands, which had tightened on the wheel. "Tut, tut. He wants to get you even though you're on your way to the airport? Even though you're leaving?"

"Let's just say that he's very upset."

In his rear-view mirror, I watched him grin. "Ho-ho. He must be. Don Juan, eh? Sure I can tell if we're being followed. You sit back and act normal. Make yourself comfortable. Trust me; I'll know within four blocks whether there's anyone interested in following you."

I sat back. He turned right, went one block, turned left, went down two blocks of congested street with market stalls at the sides, turned again.

He nodded emphatically. "You're being followed," he said. "A Ford, blue, no question."

"How many in the car? Two?"

The taxi man chuckled, shaking his head in mock reproach. "How many husbands you upset? Oh, maybe he brings his brother to help him, eh? Or hers?"

I screwed up my eyes to visualise Guimares's two thugs. "One fair," I said. "One balding? Dark jackets?"

The taxi man shook his head, flicking his eyes back and forth at the rear-view mirror. We were approaching a broad avenue now, with a big aircraft outline and arrow on the green direction signs nearby. "Only one in the car. Thin hair, yes. Dark jacket."

"Mobile phone? Cellular?"

"Mobile phone, sure. He's talking into it."

That meant trouble. If they'd been clever enough to track me from the reception to my hotel the night before, they'd be competent enough to stay ahead of me now, block my route.

"Is there another way to the airport?"

A frown. "Why?"

"The man behind could be laying a trap. If we follow the obvious, the regular way out to the airport, there could be someone up ahead. At a traffic light maybe, or a crossing. Come from in front of us."

An even more worried frown. "You sure this is only a husband? I don't like to get mixed up in some things. I got a family, you know?"

"Believe me," I said earnestly, visualising Carlos Guimares to get the tone of conviction right. "He's rich and he's upset about my attentions to his lady."

"Rich, eh? Well done. What did you do? Screw her in front of him? He find you *flagrante*?"

"The lady was most obliging. In the marital bedroom. I didn't know it but there was a camera running at the time. Some people in São Paulo seem to have funny habits. He seems to have seen the film."

"Funny habits?" The tension which had entered his voice was going back to amusement. "You don't know the half. To find yourself a surprise on video's nothing, here in São Paulo. I could tell you things you wouldn't believe. I guy I knew went to a porn movie place off the Republica, sat down in his seat and found he was one of the main performers on screen. Gave him a real shock, I can tell you." He gestured at the road ahead. "Look, I'm heading south, then doubling across back to another approach. I assume you don't mind the extra fare?"

"You get me safe to the airport, a hundred dollars is yours."

"You're a gentleman." He was even more relaxed, now. "Expensive though, isn't it? Sex is the most natural thing in the world but even in Brazil it's always expensive."

"And life's cheap."

He swerved suddenly across the highway, left, and shot laughing under the bows of a howling bus, which braked too late as it almost grazed us. I managed to open my eyes after the muscles clamping them shut seemed to ignore nervous instructions.

"In the old days," he said cheerfully, manhandling the wheel in a competitive fashion, "we could have raced them all the way to Viracopos – that would have been fun – but the new airport's nearer. For we Brazilians, motor racing's the next best thing after football."

Roadwork signs began to appear in yellow and black snakings at the side of the road but the car kept up a remarkable speed.

"Look," I said nervously, "there isn't anyone still following us, is there?"

"Oh yes." He nodded emphatically. "The Ford driver is good. He's still there; you can see him if you turn round. The next bus nearly got him, though."

We seemed to be hurtling way off route. The tarmac ran out, shale drummed under the floor, dust began to billow out on either side of us in great, dry, reddish clay-coloured clouds.

"I'm letting him get closer," the taxi man said. "That way he can't see much up front. It's a construction site."

I clung to the back of his seat. "And then?"

A chuckle. "You have to right turn on the edge of the new motorway embankment they're still working on with graders. There's just a service track on top."

My throat was dry and I had to work up some saliva to talk. "You must get around a lot."

"My brother-in-law's a grader driver."

The cab hit a huge bump which launched me up to the ceiling with a great obscene shout.

"Hold tight!" yelled the driver, ignoring my words.

I grabbed the back of his seat again, knuckles showing even whiter. Rocketing up in front of us came yellow and black railings, posts, a warning sign. Brakes threw me forward into the back of the driver's seat, centrifugal force keeled me over to the left. We twisted right, wheels locked, ran forward at right angles to our previous line of travel, accelerated again.

I turned to look out of the back window to see, in the billowing dust, a blue Ford saloon right over on its suspension, desperately scrabbling to keep a grip on the edge of a steep slope. Then the rear end broke away down the embankment, the nose reared, and it rolled over, bouncing away down to my right in stony eruptions further and further below, away from us, until it came to a stop.

There was a whoop from the front seat. "Not bad, eh? That'll give him a headache."

"Not bad," I whispered hoarsely. "Not bad at all. If you're us."

"Of course we're us. Aren't we?"

We reached the airport by further back routes that took us through shanty towns strung across open country. When we arrived, with hands that were not quite steady I gave him the hundred dollars plus a handsome tip.

He grinned cheerfully at me as I clambered quickly out of the car. "I think you'd better stay away from town for a while, eh? Until he calms down."

"Sure," I said. "I'll stay away."

But now I was lying, too.

27

I landed at Heathrow early in the morning. I'd been awake all night. Eyes full of grit, aches in the joints and bristle on my chin made me feel like a piece of used sandpaper. The airport was shrouded in grey, colourless moisture, my face and skin were hot, my clothes flimsy and creased. No one noticed me. Just another grizzled old buzzard dropping back to earth in a cold, wet country full of restless people, luggage and car parks.

I drove home carefully through driving rain. Everything looked safe and unchanged, the dense M25 traffic spraying itself elbow to elbow at whatever speed or stationary until at last the fork to the south. Then into the small, rural, charcoal-coloured road, tired hedges, brown lumpy ploughed and puddled fields until, past Pembury, a nostalgic oast cone came up like a small spire with pointing white finger. Around me the land had started to flood; there was no interruption to the road but you could see that there would be if the relentless rain went on. Then came the thirties-suburbed outskirts of my coastal town, a long decline to the dancing sea and flat Channel horizon, puffed damp stucco, featureless wet brick, huge wet derelict churches, a withering sky loaded with grey and cascading with water.

Comfortingly familiar. What Betjeman might have called sweet uneventful countryside except that he was writing about Middlesex. He would have found Marine Court architecturally hilarious but I liked it, needed its anonymity, the security of one locked door to enter unless you could scale the vertical whitewashed walls to reach the wide balcony which, had it not been raining, I would have enjoyed.

Home: inside, the books, records and films, the computer, the telephone lines and their secrets, some mail. Outside, the wind and the sea, slapping and lunging at the uncaring beach. The whole apartment block was like a hive, with scraps of life in cells of varying size, each sticky inhabitant hoping its significance would last just that little bit longer, oblivion not arrive just yet.

On the fax machine there was a single sheet. I took it outside to read.

Johnny my dear

I'm very sorry. It was a great time in Cartagena. But it's better this way. Our lives are different, aren't they? There are things best avoided. We were lucky to have what we had. Don't worry; I'm well and happy. And safe.

I still prefer the average commercial traveller.

Love

Katie

The handwriting was unmistakable.

I walked slowly into the office to see the message light blinking on the recording machine. When I pressed the button, Betty's voice came over clear, flatly factual-pissed-off.

"Johnny? You seem to be away for longer than you said. I can't stand this weather any longer. I'm off to Tuscany with the Cartwrights. It's bloody awful and I'm not coming back 'till it stops. I hope it rained on you in South America, you lucky, neglectful bastard."

There were no other messages.

I went inside and had a hot shower. Then I shaved, threw my rumpled clothes into a laundry bag, wondered whether to try and get forty winks, decided the mind was too active, racing like a Cosworth, put on a clean blue shirt, khaki cotton trousers, dark blue V-neck pullover, socks, light leather shoes. I thought about walking along the beach, for miles and miles and miles. But it was raining.

If Carlos and Tony Barnwell thought I was out of the running, they'd got a shock coming. I am, like most of my fellow-islanders, easy-going, mentally lazy, amiable enough until roused. When roused, we can be difficult people.

The telephone rang in the office.

"Johnny? Mario."

"Mario! *Que tal, pibe?*"

"How are you? Your trip OK?"

"Fine. They're both coming, the machine's as good as sold, I'm sure of it."

"Don't be a *Fúlmine*, Johnny."

177

Fúlmine was a character from the cartoon strip in the Argentine magazine *Patoruzú*. Anything he blessed came to grief.

"Everything OK in Milan?"

"The machine's fine. No problem. But we have observed a lump in the espresso blend."

"Lump?"

"Arabica. Private, it seems so far. You don't know of any reason?"

"Not a clue. Right there, is it?"

"Outside. An addict of *El Diario*."

"Mmm. No reason I can think of. Nothing in the grinder to explain it."

"OK. I'll look into it further myself, then. See you soon."

"Ciao, Mario."

"Ciao, Johnny."

So Mario had got an unwanted observer or snoop – an Arabica, in coffee-code – outside every day.

Who? Why?

The entryphone bell rang.

That meant someone was downstairs on the pavement, ringing at the main door and waiting for my answer. I picked up the entryphone receiver.

"Mr Barber?"

My mind leapt. That voice; it was the feminine, educated voice of Lawrence Edwards's 'desk'. Not flustered this time, not breathy, just cool, noncommittal.

"Yes. Who's that?"

"My name is Parks. Frances Parks. DTI. May we come up and have a word?"

The force had arrived at Fort Zinderneuf.

28

Reprise: resumption of action, one of the times devoted to something not done all at once.

Concise Oxford Dictionary

The office-shop was still littered with kit. The Dexion racking looked a bit rustier than when I'd last seen it, or more flyblown, and the mess littered by the kettle on the chipped Formica-topped table seemed to have intensified. There were more components about, more circuit boards, wiring, control boxes and dirty cups.

Outside, the passing lorries still made the shop shake and the two long windows reflected dull light from a sky full of rain. Even as I walked in and shut the door, a gust of wind filled with drops spattered the plank floor around me.

"Hi, Johnny," Richard Keane said. "Back already? Got any orders?"

He grinned combatively and put his hands on his hips, making his waterproof watch glisten sharply. Feet square on the ground, broad shoulders back, he looked more like a prop forward from Widnes stretching himself after a scrum than an electronics freak.

"Yes, I'm back," I said. "No orders." And, one combative question deserving another, "Why has that second unit not gone to Switzerland yet?"

He gestured behind him with a broad hand. On the bench stood the dagger-slide apparatus, gleaming with a new finish and streamlined casing next to a large grey box with an LED display screen to it.

"Had a small snag. Nothing serious. It's ready to go tomorrow. What do you think?"

"It looks impressive," I answered cautiously. "Does it work?"

"'Course it does. Want a coffee?"

"No, thanks."

"I've got some proper now. Real grains. Want to try?"

"If you insist."

He bared his teeth again and plugged the kettle in. "Want to see the unit work? I've calibrated it and everything."

"What's the grey box for?"

"That? That's the microprocessor with display unit. And the logger, the A to D converter. The whole box and dice. That's the customer interface, that is. You pop your bean in the right hole and up comes the moisture, in absolute grammes or percentage. Brilliant, that is. You can have trends on it, averages, multipliers and offsets, the lot."

"Lucky Swiss."

"They will be. I've done much more than I quoted for with this one."

"Oh? I hope you're charging more for it."

He looked a bit rueful. "I couldn't help improving on it."

"Didn't the first one have the microprocessor?"

"No, it didn't; I hadn't had time to buy it and connect it before the unit was stolen."

"How could anyone use the thing, then?"

He looked at me pityingly. "They'd just have to stuff the 4 to 20 milli-Amp analogue output signal into a microprocessor of their own."

"Oh. Just checking. Would it take them long?"

"Not if they had a logger. An A to D converter. Common as muck. They could stick the signal into any old laptop or a PC then and off they'd go. A lad with less than a GCSE in electronics could do it. Why? You think someone stole number one in order to use it? Actually use it? Where? What for?"

"I don't know."

His face had a dubious expression as the kettle boiled. "These big coffee companies would have to have some pretty odd reasons to steal a bean moisture instrument rather than buy one, specially since the research is ICO sponsored. Very odd." He handed me a cup of coffee which was a major improvement on the last one I'd had from him but still fairly muddy. "A specially commissioned theft, you think?"

"Could be." My eyes met his. "It's always been a daft burglary, hasn't it? Something funny about it."

"It certainly has. Something more than funny."

We grinned at each other, then his face went serious.

"What happened about that DTI bloke Edwards who got knocked down by a car? Did they get the hit-and-run driver?"

"No, they didn't." I thought of telling him about other attempts that had been made, on me, but decided not to.

"Bloody hell. D'you think it was deliberate?"

"Yes."

His jaw set. "I was afraid you were going to say that."

"I've just had a long session with a police sergeant specialising in fraud and a DTI lady inspector who clearly think I'm behind something shady connected with this. I'm not. Lawrence Edwards said that this matter was not dangerous. Poor man. It obviously is, but I don't know why. My visitors certainly didn't, either."

"Didn't Lawrence Edwards tell you it *might* be dangerous?"

"Lawrence was lying. He was on to something, something involving someone so close to home that he kept all his cards tight to his chest. Didn't come clean at all. And paid the price."

Richard put his coffee down. His expression had gone more serious. "Money, it will be, won't it?"

"Of course."

"Must be a lot of it to kill someone for."

"Coffee is the second most traded commodity in the world. There's a huge industry out there."

"Which means a lot of money."

"Yes."

"The City of London? Futures?"

I stared at him. Futures. Maurice's field, not mine. Richard's broad face stared back. I got off my chair, put down my coffee cup and walked over to his assembled instrument. The inkling of a dim idea was dawning in my mind, an idea that took images of Carlos Guimares and surpluses of Robusta coffee beans, and stolen containers of beans on their way to Santos along with it.

Richard Keane stared at me impassively, his instrument and his wizardry surrounding him.

Moisture; you put a bean in the space provided in the slide, pushed it into the microwave beam and it told you immediately how much moisture was present. In a tiny bean, or rather a sort of half-bean, that might have the right amount of moisture for a kidney-cropping toxin to develop from a fungus that depended on the amount of moisture present, or was related to it in some way.

It was a lottery, according to Lawrence Edwards; the toxin might turn up or it mightn't. Everyone in the trade knew that.

"Tell me, Richard," I asked, staring at the blank LED display. "Can you work this thing backwards?"

29

In 1940 my father assisted with the burglary of a small power station near Porto Alegre. He did it mainly to help his agent's local sales-man, an Anglo-Brazilian called Freddy Dos Campos.

Freddy had sold a National Gas engine to an entrepreneur in a small town down the coast, a man who owned the local power sup-ply company and was using the engine to drive the town's main generator. For some reason Freddy had agreed to staged payments without any hard documentary guarantees or security, trusting the fellow, so the entrepreneur was delaying payments if not actually defaulting on them.

Serfaty would do exactly the same if I let him.

Freddy's bosses up in São Paulo said that Freddy's job was on the line if he didn't get the engine paid for. Freddy was getting a bit dis-traught because the Brazilian entrepreneur showed no sign of pay-ing even though the engine was up and running. Possession is nine points of the law; Freddy couldn't work out how he was going to get paid.

My father rather liked Freddy Dos Campos, who was engaged to a pretty fiancée and who was doing quite a decent job with my father's equipment. He used to tell how Freddy once persuaded him to attend the New Year's Eve party at the local English Club, a place my father, who liked golf clubs but was wary of the expatriate social side, would not naturally have attended. The thing that really impressed my father was that the members of this English Club every year made a special, powerful New Year's Eve punch in a huge tin bath. The ingredients included several bottles of Owbridge's Lung Tonic shipped out specially for the occasion to give a bit of bite to the blend of rum, gin, granadilla, wine and other constituents that made up this annual brew.

My father was no great drinker at all but he really liked that punch. It was a strong counterbalance to the throat his pipe smoking gave him. "There was something," he used to say, "about the way the

Owbridge's Lung Tonic caught the back of your tonsils that made it excellent. Took the fur right off them. Really cleared your throat."

Anyway, he and Freddy decided that the only way to put pressure on the entrepreneur was the old spares-crunch routine. They decided to nip in and pinch the governor off the top of the engine when the place shut down at night. There was no spare governor in the plant because it was too big an item for normal spares; who ever heard of the governor wearing out within the first few years?

They had a good dinner somewhere then drove down the coast, stopping on a hill outside the small town in question. They waited until about two in the morning, when the power station shut down and all the lights in the town went out, then they got out of the car and picked up a tool kit from the boot.

My father said that Freddy also pulled out a big revolver but my father said if Freddy was going to take that along he wasn't coming, so Freddy put it back.

The power station was not much more than a big corrugated barn. It was completely silent and empty, the main doors padlocked. They broke in through a side door and soon got to the engine, which was the classic type with a big speed governor, the sort with heavy balls on hinged arms that rotated, relying on gravity and centrifugal force to move the regulator collar up and down with speed. A few nuts to unscrew, a bit of careful uncoupling, and it was off. They scrambled back to the car and drove home in jubilation.

The next morning they arrived at the office in relaxed mood, rather late. The Brazilian was waiting for Freddy, dancing up and down in agitation. The whole town was without power. He had contracts to fulfil to local companies, quite apart from the domestic side. The Town Hall officials were making very nasty noises. The governor had gone: how quickly could Freddy get another from England, air freight?

Freddy pulled a long face. England? A spare? Air freight? Didn't he know there was a war on? Getting things like that, engineering parts, was a long haul from England these days. A matter of months rather than weeks.

The entrepreneur jumped up and down in further agitation. He had to have another governor. Had to. The town's power was at a standstill. Sweat poured down his face. He could never have foreseen that some maniac would steal a thing like the governor. People without electric power or light would threaten him nonetheless. This was a dire emergency; his business and his life were on the line.

Freddy nodded, slowly stroking his chin. He quite understood. Indeed he did. Of course, he said, looking at the entrepreneur steadily, it might be possible to deliver another governor very quickly, within a matter of hours even, if the entrepreneur could see his way to settling his account with the company.

My father said that that entrepreneur's face, as the penny dropped, was a picture. My father treasured his expression as an experience that went along with the impact of the piano on the cobbles in Cairo. The man let out a howl of rage. He would have grabbed Freddy with the intention of throttling him had my father, who was much bigger than the entrepreneur, not been there, grinning, genially leaning against the office door.

The entrepreneur paid up. He got his governor back. He said he would never deal with Freddy again, never, ever.

Freddy said he didn't care.

That's the whole essence of dealing people like that. The law is useless and you mustn't try to fight with their weapons. You've got to use yours. Weapons you understand and can control but which have the right impact on the bastards you're after.

My father and I never entirely saw eye to eye on politics or business but he was good on dealing with chisellers.

30

Maurice Butler is tall and unathletic, given to golfing references and jokes culled from old Morecambe and Wise shows. He wears Savile Row suits and Armani spectacles with fine, flexible rims. During the week, immobilised in the City, he stares at PC monitors whilst welded to telephones both mobile and fixed. What he does with his spare time I have no idea but Betty is suspicious, which has suited me. He drives a big BMW to get himself to and from Betty down in St.Leonards, mid-week and weekends. Maurice still thought that the Burton part of St.Leonards has a certain stylish cachet despite the blatant evidence, so he and Betty used to eat regularly at Rösers, the top south coast restaurant right by Hastings pier, until it closed. I think they did it just to satisfy Maurice's belief that the place does have some class and to show that they have money.

When not otherwise sequestered by Betty for shopping, outings and social purposes, at the weekends he motors out on a still powerful vintage Norton, all dressed up in crash hat and oily custom-made colourful leathers, which is a very bad sign. Otherwise he plays golf. They have a place in Tuscany as well as Maurice's regulation warehouse flat with a view over Docklands, which Betty says she detests; she thinks it's the acme of isolation. She preferred to stay in their flat on the friendly, accessible coast, she said. We all have our definitions of isolation.

Maurice deals in several things but I was after him for coffee, which he said, when I first met him and Betty at a cocktail party, was a speciality of his. I had no reason to doubt him. After oil, coffee is the most traded commodity in the world. He is a commodity dealer. Coffee is big time dealing.

It was time to use the contact. Time was of the essence. Misgivings about the effect on Betty would have to take a back seat.

"Maurice? It's Johnny. Johnny Barber. Hi. How are you?"

"Johnny! Johnny Barber! Hi! Great to hear you." Maurice was affecting a tolerant amusement at this intervention during his hectic working day. Doubtless his remarks would be overheard by ranks of dealers around him. "I thought you were in Antofagasta or somewhere like that. Where are you?"

"Back home, Maurice."

"Great. We must get together now you're back. Do dinner. How's the old sex life in Marine Court?"

"Still abundant, Maurice, still abundant. How are things with you?"

"Seething, my old son, seething. The City never sleeps."

The hint was clear. I got straight to business. "Are you still one of the coffee kings of London? Still the big business, is it?"

"I am, we are, it is. Whatever." Interest returned to his voice. "Why do you ask?"

"I wondered how coffee futures are shaping up."

There was a silence, just fractional, then Maurice replied cautiously, in a lower voice. "Odd your asking at this time, Johnny. Why the sudden interest?"

"Just curious. Just got back from São Paulo, you see."

"Really? Any hot info? Want me to buy some futures for you? Prices are very depressed right now. Lots of product available. Coincidence?"

"Prices? What of? Arabica or Robusta? Which countries? Which types?"

"Most. Several countries. Various types. South American in particular. Especially Robusta, which is never great shakes."

"So there's a surplus?"

"There is." Maurice, I could visualise, would be nodding wisely at the other end whilst casually adjusting his Armanis with his free hand. Maurice liked to cultivate an owlish image when dealt with as an expert. "But within a surplus you can get shortages of certain kinds or qualities, hey, like wine. It might be a good year for Bordeaux once again but my advice is to leave it. Australian's still my tipple. For value, anyway."

"Australian's too heavy for an old cove like me, Maurice. What's up with the Robusta, then? Can't the ICO rig the market?"

"Dear, dear, Johnny." He was only mock reproachful as his

interest was maintained. "Tut, tut. What are you suggesting? They won't thank you for saying things like that. Straight to court, you'll go. The jug for you. You're maybe thinking of the ICA, the International Coffee Agreement, but that cartel went phut a few years ago and the Association of Coffee Producing Countries, the ACPC, took over. Not had too much success, though, Johnny dear boy. From an ICO recommended price of two dollars per pound for Arabica, the price is currently at ninety-two cents." He put on a concerned voice. "Bad news for producers, Johnny, really bad news. Way under par, they are right now. Way under par."

"What makes the price of a commodity in surplus go up, then? Apart from someone buying to rig the market?"

"Guess." The voice, still pitched low, had gone sharp.

"The prospect of a shortage?"

"Johnny, my old friend just home from São Paulo, is there something you should be telling me? Brazil is the key to all coffee prices. And Brazil is currently in massive surplus. Anything you'd like to get off your chest, is there? Something you're teeing up for a real swing? A great big boomerdanger with your best wood?"

"My advice, dear Maurice, is that you may be about to see a sudden jump in some prices. Due to a panic."

"What sort of panic?"

"Maybe a panic to do with a fungus."

"A what?"

"Fungus. As in mushrooms, Maurice. Don't put any of my money on it. But if you were looking to buy Betty a diamond tiara, a flutter on Robusta wouldn't harm you. And Arabica as well. Although I'm off to Milan right now, I'll be back in touch. The price of this little tip-off, Maurice, is instant information when I call for it. Otherwise you've got an exclusive and the floor is yours. OK?"

"OK, Johnny. OK indeed. Much obliged. I'll be watching. But it sounds as though you may be ahead of me. Anything particular I should be watching for?"

"You ever hear of Admiral Cochrane?"

"Er, vaguely. Sort of Hornblower, wasn't he? In Chile or Brazil or South America somewhere as well? Naval hero? Cocked hat

Admiral? Bit before my time. You serve under him or something, Johnny? In your maritime youth over there?"

"Saucy old Maurice. Cochrane was indeed a naval hero. Early nineteenth century. Royal Navy to start with then perforce South America, Chile and Brazil, when he was outlawed. Sometimes an interest in history provides lessons. Cochrane got jugged by a nasty judge called Lord Ellenborough. Twelve months in chokey and absolutely ruined due to a Stock Exchange scandal involving a false report of Napoleon's death."

"Really? How come?"

"Boney's demise at the hands of Polish Cossacks was reported by an alleged party of French Royalists landing at Dover. The death of Boney meant the end of a very expensive war for Britain. So London Stock Exchange shares shot up, particularly some Cochrane held. Speculators sold, report turned out to be a hoax. Boney wasn't dead. The shares went down. A lot of people got burnt and were furious. They landed Cochrane with the hoax. Look for a bit of coffee news like that. About fungus, Maurice. Fungus that produces toxins." I let it sink in for a moment. "This fungus could make genetic modification, salmonella, e-coli, mad cow disease and foot-and-mouth look like mere nappy rash."

"My, my, Johnny." The bantering tone had gone out of his voice. "And I thought you were in the machinery business."

"I am. And am off on it. Now."

"Go carefully, Johnny my son. And thanks."

"I will. Love to Betty, Maurice."

"And mine to your latest, Johnny. Whomsoever she may be. And all who sail in her."

I landed in Milan that afternoon and went straight to Mario's factory. He wasn't in his office, he was down in the workshops. I could hear the high-pitched screech of a hammer mill biting into fluff pulp, the rattle and clip of cutters and rotary dies, hiss of pneumatics, clack of packers and similar sounds. His office was occupied by a new girl, dark, full bosomed and ripe, who stood up as I entered and smiled a brilliant smile.

"Mr Johnny Barber! Welcome! I have heard much of you."

"Really?" I grinned as we shook hands. "Not too bad, I hope?"

"Not at all. I am Chica Morelli. Mario's secretary."

"Lucky Mario."

"Ohhh." She gave me a reproachful look, one that implied things about political correctness and modern office manners in the wake of feminism but it wasn't too severe. I walked over to the inner window. Down on the workshop floor the line was in full spate, racketing on like a sleek threshing machine, cams and applicators and shafts whirling eccentrically or humming with power contained by bearings. Mario, well-dressed as ever in sports jacket and flannels, was standing in front of it talking to two mechanics and watching a couple of lads taking bags off the end of the packer. He looked up, saw me, and waved. I waved back.

"Look at that," I said to Chica. "New rotary drum former and all. You'd never believe that was old Duvivier's line now, would you?"

"No, it looks like nearly new," she said, almost proudly, then laughed. "You are the same as Mario. You think that is a beautiful sight?"

"Marvellous. Nothing like it."

"You think you have sold it?"

"Twice over. I'll go down and congratulate the man."

I had to admit it looked good. As I approached Mario signalled the guy at the control panel to speed up and the rate increased to around three hundred or more pieces a minute. The whole line began to sound right – you always know a good machine by the noise – and the lads at the packing end began to struggle to keep up; girls always pack much faster than men. Mario beamed as I put my thumb up and then signalled the guy at the control panel to slow down again as we shook hands.

"We haven't the space to run too long here. I have to keep the place clear for tomorrow, when Serfaty comes." He gave me a careful stare. "How's things, Johnny?"

"Fine, fine. You?"

"Very well."

I jerked my head towards the doorway. "Man still out there?"

"Not today. Seems to come and go irregularly now. Any ideas?"

I shook my head. "I haven't robbed any banks lately. Whose husband have you upset?"

He chuckled. "Flatterer. Not a chance. My fourth is due any minute and this machine takes all my time. All of it."

"Not even Chica?"

"Especially not Chica. I never mix work and pleasure. At least, not that way. My work is my pleasure these days."

"So who the hell is taking such an interest?"

Mario shrugged. "I don't know. I thought maybe something to do with you. From Switzerland?"

"There's nothing that sticks out, right now. Nothing."

"The South Americans? Serfaty? Arochena?"

"What would they watch us for?"

He shook his head. "I do not know. But I can tell you that Serfaty has been making some remarks about you."

"What sort of remarks?"

Mario smiled cautiously. "I think he is suggesting that you have upset some people in Brazil. Powerful people. He did not want to talk about it on the phone. He knew that you had gone to Brazil. And he made some oblique reference to the way you went to Cartagena." His eyes rested on mine for a moment. "A lady might be involved? If I know you, Johnny?"

"Oh, ho. Serfaty seems to be as curious as the proverbial cat. Prurient bastard."

"This is a small world. People in our business know each other. Without doubt, Serfaty will know that Arochena is in the market. His spies will have followed your movements. They seemed to think that you wouldn't be back. That's what Serfaty implied."

"Heavens sake. I'm flattered by all these attentions. Just for a baby diaper machine?"

The eyes hadn't flickered. "Anything more I should know about?"

"Nothing, Mario. You have my word."

He relaxed a little. "Come and have a coffee. We can go through the technical specification and make sure we're both completely prepared for tomorrow and – what is the expression they use now – singing from the same hymn sheet?"

"Amen to that."

We worked up in his office, where Chica brought us excellent coffee. I didn't say a word to Mario about my coffee capers in Colombia and Brazil because he didn't need to know. He had more than enough on his plate getting ready for Serfaty, finalising all the machine details. Mario was thorough, precise, disciplined; there were no La Scala stage-operatic aspects to him. When we finished it was getting late. Chica had left and there were only two men down on the shop floor, cleaning up and polishing the twenty-metre-long machine. Mario asked me to excuse him from dining together that evening; his wife was on the verge of producing.

"Of course," I said. "I'm due an early night myself."

Back at my hotel, just after I'd washed and was preparing to go downstairs to get something to eat, my mobile phone rang.

"Johnny? It's Maurice. I'm raising a G and T in your direction. You made me some money today."

"Yes? Bit of movement, was there?"

"Movement? Major turbulence is more like it. From late morning onwards, over news from Brazil."

"You don't say?"

"Did you know – yes, I bet you did – that bandits sometimes pinch container-loads of coffee on their way from the plantations for shipment at the port of Santos?"

"I believe someone did mention it."

"It seems they hijack the container lorries. Anyway, according to this news flash this morning the police got a tip-off and recovered a whole fleet of missing truckloads inland somewhere."

"A tip-off? How timely."

"Yes? Well I don't know about timing but there was great jubilation except that for some reason some busybody who accompanied the police insisted on checking the contents carefully. The sacks of coffee beans, that is."

"How efficient. And unusual."

"Very. And what do you suppose they found as a result? Let me hear, Johnny my boy, what you think they might have found."

"That some of the coffee beans, some of them but not all, were infected with a toxic virus?"

"Johnny, just what kind of machines have you been selling down there?"

"I'm right, then."

"Indeed you are. So the whole kit and caboodle has been impounded for investigation. And – this is the keen part – the press statement alluded to fears, rumours circulating in the interior, that this fortuitous event, ha-ha, might be confirmation that a high percentage of the current bumper crop is possibly affected, giving rise to–"

"Shortages?"

"How do you do it? How? Why didn't you buy in when I offered? There's still time, I reckon. Prices could escalate when trading starts tomorrow. The rumour has it that it's not just Brazil that's affected."

"Has there been a lot of money involved, Maurice?"

"How long is a piece of string?"

"All right, I'm not being numerate. Enough money to kill for?"

"How much would you kill for, Johnny? A million? Two million?"

"It'd have to be at least that."

"Then there's been much more than enough to kill several people for, in some trading cases I could mention. Want to get in on it tomorrow?"

"Thanks but no thanks. I'll stick to machinery. But do keep me posted, won't you, Maurice?"

"Posted? I'd like to run out there with a forked stick, myself, just to find out what you're up to."

"You mean Betty'll get a tiara?"

"Will she hell. I'll make much more than a tiara out of this. Besides, Betty's still in Tuscany with the Cartwrights, making me commute to Pisa every weekend. She says she won't come back until the rain stops. What are you doing, though, Johnny? Just what in hell are you up to?"

"Earning an honest crust, Maurice. In industry. Not like the City of London at all. We are plain, horny-handed engineers here."

He blew me a raspberry and signed off. I went down to eat pasta followed by veal.

On my own. Thinking.

32

The next morning everything went very well. We set out in Mario's Alfa to collect Serfaty from a swish city-centre hotel. He was unaccompanied and friendly, very friendly, to Mario. And polite to me. Polite, and surprised. So high did his eyebrows go that I had to grin at him.

"I'm back from Brazil, Sr Serfaty. As you see. You look surprised."

He gave a sort of brief bow and smiled back, one of his dark, oxblood-coloured smiles. "I am very pleased to see you, Mr Barber. There are times when it is a pleasure to be proved wrong."

"How kind."

Mario looked puzzled but said nothing. We drove out to the factory, went straight on to the shop floor, watched Mario give orders to his men and apprentices. Motors began to hum, rolls of pulp and tissue to rotate, shafts to turn. Serfaty turned to me.

"He's a good engineer, isn't he?"

"Excellent."

Serfaty nodded, as though reassured. The hammer mill ran up to speed with a whoop and then, at a sign from Mario, the pulp roll feed edged three layers of stiff white cardboard into the mill inlet. There was a high-pitched scream as the hammers bit into the incoming material. The whole line started to turn over, dies and shafts and gears and applicators, pulp and tissue and nonwoven and glue and elastic and plastic and superabsorbent powder reeling and folding and plying at the command of each mechanism. We strolled down to the end of the line where the two apprentices were receiving the stacks of products being pushed out into plastic bags, turning to seal the bags in a heat sealer.

Serfaty picked a product out of the horizontal stacker as it turned past us.

"All this technology," he said to me, baring his teeth in a grin, brandishing the folded plastic exterior, "to produce diapers for babies to pee and shit into, then to be thrown away."

195

"That's modern economics," I said cheerfully. "Everything disposable. Everything replaceable. The world would stop without it."

For some reason Carlos Guimares's face came to me as I said this, in a quick mental image. What was it he'd said to me when I said that no one is irreplaceable? The denial had been emphatic. That's a nihilistic belief, he'd snapped at me, Katie would reject it utterly. We are all unique.

Did she really have some sort of hold on him, however tenuous, with her New Age beliefs? Was their relationship far from the feudal one I'd always imagined? Carlos was ruthless, predatory and relentless but such men always have their weak spots. The late Sir Jimmy Goldsmith was superstitious, had lucky and unlucky clothing, loved sex the way Carlos did, maintained several domestic establishments, took up political and ecological crusades. Carlos was just as likely to be bitten by some sort of Messianic bug, something political doubtless, surely right wing, with Katie's Jungian, or more likely Nietszchean, philosophy behind it. A transient like me had no insight into the depth of feeling between Carlos and Katie, no proper feel for their day-to-day relationship.

So if she had some sort of hold on him how far did it go? Not far enough to insist on access to me, evidently. If she really wanted such access, which I was sure she did. She'd said she'd help me.

On the other hand, there was that fax.

"You don't need to run the machine any more," Serfaty said. "I've seen enough."

I stepped back and signalled to Mario with a cutting motion of my hand. He gestured to one of his men and the noises all started to die down until only the wheezing of a pneumatic cylinder on the packer impinged on the ears. The machine came to rest. Mario and Serfaty and I trooped up the staircase to the office, where Chica prepared coffee.

"To business," Serfaty said, sitting down at the big birch table Mario used for meetings. "To business, gentlemen."

The business turned out to be simple and didn't take more than an hour to complete. Serfaty agreed to buy the machine. We drew

196

up a standard form of contract with one of my Swiss companies. He wanted two hundred thousand dollars to be put on top of the agreed price – to be over-invoiced in effect – and after the funds were received from Colombia, this excess 'third party commission' was to be transmitted by me to an account of his specification, abroad. The Cayman Islands, to be precise.

The money was not for him personally, of course, he said earnestly, it was to go to a family business account, for the future security of the company.

Of course. My grandfather rides a bicycle, too.

He also wanted us to guarantee that the machine was now his, to commit ourselves to this sale. He signed the contract with a flourish.

"As soon as the deposit is received into our account," I said, putting my signature to the contract as well, "the line is yours."

Mario gave me a slightly worried look.

"I shall give instructions to my bank this afternoon," Serfaty said.

"No problem then. You are ahead of the pack."

His eyes rested on me. "I would not like to think that my trip has been for nothing, Mr Barber," he said.

"I'm certain it won't have been. Mario would like you to be our guest for dinner this evening and the happy conclusion can be celebrated then."

Serfaty nodded slowly. You could see he wasn't that happy. Men like Serfaty like to delay making the deposit payment for as long as possible, leaving you thinking you are committed by a signed contract but in reality just dangling. They try to pretend that it takes a long time to make transfers, that banks delay things, hold on to the money. It's usually lies. A transfer is electronic, faster than you can blink. Import restrictions and politics cause delays, particularly in places like Brazil and Colombia, but not banks, not if given clear instructions. Mario and I had agreed to stick to the rules of the game rigidly: the first to put his money down would get the line. I was not going to be at that dinner, I was heading over the border in a rental car to pick up Euripides Arochena in Switzerland. Our next demo would follow exactly the same procedure, next morning, when I brought Euri to the workshops.

"If," said Nassim Serfaty, "you can please arrange to take me back to my hotel, I shall make the necessary arrangements."

"Splendid. I look forward to seeing the line in place in Colombia, Mr Serfaty."

He gave me another of his steady, surprised looks, shook hands, and went out shepherded by Mario, who had agreed to drive him back into the centre of Milan. Chica Morelli came in and looked at me enquiringly.

"It's OK," I said. "He'll buy. We just need his deposit. An order is not an order until the customer puts his money down."

Chica's eyes widened. "What about the Brazilian? Will you cancel his visit?"

"Good God, no. The Brazilian is our insurance."

"Insurance?"

"Sure."

"But you can not sell the machine twice?"

"Until the money is in our account the machine is not sold at all. There's many a slip 'twixt cup and lip, Chica. Excuse me now. I must be off. Arochena has arrived in Switzerland and I have arranged to meet him in Lugano. He's doing some other transactions whilst on his visit."

Next morning I was back with Arochena. He was, if anything, slightly more querulous than he'd been at our meeting in the park in Belo Horizonte. Throughout the car journey he recounted how the Kellerman people were steadily infiltrating, interfering, behaving without scruple. This was probably the last project they'd allow him to complete on his own. Many of the others were being 'reviewed' as they called it despite his earlier decisions. It was humiliating.

I made sympathetic noises. I'd had a project 'reviewed' myself, by Robinson and his mates at the DTI, and it didn't make me happy, either.

Mario did his stuff excellently once again. The machine ran like clockwork. We retired to the office to sit at the big table, where Chica had prepared coffee. Before I could sit down, Mario held up his hand. There was an anxious expression on his face.

"Sr Arochena," he said, "would you just excuse Johnny and myself one moment? There is another matter I must just clear up before our discussions."

"Of course."

Mario and I retired to another, inner office. He waved a piece of paper under my nose.

"Serfaty did give instructions to the bank to credit your account with the deposit. These are the transfer copy confirmations he passed to me at dinner last night. They're kosher. He's bought the machine. It isn't for sale any more."

"Mario, trust me. If Serfaty's money is confirmed into my account, he'll get the line."

"It's bound to be. This kind of instruction is for keeps. We should tell Arochena, shouldn't we?"

"Not yet. Not until the money's in."

"Johnny, what game are you playing?"

"Trust me, Mario."

"Serfaty could be very dangerous if double-crossed."

"No one is double-crossing Serfaty. Leave Arochena to me. Go home to your wife. She's due any minute, isn't she? You've done your part and you weren't home for dinner last night. The machine is sold. I'll do the commercial side, as I always do. We work well together, Mario. Don't we?"

He hesitated. "You didn't tell me you were playing dangerous games in Colombia and Brazil, Johnny, did you?"

"What dangerous games? What's Serfaty been saying to you over the dinner table?"

He smiled wryly. "He says that the man who fools around with the mistress and long-term confidante of one of the most powerful businessmen in Brazil isn't likely to last for very long. He says he was surprised to see you here. He never thought you'd come back from Brazil in one piece."

I laughed. "So that's why Serfaty has been so solicitous about my health. My goodness, he must have done some fast checking that weekend I was in Cartagena with Katie. He really wanted to buy this machine all along. If I'd not gone to Brazil, we'd only have him as a customer and he'd be in a much more powerful position."

Mario's face had gone serious again. "He's got good sources. Don't underestimate him. Johnny, according to Nassim, you have been doing the *cucaracha* with a lady whose boss will stick at nothing. This man Guimares is not to be fooled with, you know? People have had accidents, disappeared. She's his right hand lady, and much more. You know that?"

"Tell me about it. I've known Katie for ten years, Mario."

"Maybe. But Guimares has steadily got more and more powerful, according to Nassim. He was a successful businessman before but now he's very heavy, into politics, big deals, you know what South America is like? These are tigers. Women and money mean everything to these bastards. You threaten their reputation, the old macho behaviour comes out like we here don't know it. We Italians can behave tough but a powerful South American – shit. You're not going back there, by the way, are you?"

"Brazil isn't Colombia, Mario."

"No? You think the police there are nice to criminals, if they think they're criminals? You remember what they did to those stray kids on the church steps? Rat-tat-tat and it's all over. No orphan problem any more. You remember the squads taking criminals down back alleys? It isn't Europe, is it? A man like Guimares can pull strings you wouldn't believe could be pulled."

"Tell me about it." An image of the blue Ford rolling over down the dusty embankment came briefly into my mind's eye, like a sharp camera-shot from an old film, and I had to blank it out quickly. "Stop worrying, Mario. I'm a big boy now. And I'm here, not in Brazil. Go home. I'll wrap up this business and see you this evening, after I've taken Arochena back to Lugano. Let's have dinner together – if you're not pacing the hospital passages with a pocketful of cigars."

He still looked worried. "You can't sell the same machine twice, Johnny, and I haven't got another."

"No. But you soon will have, knowing you. Especially when you've got four children to cater for."

200

He grinned. "That's true. There's a line in Jordan I'm interested in."

"So trust me. That's our whole business, isn't it? Based on trust?"

He nodded slowly as his grin faded. "You're right. Sorry Johnny. Look, if you need anything, ask Chica, eh? She's pretty competent; I'm giving her more responsibility these days."

"She's pretty, for sure."

He gave me a jab in the ribs. "Enough of that. Stick to Brazilian cuties, not my staff. But not Brazilian cuties who belong to robber barons, eh? And for me I'd be happier if you left all Brazilian cuties alone for a while."

I smiled at him. "I'm touched by your solicitude, Mario."

His face was still slightly creased. "We make a good team, you and I, Johnny. I'd be really upset to lose you. There is something about you these days which has changed. I can sense it. This is Serfaty's machine, though. Are we agreed on that? I'll leave you to deal with Arochena how you like but I want your assurance. Please."

I stuck out my hand. "Agreed. You have my assurance. See you for dinner."

He smiled apologetically, shook hands, and left. I went back into the main office where Chica was hovering attentively and sat down opposite Euripides Arochena.

"Sorry about that, Euri. Mario's wife is expecting any minute and he had to go."

"Ah, new children," he sighed heavily. "Lucky man. How I wish I was that young again. But I have seen the machine so his absence is no problem. It is excellent. I think that now you and I have to make some arrangements."

Chica gave me a harassed glance.

"Fine." Ignoring her, I looked at my watch. "It's not too far from lunchtime, Euri. Why don't we go down the road and discuss final details over a bite or two? There's an excellent trattoria near here."

"How civilised. It is a pleasure to do business with you, Johnny. Unlike those bastards at Kellerman's. Do you know that one of their accountants has already had the insolence to query some of my personal expenses? Would you credit that?"

"Disgraceful. Come on, allow me to buy you lunch."

"You're a gentleman, Johnny."

We stood up and I let Arochena precede me out through the office door. Chica caught hold of my sleeve. "What are you going to do?" she whispered. "The transfer from Serfaty is certainly already into your account."

I patted her hand in my most avuncular manner. "Don't worry, Chica."

"But what? Won't you have to tell Senhor Arochena that his trip has been for nothing?"

"Leave it to me. There'll be another machine, soon. Our business is based on trust."

She looked into my face, hard, then slowly shook her head. "Suddenly," she said, "I feel sorry for poor Senhor Arochena."

33

"So this is where you and Lawrence Edwards met," Frances Parks said, nodding at the waitress who put down her espresso yet simultaneously cocking an eye towards the passing people on Northumberland Avenue.

"This is it," I answered. "With William Pulford."

It was a much duller day than the one on which I'd met Lawrence and the people didn't seem to be so brisk. They moved with more caution. I put a cube of sugar into my cappuccino and watched it sink through the chocolate-crumbed foam into the source of the trouble.

Her face twitched at my deliberate reference to Pulford but she didn't respond to it. "How did Lawrence seem that day?"

"Tired. His usual pedantic self, but tired. As though he'd been up late."

She nodded slowly, as though that fitted in to something. I waited but she didn't elaborate.

"Has Barry Henshaw come up with anything about the hit-and-run yet?" I asked.

She shook her head, making her brown hair ripple a bit. She had a very similar sort of get-up to the time she'd visited my flat. Smart, professional, grey-suited, white-bloused. Like a uniform, or maybe armour.

"Not getting very far, are they? The police, I mean. Lawrence didn't have a high opinion of them, either. Said they'd never find the bean analyser. And they haven't. He was right. Nothing on the caravan explosion nor the hit-and-run to boot. Not up to much so far, are they?"

She took a delicate sip of her espresso then put it down. "Maybe not. Maybe they're better than you think." She smiled suddenly, making her face lighter and more attractive, as it did when she was in my flat. "Barry says you did an amazing badge job between Sweden and Italy once," she said, as though that were relevant.

"Badge job?"

"Sure. A badge job. You arranged to ship a machine from Italy out to Sweden, change its maker's name plates and ship it back at twice the price. As a Swedish machine."

"Me? Why would I do that?"

"So that the Italians who'd got an EEC investment grant for a hospital project could buy the Italian machine they wanted but get all the kick-backs – all right, third party commissions – they wanted by importing the thing. Money salted away for them in Switzerland, you know? They could only do that by importing a foreign machine. And you, of course, prospered too."

"I can't imagine where Henshaw got that idea."

"He says the machine is still standing unused in a factory in the Mezzogiorno. A typical EU scam. You have a friend in Milan you collaborate with on such deals. A guy called Mario Chiari."

"Amazing. I'm afraid he'll have to be very careful about what he says. I'm sensitive – and litigious – about such things."

She smiled even more broadly. "Oh, I'm not interested in your foreign entanglements. I'm not here to put the world to rights. Especially not stupid EEC investment capers. My brief is nice and insular. And about Lawrence in particular."

"Limited objectives, eh?"

"Precisely."

"Tell me: is there a Mr Parks?"

She looked startled, then glanced at her ring finger. "No," she said, "there's never been a Mr Parks."

"My apologies, in that case, for calling you Mrs."

"No offence taken. Understandable, in the observant circumstances."

"Why the ring?"

"Camouflage."

"I understand."

"Do you? I wonder. I know you're not married," she said, slowly crinkling a small twist of paper beside her plate, as though it had contained all she needed to know about me from her files and could now be dispensed with.

"Not now, no."

"But you were, once."

"Yes."

"You've not tried again?"

"Once bitten, twice shy."

"You have children?"

"No."

"You've never thought of emigrating?"

"What for? I can go anywhere I like from here. Perhaps, when this is all over, I might go away for a bit."

"When this is over? Surely it is all over, isn't it? The bean research is cancelled. Isn't your Italian machine sold?"

"The machine is more or less sold. But there are matters to clear up."

She frowned. "What matters?"

"Just private things."

Her expression became more interested. "That extraordinary block of flats," she queried, "made to look like an old ocean liner. Why do you live there? I mean, I'm sorry, I would have thought you were a much more social animal than that isolated place allows."

"Do you? I'm there because up to now it has suited me. An unremarkable place where many people are unnoticeable. Anonymous. Perhaps it is getting time for a change. When all this is over and I've done my trip, I might look elsewhere."

"What trip?"

"To Brazil."

"Brazil? Why?"

"I told you: there are private matters to clear up."

"Where will you stay?"

"I haven't decided yet."

She paused for a moment. Then: "If you left your flat, where would you go?"

"I haven't thought about it until now. Somewhere inland, perhaps, with a view of country. Or a small town. The seaside has a terminal feel to it and I'm not ready to terminate yet."

"Not South America?"

"South America is fine to visit. It can offer a life of applied hedonism. But there are disadvantages."

"Why would you not want to live a life of applied hedonism?"

"Something Puritan within me."

She smiled. "I can understand that."

I decided not to ask her where she lived in return, make any more personal enquiries. It would be better to let her feel she was controlling things now.

My hunch paid off.

"Is there a future in what you do?" she asked.

Just like Katie, I thought. Even Betty. Are all women the same?

"Are you aiming to replace Lawrence?" I countered.

She thought for just a fraction of a second. "Possibly. Well, probably."

"Am I speaking to just you or is Barry Henshaw a party to our conversation?"

"That depends on whether he can indict you in some way or not."

"My goodness. We are being very frank. The future is something I've only just started to think about once again. One of the reasons I went to live in the ocean-liner apartment block was that, ten years ago, I passed through something of a crisis. My job was cancelled. My wife had left me for a market gardener. I met a Brazilian lady at a party and we were attracted to each other. It was more than a passing affair. She caused me to rethink what I was doing from first principles and to see that I had got myself into the classic middle-executive, middle-range treadmill. My life was not in control. It was time to do something about it – now or never, so to speak. It so happened that shortly afterwards an Italian businessman with whom I had friendly relations came up with a proposition to me. One which the firm I had worked for would never have entertained. I had exactly the right experience. I agreed to collaborate with him while developing my other contacts as well. That was, and is, Mario Chiari."

"I see."

"Do you? It wasn't a lightly taken step, let me tell you. I left the life I had been living and embarked on something entirely different.

It has been enormously successful commercially. Until now, I have never looked back or forward. It was only recently that Lawrence found it useful to pick my brains."

"Within limits, of course?"

"Of course. Another coffee?"

She shook her head so I ordered just one for myself. "Why was Lawrence so chary about this coffee bean thing? I mean, why did he play the cards so close to his chest?"

She had to think before answering. I suppose she could hardly say that the DTI was riddled with informers reporting to Tony Barnwell and maybe Lawrence had had thoughts about that.

"It's very hard to understand," she said. "I'm still trying to find out."

"It seems to me that he sent me off into the blue because he must have thought I'd trip over something in Colombia or Brazil. So this end wasn't maybe so important."

"I think it's possible he was thinking about Colombia," she said.

"Why?"

"Lawrence had his little idiosyncrasies. Maybe he thought your enquiries in Colombia would yield a result once you started asking about."

I managed to avoid wincing at the word idiosyncrasies. Things you'd punch a man for, you let by from a woman.

"Yet this end turned out to be the lethal part," I answered, trying to cover up some ideas that started to filter into my mind. "Despite what Lawrence said."

"That's possibly just a result of distant stirrings by you."

No, I almost answered, that couldn't be related to Colombia because Lawrence was already dead before I got to Colombia, let alone Brazil. Something here got to Lawrence and Pulford first. And Brazil, just as Maurice said, is at the centre of anything to do with coffee. Colombia wasn't important.

I didn't voice my thoughts, though. You must never let your guard down with people like those.

Frances Parks was watching me expectantly, as though trying to follow the invisible train of thought in my head.

"Well, this is all speculation," I said, briskly. "We may never find out. It may just have been an accident. If I can help in any further way," I turned my voice earnest, "please do let me know."

She smiled a rather disbelieving smile. "Within limits, of course?"

"That depends on what help is needed. And on potential indictments by your colleague. Ah, here comes my second cup of possible Balkan Kidneys." I looked at the cup thoughtfully as it was put in front of me, then up at her. "You know, for all his knowledge, Lawrence didn't seem to feel the least bit threatened by the toxic syndrome at all. He downed coffee in quantity at our last meeting. So did William Pulford. As though they didn't really believe in any danger from beans. I wonder if there is any relevance in that?"

Her smile broadened.

"Perhaps I might have a second one myself, after all," she said.

34

Instrument: tool, implement, esp. for delicate or scientific work; formal, esp. legal, document.

Concise Oxford Dictionary

They have knocked down the offices on Broadway where I learnt how to export machinery. New Scotland Yard stands there now. Its triangular metal sign rotates slowly, accusingly, on the site of what was a sooty, late Victorian block encrusted with classical mouldings. Outside, the grimy broken pediments and sills were chalk-splattered by pigeon droppings that ran over edges like streaky icing across a black birthday cake. Inside, dark brown or green walls gave way to passages of crackled white tiles like an aged public lavatory. A flock of different businesses roosted in Broadway Court, from large mahogany-lined enterprises to desperate one-room traders anxious for a respectable address.

I worked on the top floor overlooking Epstein's disturbing figures above St James's Park tube station. Westwards I could see Victoria Street and the stews of Strutton Ground. There I learnt everything there was to learn about documentary credits, import licences and bills of lading.

These were now my weapons.

The offices occupied an attic suite under canted head-cracking ceilings, walled with open shelves full of dust and old files that threatened to choke the place. In the winter the dormer windows rattled and sang with the wind; rain squeezed through the loose sashes to form inside puddles on grimy yellow sills. The firm had been there for donkey's years, selling textile machinery to far-flung places who now made their own contraptions for scraping, cleaning, winding, warping, reeling, weaving, knitting and sewing textile fibres.

It was a filthy perch. Grit sifted in continually. Draughts stirred the dust in piles of tattered manufacturer's leaflets and catalogues, some of them quite heavy volumes bound in old, rock-hard covers sturdily confident of an unchanging product range in an unchanging textile world. Much of the machinery depicted was made by northern firms who had not redesigned their work for over forty years; built on the principle of a cast-iron frame to which attachments were easily added, they seemed indestructible, capable of absorbing endless additional gadgets and afterthoughts.

Beneath the dormer windows, under sloping geometric roofs, clerks sat at desks facing each other. They tried to keep warm in winter by moving old single-bar electric fires, with rusty filaments that popped and phutted and smelt of burning dust, to strategic positions near their feet. The draughts were unpredictable; some clerks wore woollen mittens while they worked. Everyone had to clean off the gritty working surfaces every morning. There was no point in complaining because everybody knew, back in the mid-sixties, that the place was for the knacker's yard.

In those days machinery was still packed into huge wooden crates, expensive timber boxes, for shipment. The container was just starting to change the way everyone thought about shipping. No one could foresee how you might just sell containerloads of things using bills of lading as documents of title – *instruments*, as they are called – to containers that might contain God knew what inside.

Perhaps nothing inside.

Or not exist at all.

On winter afternoons, after four, when the lights were on and London glowed outside, it was still possible to imagine what life in Edwardian times might have been like. The office boy coming round with files or to collect mail, a smell of tea brewing in the passage, shipping clerks slipping out to place bets or buy The Pink 'Un in the cold wet street below. The managing director, who had started in this, his family's business as an office boy in 1912, might come in shouting angrily about an error in a bank draft or because a consignment had missed the weekly Royal Mail packet to Buenos Aires from Southampton. Documents might have to be re-presented or a Letter of Credit to be extended by cabling embarrassed requests to supposedly inefficient foreigners.

The language of business was still packed with obsequious courtesies and derivative Latin. Months were instant, proximo or ultimate. Remittances with musical names like tenure drafts flew to and fro. The firm never wrote back on a subject; it reverted, like a cultured plant going back to the wild. No one tried to find anything out; they endeavoured to ascertain.

Shipping documents, like old black-and-white five-pound notes, were much more impressive then. They were fine-printed, scrolled, headed with magnificent artwork based on Victorian steel engravings. The Bills of Lading of each shipping company were like titles to a grand property in the foxhunting Midlands, flowered with multi-coloured flags and exuberant bunting above whole gazetteers of finely printed clauses. How much duller, now, the computer-generated documents of modern commerce, dry, sober, the outcome of efficient rationalisation and computer memories full of standardised fonts and easily-emulated design criteria.

It is not surprising that Letter of Credit fraud, backed by bogus bills of lading, has become so common, such a daily occurrence. Ask the banks, ask the International Maritime Bureau, the lot run by Eric Ellen I mentioned to Frances Parks and Barry Henshaw; they'll tell you. In confidence, of course.

From the spares department in Broadway they exported shuttles, jacquard cards, tufting needles, pickers, bobbins, non-reedy reeds and sliver cans with kicking bands. They used the clerical methods of an industry, those manufacturers of looms, carding engines, spinning frames, tufters and winders, whose demise was imminent. They thought that computers belonged to the literature of Babbage, to space-age fantasy. The game was lost but they did not know it there in Broadway Court. They were finishing an innings, scoring the last few runs for an old club side whose pavilion was falling apart.

The principles, though, have remained the same. The training you got in those old places was something you never forgot. When Lawrence Edwards used to talk to me about bills of lading and documentary credits he knew he was speaking to a pro. It's much simpler now than it was then. Much simpler, and much easier to subvert. Documents are like rules; there to be used for your own ends when you're desperate.

I remained at Broadway Court until the demolition men moved in. They worked their way across the roofs, bashing in the slates with picks and cascading the rubble down into the crackled white-tile passageways below, steadily exposing the interiors to the weather. The firm was last to leave the building, which was nearly all dust and rubble, splintered joists and shattered ceramics by the time it vacated the place. I resigned round about then. I heard that the firm struggled on in modern premises for a while until, like an aged man dug out of his dirty old den and exposed to the glare of clean sanitary conditions, it died.

You have to fight your battles with weapons of your own, on your own ground. Mine are not speed governors or spare parts. Like those of a lawyer, they are pieces of paper and invisible quantities of money, dumb figures on printed statements glanced across the world. Dumb figures, which have their own impacts.

Mario had provided me with the immediate weapon I needed. As Euripides Arochena and, through him, Carlos Guimares would come to know.

35

I had the good fortune of the foolhardy. Another Brazilian currency crisis had receded. Argentina was all the news. The last crisis was, to Brazilian optimists, now part of another past quickly to be forgotten in the same way that Brazilians always hope their financial past can be ignored. They prefer to see life in the light of one more bright, sharp, Carioca dawn, heralded by sambas and the trumpets of football trophies. Import licences were re-issued, transfers were no longer blocked. Euri Arochena moved to conclude his contract with an urgency which, to my instinct, was impelled by approaching nemesis.

He wanted his cut quickly, in other words.

I received and transmitted documents, kept close to my Swiss collaborators, rigorously observed the fine print and the sub-clause. Banks have an obsession with minutiae, the crossed t, the dotted i, whilst broader, more fateful issues pass clanking by, leaking steam and energy. But banks are, after all, merely obeying instructions, obeying them to the letter, making sure their client cannot claim some clerical negligence in the aftermath. A bank is merely establishing that, within the law, it has done what it was told.

It took nearly three weeks before I got back to Brazil. No further news came from Katie, no reply on any of her numbers. It lent urgency and justification to everything I did, but three weeks is a long time, even if you are rather enjoying a skilful game of nefarious revenge.

From time to time I tried, but Betty didn't reply to any of my calls. Tuscany was retaining its attraction.

When everything was done I flew down to Recife on a charter from Madrid, changed planes, took a local flight down to São Paulo, checked in to another hotel, a small one, in another district from the last one. I used a pay telephone box in a very public mall to make my calls.

Still no Katie.

It couldn't be that she was really that upset about the timing part, my little deception, surely? Even if she were, she'd have it out with me, bite my head off in a furious phone call. But there was no answer, anywhere.

I will help you, Johnny?

I thought I was about two or three days ahead of the notices that would go out advising of the disappearance of a machinery shipment to a firm in Belo Horizonte, Brazil, called Texteis Arochena. The notices would say that the bill of lading used for collection at sight against the confirmed and irrevocable letter of credit opened by the buyer referred to three mythical containers on a non-existent Panamanian vessel. The container specifications detailing which bits of machinery were in which seemed marvellously genuine – I'd used the ones sent to Serfaty as a model. The beneficiary's Swiss branch address had an authentic ring even if, for anyone who might check, that street didn't go up to those numbers. The shipper was a nominee business branch in Lugano and the address in Clapham of the British principal was a derelict flat over a curry house that specialised in tandoori takeaways.

When sheer greed motivates your customers you can get away with all sorts of things. Ask any con man.

None of the documents had my name on them. No one apart from Euri Arochena could testify that the transaction related to me, that the phantom machine was anything to do with Mario or me. Euri had placed an order in Switzerland for a machine. Whose machine and where it was could only be established by word of mouth, by Euri actually pointing to me if he dared do so and lose his chance of putting away his half million dollars. They say it happens every day but the people who do it disappear.

I had no intention of disappearing.

I collected against another letter of credit for Serfaty's machine – which was put through another company entirely – and paid Mario, with the usual reserve for him into his account in Switzerland. The machine was still on the high seas bound for Baranquilla. I sent Serfaty his two hundred thousand dollars, to the account in the Caymans he'd specified.

214

I heard nothing more from Frances Parks or Barry Henshaw about their investigations into William Pulford and Lawrence Edwards's deathes and I had no intention of contacting them again while I was so occupied. My flat in St.Leonards saw little of me and its telephone was not used for outgoing calls. Nor was my mobile. I speculated a bit about Frances Parks, the carefully clad lady with her defensive wedding ring, and decided that the relationship could develop, like that with Lawrence, into something indefinably interesting once this was all over.

I didn't put in a claim for expenses to Robinson at the DTI; I decided that could wait. I had other points to make.

Maurice phoned me a few times from the City. He cleaned up well on the coffee commodity market before it started to calm down again. Reports now said that the problem of the fungus had been very exaggerated, that stocks were good, prospects for production good and there was no cause for alarm. The whole thing had been a storm in a coffee cup. The media were preoccupied with genetically modified maize and violent animal rights campaigners rather than kidney-cracking coffee beans. Apart from one or two vitriolic newspaper financial columnists' comments, there was very little published about the scare.

Tony Barnwell announced a new trade agreement with Brazil and got good notices in the business and political press.

Someone made a bomb while the coffee panic lasted, according to Maurice. Great trading went on. The Enron scandal had taken eyes off the ball.

The day I arrived in São Paulo I phoned Carlos Guimares from a public call box. The same frosty dame answered.

"It's Johnny Barber here," I told her. "To make an appointment to see Senhor Guimares."

"Mr Barber?" The frosty voice sounded incredulous. "You mean you have returned to São Paulo?"

"I have. Tell Senhor Guimares that I have a bearer bank draft for him for one million six hundred thousand dollars drawn on a Jersey bank account. The money is owing to Texteis Arochena, your subsidiary via the Kellerman finance group, due to an error in shipping documentation. Actually, I expect it's Kellerman's money rather than Arochena's, so it belongs to Carlos directly. On certain conditions, he can have it back."

I could practically hear her swallowing. Or gulping. "Senhor Carlos is not here right now. I – I have no idea what you're talking about. Our finance director will, I am sure, take the draft for you."

"Carlos never is there, is he? Your finance director can go fish. I want to see Carlos in person. Tell him that I will hand him over the draft in the presence of Katie Gonzalez. In person. No other circumstances will be acceptable. No one else is to be present and no authorities to be contacted. Otherwise no deal."

"I – I will have to try to contact Senhor Carlos."

"You certainly will. I'll wait if you like. Where is he, next door? Or just across the desk from you?"

"Where can he contact you, Mr Barber?"

"He can't. I will phone again this afternoon at five. I want to see Carlos and Katie tomorrow. No one else. No tricks. Otherwise I leave São Paulo tomorrow, keeping the money."

"Mr Barber –"

"Five o' clock. This afternoon."

I rang off. Even public call boxes have their hazards. I could have insisted on some remote meeting-place, some busy street corner, but I didn't want that. I wanted to rub his bloody nose in it right there in his own office.

At five o' clock the frosty dame put me straight through to Carlos.

"Hello, Johnny." The voice was cool, controlled. "I believe that criminal fraud carries very severe, very long jail sentences."

"So does criminal theft of scientific instruments and deliberate impregnation of coffee beans with the correct amount of moisture to generate toxic fungus in the furtherance of even bigger criminal fraud."

"Come, come. Why would anyone do such a thing?"

"To clean up on a difficult, over-subscribed commodity market in which there is a massive surplus of low-quality product."

"It would be very difficult to establish such a theory. And impossible to prove in practice."

"Not as difficult as proving criminal fraud against a phantom company with no directors and with which I have no connection."

A pause. Then: "So where do we go from here?"

"You heard my terms, Carlos. You produce Katie. At your own office. Tomorrow. For that I will pay you one million six hundred thousand dollars. Just to see her."

There was, suddenly, a chuckle at the other end.

"You do have some style, Johnny. I have to admit that. Tomorrow morning, then. Say eleven o' clock?"

"Eleven o' clock. No one else. Otherwise your cash is gone."

"I understand."

I put the phone down and left the mall quickly. Where the hell had he hidden Katie? And how persuaded her not to respond to me or try to contact me apart from that one telefax?

So far Carlos had done all the winning. It was time for a round to go to me, but I slept badly and didn't eat much. No one bothered me or even seemed to notice me. I was travelling on my own passport and would use my usual credit card to settle my hotel bill. That much confidence I had but, in Brazil, Euri Arochena's word might go a long way further than mine – if he dared to use it.

Somehow, though, I felt elated. Buzzing.

I dressed carefully the following morning, trying to look as well-groomed and relaxed as possible, ate a leisurely breakfast avoiding the papaya, read the papers which were mostly about domestic matters, football or economics, steadied my nerves with an extra shot of black coffee, then took a taxi to the Centro Empresarial where Carlos and Katie had their offices. The commissionaire in the foyer was impassive as he phoned the news of my arrival upstairs. I went across the marble floor to a lift, up to the tenth floor, was met by the owner of the frosty voice, a bronzed matron in a smart pleated outfit who stared at me with unconcealed curiosity but kept her distance as she ushered me into a suite with great glass-windowed walls that overlooked a park and busy boulevard beyond.

I kept my distance, too. Impassive, I was.

"Senhor Carlos will be here shortly," she said.

I remained standing, looking out at the park. The room was cool and well furnished, with a low coffee table in front of a pale leather settee. There were four doors, all panelled in a pale figured wood I didn't recognise but it matched the leather. One door opened and in he walked, Carlos, dressed in rather similar colours: a pale fine-woven suit, pale crocodile shoes, cream shirt, and tan tie. Expensive. He held out his hand.

"Johnny Barber." The voice was still calm, controlled, the English without accent. His face was pale brown like everything else around us, above it thick wavy hair turning grey but perfectly brushed, cheekbones broadly set, the eyes dark brown with clear whites looking straight at me, the mouth full, sensual. "We meet at last."

I took the hand, shook it briefly, found it perfectly dry, dropped it. "Carlos Guimares. So we do."

"There are people looking for you. There are cautions about you. I have not told them you are here, as you requested, but I thought I should warn you."

"I'm not frightened of meeting them."

"No?"

"No." He wasn't going to rattle me with the idea of official pursuit.

"But you do admit that you have one million six hundred thousand dollars of my organisation's money, obtained by documentary fraud and criminal deception."

"No, I don't. I should be sorry to hear that Euri Arochena placed an order with a company that deceived him but he didn't buy the machine I had on offer. I sold that to Colombia. He must have placed an order with someone else. Someone who seems to have made an error in documentary procedures. The Swiss can be surprisingly inefficient, despite their high reputation."

"You might have trouble defending that position. It could take a long time, during which you would be in unpleasant circumstances, find it very expensive, and even then probably lose your case."

"You might have trouble denying that you and Tony Barnwell

218

arranged to steal a high frequency microwave moisture sensor and use it in reverse."

"I cannot think what you mean."

"You used the instrument to put an amount of moisture into coffee beans so as to create the right conditions for toxic fungus to form. It was intended to be used the other way, to detect such conditions quickly, in order to help prevent them. Laboratory gravimetry would be too tedious, take too long. You made money while the market panic took place. It is even possible that you and your English accomplices killed two civil servants who had become suspicious. Principally a man called Lawrence Edwards and someone called William Pulford, who he enrolled to help him."

He smiled broadly. "Absurd. A farrago of utter nonsense."

"Investigation, particularly of those who profited most by the market panic, could take a long time, during which you would undoubtedly be in unpleasant circumstances."

"You're bluffing."

"So are you. And you want your money back. If I were to be prosecuted, you'd never get it." I shook my head at him. "It would be ridiculous, wouldn't it, to pass by the opportunity to regain one million six hundred thousand dollars missing from your business simply due to an obstinate refusal to present one woman executive in person to the man returning the amount? What would your shareholders and banks say to that?"

His voice dropped. "You still value her that much?" he muttered.

"My motives are complex. Pride is among them. But have no doubt that Katie's welfare is paramount."

"Once you have seen her what will you do?"

"Return your money." I pulled a manila envelope out of my inside jacket pocket and gestured with it.

"And then?"

"It depends on Katie."

He nodded slightly, as though satisfied. Then he stiffened himself, turned to one of the doors and tapped on it in a marked pattern of raps. It opened and two men came in, casually dressed, alert, on the balls of their feet, to stand behind him.

I recognised my two pursuers from the last visit at once; even the clothes were exactly the same. One had a scar healing on his forehead. Possibly a bump from a car, rolling over and over.

Their eyes took me in contemptuously. Their expressions said I'd be a pushover this time.

36

Fraud; Deceitfulness (rare); criminal deception, use of false representations; dishonest artifice or trick.

Concise Oxford Dictionary

A *salacacabia*

I shook my head sadly. "You never can keep your word, can you, Carlos? Not even safe passage to the airport. Now you've broken it again. I said no one else was to be here except you, me and Katie."

He stood square on to me and held out his hand. "I can have the draft taken from you, now. I suggest you hand it over to save distress. You may then leave to face your prosecution."

The two men stood behind him, impassive, but waiting.

I grinned as I passed the manila envelope over and watched him scan its empty interior. "You don't think I'm that stupid? There is no banker's draft. I never believed that you'd let me leave if you had it. You'd do what you did last time." I let the facts sink in for a moment while he stood silently, impassive. "You can still get the money, though. I'll wire transfer it when I'm satisfied. And safely away."

The hand holding the envelope dropped. His face flushed and his voice went tense and threatening. "Without the draft there is no deal."

"Then there's no deal. You lose."

His eyes were reddening. "You expect me to accept your word? After I have agreed to settle my side of the bargain?"

"Some agreement, with those two goons behind you." I smiled, just to rile him. "I had to accept your word on my last visit. And you didn't keep it. I didn't expect you to keep it now, either. You fell for my nice little lure of bearer cash, Carlos. Now it's your turn to have to accept my conditions. Not exactly an onerous demand, is it, to produce Katie to get your money back? Or is it? Is she still alive?"

Women and money, Mario had said. Women and money were more important to these bastards than anything else, discounting power except in so far as the possession of women and money is perhaps a definition of power. Sir Jimmy Goldsmith was the same as Carlos in many ways. Yet some of their women – in this case one of them – had influences, could stipulate conditions which appealed to deep-rooted superstitions within these sorts of men. Katie would be one if anyone could. Carlos was the kind that had Beliefs with a capital B, could take up philosophies, follow random theories and semi-religions, at the drop of a skirt.

"You have lied to me." The voice was flat, accusatory, as though I had acted like a moral outcast, not him.

"So did you to me. I said alone here, with only Katie, and you agreed. Your goons were not part of the deal. I changed my mind about the money because I knew I couldn't trust you. A bearer draft would have been much too dangerous, what with these hoods you employ and your propensity get rid of people by using cars or other methods. I was right, wasn't I?"

"You lied."

"You're pretty economical with the truth yourself. I give you my word: once I've seen Katie and satisfied myself she's OK, you'll get your money. I'll wire it as soon as I'm back in Europe. I have a flight reserved for tonight. Via Zurich. I can send the money tomorrow morning. If I want to, that is."

He glared at me. Even though my pulse was thudding, I was starting to enjoy the expression on his face. This was hard for him to swallow. He, Carlos Guimares, not to be in control?

"This is unacceptable."

I stuck my hands into my pockets. "Let's ask Katie, shall we? Unless you've lied even more to me and can't produce her. In which case I go straight to the police and tell them the whole story, detail the complete *salacacabia*. If I promise Katie I'll return the money, when I see her, that should be enough. You'll never get it back any other way, I can assure you. I've put it where no one will find it and only my signature will release it."

At that he paused again, as though considering deeply. I saw a

222

slight flicker of humour pass over his face and wondered what the hell he thought was funny. There was a silence while his features, normally fairly immobile, tightened and flexed very slightly. Then he nodded, a faint reluctant nod, said something sharp to the two goons and watched them leave by the same door as they had entered. He looked at me for another long moment as though still considering something, turned without another word and went out, not through the door he'd come in.

I was left alone.

What would he have told Katie, I wondered, if I really had the bearer draft, and he had forcibly taken it? That I'd gone, been bought off, without seeing her? What terrible fate, what elimination, had I just avoided? How quickly could he readjust to circumstances, re-set his strategy so as to assuage his pride and benefit from the change in events? There was a pause while presumably he found or briefed Katie. A few minutes went by. I stared out of the big glass windows, trying to look unconcerned for the benefit of what I believed might be surveillance cameras covering this room, then decided there might not be, not if he'd decided to have his two henchmen frisk me by force.

But you never knew.

On the other hand, money talks. One point six million dollars of it talks quite loudly.

His door opened and Katie came in, alone. Her head was up proudly and she was stylishly dressed in flowing cotton, carefully made up, coiffed, high-heeled, the epitome of the elegant Brazilienne. My pulse, already unstable, picked up at the sight of her.

She gave me a wicked but slightly tremulous smile.

"Well, well, Johnny. What trouble you can cause, you English pirates."

I stepped across to her and kissed her, respectfully but thankfully. My heart rate steadied just a little. Katie looked like everything memory held for me: a fine ripe woman in her forties with all a woman needs.

"Katie. Thank God, you look great."

I meant it.

She disengaged herself. The look she gave me was long, steady, composed.

"What are you doing here? Why have you come back? I sent you the fax, didn't I?"

"You did, but how could I believe it? I had to come to find you. I was worried about you. Did you know that Carlos intended those two thugs to frisk me, and worse?"

She shook her head calmly. "I told Carlos before he came to this meeting that if any harm came to you, especially from them, I would break every promise I made to him."

"Carlos didn't listen."

She frowned. "You do not know what influence I have with Carlos. He has certain convictions. You have been very lucky, also. I think that Carlos has come to believe in your luck."

"Perhaps he has, perhaps not. I wouldn't buy a pension on the basis of it. Did he tell you that I have promised to pay him the sum of one million six hundred thousand dollars just to see you, Katie?"

"He said you'd say that. But you stole the money from him in the first place."

"I could easily have kept it."

"Could you? I'm not so sure."

"Be sure. And trust Carlos to try and turn my victory to ashes. He can't bear to lose, can he? Even if he still has you in his power, to be made to produce you to me like this must really bug him. I could easily keep the money and can still do that. Where has he kept you? In a stone tower with a dragon to guard you, your body available to him at his whim?"

She smiled. "What a foolish man you are, Johnny. Of course not. You are no knight-errant. I have been in Brasilia on a special project."

"Speculating in coffee beans, perhaps? Odd that you should disappear so soon after what we agreed."

"Carlos is not what you think. He is a most attentive, considerate man despite his – his infidelities. Which are no worse than any other man's."

"But freedom doesn't come into his thinking."

"After Cartagena I promised not to speak to you until Carlos told me it was safe. Now he says it's safe. Your interference can not harm him."

"He can't get his money back without it."

She shook her head reproachfully. "How you lied to me, Johnny. You told me you really wanted to see me in Cartagena, that you cared for me, while all the time you were snooping on Carlos for some British agency. You used me as a means to an end."

"Oh? Do you really want to believe only that? Should I only believe that you came to Cartagena to pay Carlos back for his infidelity, to show him that you too could have flings when you wanted? Should I believe that our meeting was nothing but selfish self-interests, not fun and life and liberty and love and wanting to see each other?" I gave her a straight stare. "Should I remember that look of recognition when I mentioned Texteis Arochena, a look that told me later that you knew Carlos had bought it but you said nothing to me about it? You could have warned me, Katie. Should I just remember your loyalty to him? Or should I believe that you came to Cartagena because we are old lover-friends, will always be old lover-friends, despite anyone else? That one bit of my heart wanted it because it is owned by Katie Gonzalez? Always will be."

Her face clouded. "You devil, Johnny. You've always been good with words. For a shallow man, as you so often claim to be, you have resources you use unfairly. I said once, years ago, that we could have been a couple and I was interested that you accepted that at the time. Didn't you?"

"Yes. We've always had a – a sort of domestic acceptance."

"But of course, although you did not say it, we knew we could only have been a couple if things had been different, if our lives had taken different courses. You were silent, as you sometimes are, in your English way. When I came home this time, Carlos told me of the real reasons for your trip. The couple idea is not possible for us, can never be. You will never come to South America except as a pirate, amorous or commercial, and I would never live in England, never." She shivered at the thought. "So we must be realistic, mustn't we?"

"If you say so."

"You know so. Do not try to put all the responsibility on me. My life has to be here and yours has to be in England. I have my freedom, do not worry about that. I have chosen what I choose."

"No pirates, then?"

She frowned. "I did not think of you as a pirate, before. You have changed. You were much more ingenuous, once. Almost innocent. You will say that the change is due to me and maybe also Carlos but that would be unfair. It was due to other things, many other things, to do with your work and the end of your married life and your stupid machines." Her vehemence abated and she spoke to me more softly. "We have had a great time, Johnny, but it is over. I have to make choices and they are obvious."

For a moment I nearly retorted with a flippant remark about the way her choices had been forced, so stung was I by this dismissal, but I bit the retort back. It was always too easy for me and Katie to argue, like people who are close to each other, who matter. Like married people, for instance.

"Over? Then there's nothing more to say. You're a great girl, Katie, and I'm eternally grateful to you." I looked away, out of the windows at the distant sunny park teeming with people. "In life there are very few who matter and you're one of them. Always will be."

"Brave words, Johnny. Bravo."

That angered me. "You really don't believe I've ransomed you for one point six million dollars, do you?"

"Not really, no. But I'm flattered that you believe it. And that you will be safe."

"Jesus. I could have been away on the other side of the earth, with the money, by now."

"You would never do such a thing, or live such a life. It would persecute you. You will give it back, won't you?"

"If you ask me to."

"I'm asking."

"Then I will."

When I turned back from the window view, I saw her eyes were full of tears. I walked across and kissed her again, gently, feeling her lips hot and soft. I tried to put my hand on her waist but she moved away.

When she next spoke, her voice was slightly hoarse. "Let me give you a piece of advice. Will you take my advice, Johnny?"

"Of course."

"Do not get too much of a taste for doing these things. You are not Carlos. It is not your natural milieu. You did not start this way and you lived a conventional life for too long before this. You and your stupid machines are not right for the world that Carlos moves in."

"Me and my stupid machines have forced Carlos' hand. Me and my stupid machines are not quite as helpless, or as dull, as you think. Without them I would never have seen you again. And knowledge of conventional life is a good basis for a buccaneer."

She smiled gently. "You are hopeless. Incorrigible. A dreamer, always hoping that the past can be made to work for you. You won't change, will you?"

"Nope. Neither will Carlos."

She nodded slightly. "I agree. But as we get older, we have to close some doors. It hurts to close them, but we must. Young people can ignore things we have to accept. I will not forget you, either. Goodbye, Johnny."

"Farewell, Katie. I'm really sorry that a coffee scam of Carlos' turned out to be more important than me. But I understand; Proserpine has to go back to Pluto. That's the way the legend ends."

She suddenly put a hand to her face, partly covering her eyes, turned and was gone, as though the door opened and shut without her touching it. I found myself staring at its blank pale surface like a traveller at the end of a desert.

The room stayed empty. No one came in. After a while, as though breaking a spell, I managed to open the door I'd entered by and pass through to a marbled vestibule and the lift. Suddenly I was downstairs, having no consciousness of the lift journey, and walking into the spacious main lobby of the building. Behind his desk, the hall commissionaire stared at me impassively.

Before I could reach the exit doors, the two hoods were standing in front of me, barring my way.

They said nothing. I stood and waited. After about five minutes, Carlos came into the lobby and stood beside me. His manner was calm and composed. He had a piece of paper in his hand.

"Arochena is being investigated by our foreign exchange police section," he said, in a matter-of-fact, disapproving tone. "They arrested him a couple of days ago. It seems that over a long period he has committed many fraudulent breaches of our regulations. Has stashed a fortune away in foreign accounts. On his last trip to Switzerland he went too far. Not only that, the purchase he made from you was unauthorised."

"Dear, dear."

He frowned. "Always the flippant retort. You are out of your depth here, Johnny. It would be better if my money is not entangled with Texteis Arochena and his distressing business." The piece of paper was handed to me. "Please remit the funds to another account. The details are on this note."

I looked at the paper. "Lichtenstein?" I asked. "A company account, is it? Or personal?"

"That's an internal matter."

"No way, Carlos. If I remit the money to this account there will be no evidence that the money was ever returned. I'd still be on a hook."

He nodded approvingly. "Well thought out, Johnny. But by the time you are on your plane this evening, my international office in Geneva – a high-profile office by the way – will have made the necessary recovery and remitted the funds officially, via our national bank. The documentation will state that the machine exporter, who made an error, has returned the money. This will be in order to provide all the evidence required. I'll fax you a copy of the transfer and you can send a confirmation document as required by the official exchange control authorities, to confirm the source."

I considered this for a moment, then nodded. "If you want to launder funds, that's your business. As soon as I have the transfer copy evidencing my official return of the money, then I'll remit to your account."

He paused. Then: "How much did Arochena get you to include as his personal commission? In that one point six million?"

I shrugged. "Half a million, it was."

"That's about the right answer." He nodded at the piece of paper in my hand. "What's your usual margin on that sort of transfer?"

"Whatever the transaction will stand. From four up to fifteen percent."

"Fifteen percent maximum? That's two hundred and forty thousand in this case. Let's call it half of Arochena's greedy take. Two hundred and fifty thousand."

"Eh?"

He grinned. "Remit the funds less quarter of a million, Johnny."

"Why?"

His grin broadened slightly. "Proserpine, is she? Pluto, am I? What are you, a pomegranate? And a *salacacabia*, you said. My goodness, a *salacacabia*. Of Apicius, I recall. Roman, isn't it? '*An uneatable soup of great pretensions, requiring enormous preparation, yet lousy to consume.*' I haven't heard that word since I studied the classics in my youth." The grin ended. "It's a pity, Johnny. You have talents. We might have done well at something together."

I nearly said we have, and she's called Katie, but thought better of it as I realised he'd listened to every bit of my conversation with her.

Instead, I said "Oh? You mean my knowledge of the classics is worth quarter of a million?"

He smiled faintly. "I am prepared to trust you to keep your word. I also need your discretion on these matters. You keep quarter of a million. For your expenses, your discretion and for my satisfaction. That way I know you'll keep quiet."

"But you won't keep quiet, will you? You'll tell Katie that I took money to stay away from her, won't you? That you bought me off. You won't say that having failed to kill me, it was forced on you."

"Maybe. Maybe not. Maybe the money is her suggestion. A

farewell gift. You do not know what passes between us. And anyway, does it matter, now?"

"I suppose not."

"I have your guarantee of discretion?"

"I'm no copper's nark. But Tony Barnwell isn't part of this deal."

A faint smile. "I think you'll find Mr Tony Barnwell has his own suit of armour."

He held out his hand. I shook it.

"Goodbye then, Johnny."

"Goodbye, Carlos."

He turned in a final movement, nodded at the two hoods and they stood to one side, leaving the way to the door clear.

"Johnny?" His face had gone serious again.

"What?"

"Don't come back."

37

Cuba

Strange that on the journey to Zurich, awake all night in the gloom of the aircraft, I should have Elmore Leonard's *Cuba Libre* to finish reading, relieve my seething mind.

Until 1942 my father used to visit Cuba quite regularly. He travelled round the up-country sugar mills selling chain drives and cane conveying and handling systems to them. It was exhausting work, driving a hired Chevy over miles of rough roads in sweltering heat and staying the night in flea-infested hotels or mill guest houses where a line of squashed bugs along the wall by the bed warned of what you could expect if you got under the sheet. To avoid being bitten beyond endurance he frequently tried to sleep in the single wicker armchair most rooms boasted. He became an expert on sugar cane conveying and in later life gave lectures on the subject in places like Guyana, South Africa and Mauritius. It was a hard apprenticeship but not nearly as tough as the one he'd started at the age of fourteen in the foundry of the Metropolitan Cammell Carriage and Waggon Works, six o' clock in the morning until six at night, with an afternoon off for night school. After the days of his apprenticeship, my father bore the rest of life with philosophical stoicism and good humour, finding most things not nearly as bad as those of his youth in much the same way I felt about boarding school.

On his last visit, one of the cigar makers, the head of one of the finest quality Havana producers, greeted him with enthusiasm and admiration.

"Churchill," the wealthy Cuban manufacturer exclaimed. "Winston Churchill! He is the greatest man alive! Heroic! Magnificent! My esteem for him is the greatest possible. I have made a special cigar for him. When will you next be in England?"

"As it happens," my father answered truthfully,"I have been ordered to go home next month."

His return was fortuitous. American manufacturers jealous of Britain's hold on some Latin American markets had complained that Lend Lease was providing an unfair advantage, so as well as getting ripped off by one of the worst loan deals in history, Britain was forced to withdraw its export efforts in Latin America.

Without this example of yet further American mendacity my father might have been kept away from home much longer. As it was, he was ordered to return. I was born the following year. It's an ill wind...

"Splendid!" said the Cuban. "I have had a special cigar made for Mr Churchill as a token of my esteem and my support for his superb resistance to Hitler. I was wondering how to get it to him. Please will you take it with you and present it to him on my behalf?"

He produced an enormous cigar, with a special box made to fit a great torpedo of finest quality tobacco. My father's eyes bulged.

"Winston and I," he said, "do not meet very often, I'm afraid."

"Nonetheless, when you are back in England you could see that he gets it?"

"Of course. I should be honoured."

It took a long time to get home. My father's cargo boat was torpedoed half way across the Atlantic and, sinking, put back to New York. He was held on Ellis Island as an illegal immigrant until special permits came enabling him to travel to St John's, Nova Scotia to join another convoy. There was nowhere to stay in St John's because every house had been billeted with those waiting for the convoy to depart. He walked, in freezing snow and thin tropical clothes, down a long street, carrying a heavy case and knocking at door after door until some kind soul let him sleep under the kitchen table – the top was already occupied – where it was warm. The ship to which he was allocated as a passenger was an ammunition ship. All the doors were bolted open and there was six inches of sand on most decks, intended to absorb the force of an explosion. Throughout the voyage my father played cribbage with the Welsh chief engineer down in the oily but warm engine room and at night plotted the ship's course from the stars, using navigational knowledge from his

Royal Flying Corps days. He reckoned the convoy went a long way north, into the Arctic Circle, to avoid U-boats. It was bitterly cold and if you survived the blast of the ammunition ship going up, you wouldn't last more than a minute or two in the water. When they finally got to Belfast and were being discharged he showed the course to the captain to see if he'd been correct.

"You should be arrested," growled the captain, with a grin. "That's highly secret information!"

My father was no Tory but he admired pugnacity and hated fascism. When he got home, he wrote a careful letter to Winston Churchill.

"Dear Mr Churchill," he wrote. "I have just returned from Cuba after a rather trying journey. A Cuban cigar manufacturer gave me a magnificent cigar to send to you on my return. It is a mark of his esteem for you and he was most anxious that I should convey it to you. It is truly a superb size and of the highest quality. I would send it to you but I know that your security measures are, quite rightly, of the tightest nature. The cigar would simply be pulled apart and destroyed to see if there were some trap built-in with a view to injuring you, or worse. I am, therefore, smoking the cigar as I write this letter. I can assure you that it is the finest cigar I have ever smoked. I am enclosing the name of the Cuban manufacturer who wished you to have it as a measure of his admiration for your resistance to Nazi aggression and atrocity. With my compliments, yours faithfully, etc."

He was rather pleased with this missive and the cigar, he said, really was terrific.

About a month later my father got a copy of a letter in the post. It was from Winston Churchill to the Cuban cigar manufacturer. It thanked the man profusely for his gift and said that he had always regarded Havana cigars as the finest, especially after his early days reporting the Spanish-American war in Havana and up-country in the late 1890s. The letter said it was the best cigar Winston had ever smoked. It had enriched an evening that he would treasure as long as his memory continued to function. He would never forget this generous gift and expression of solidarity and support from so distinguished a member of the Cuban people.

233

My father liked to tell this story even though he said that it was probably all the work of a private secretary of Winston's. The great man would be too busy to deal with such things personally. Yet even as he said this, his eyes would go reflective. You could tell that there was doubt in his mind. I think that he felt that maybe Churchill had read his rather presumptuous letter and, with the puckishly aggressive humour for which he was famous, had decided to upstage him. My father always told the story with philosophical good humour yet, as he sucked the flame from his lighter down into the bowl of his pipe, puffing smoke from a tiny blowhole between his lips to fill the air around him with layers of wispy blue, you could tell that there was something that rankled. He may have smoked the cigar, enjoyed the sensual pleasure, but Churchill had the last word.

Having the last word was important to a man like my father. Even after his perilous journey Winston clearly had it. That rankled. It rankled a lot. I'm pretty sure that in 1945 my father voted Labour along with most of the country and chucked Churchill out. In my father's case there might just have been a personal element along with that of socialist principle.

Sort of trumping an ace, if you know what I mean. It's a male territorial imperative.

38

The same dreary arrival. It was raining. The same dreary drive back to the same wet seaside streets. My flat was calm and cool, almost restful. I picked up the phone as soon as I'd washed, shaved and got my wits back together.

She answered this time.

"Betty? Hi. How are you?"

"Oh, hello Johnny. Fancy hearing from you. Quite a surprise. And at the wrong time. Been away again, I suppose, to South America, have you? Hope she was nice. Why are you calling me? Not satisfied enough?"

"Betty, I've been trying to phone you. But you've been in Tuscany."

"Yes, I have. And it's been really heartwarming to hear how you and Maurice are getting on so well. Quite the business partners now, aren't you? With just that bit extra in common. Emphasis on bit, you know? As in 'on the side'."

"Look, it isn't quite like –"

"I really am pleased you're making so much money together. Well, you're making it, and so, incidentally, is Maurice. That's what you wanted, wasn't it? All the time. And I was so naïve."

"No, Betty, it wasn't anything –"

"So much money that Maurice has decided to move from Docklands and we're going to live in a new place in Islington. Together all week. When we're not in Tuscany. We're selling up here and getting out of this dump. This bloody dead end. I expect you will too, won't you, now that you and Maurice have made such a killing? Where will you go? Buenos Aires, like all co-respondents? I gather it's more like Brazil for you, though. All coffee scams and brown-skinned Cariocas?"

"No, I'm not moving. I haven't made the killing you're talking about. I never invested in coffee futures. It's not my scene. And it wasn't for that I –"

"Oh, come on, Johnny, you've had double value from Maurice. Knocked off his wife and picked his brains to make yourself a fortune. Don't tell me anything else. You're a clever, shady, opportunist bastard. And lousy in bed. The Tuscans are in a different league when it comes to both flattery and action, I can tell you."

"Betty, believe me – "

But the phone had gone dead.

I stared at it for a while, wanting to try and call her again. The room was quiet. My clock – *Johannes Barber Londini Fecit* – had stopped. Ranks of books looked down at me. The room was calm, a white box, nothing vernacular like mock beams or bogus inglenooks. A sort of uncompromising modernity.

I put the phone down slowly.

Then I got up, opened the case doors, and rewound the clock.

39

"I'm very glad you were able to drop in for a chat," Frances Parks said, waving at a chair in front of her desk. "There are just a few things that need to be cleared up and it's much easier here, where all the ev – er, information is in place."

She looked just the same as ever: neat, controlled, more impersonal this time than at the coffee house. Next to her Detective Sergeant Barry Henshaw stared at me impassively from behind his broken nose. Greetings had been formal rather than effusive. There were, clearly, issues still hanging in the air.

I sat down.

The office was in an anonymous building on Victoria Street. It always takes me back, when I go to that area, to those old Broadway days and the significance of all that industry, that trade in machinery, that activity and brawl, going under slabs of civil-service and police concrete. No wonder the country's in such a state.

"You've been travelling quite a bit. To Brazil," Frances Parks said, with just a touch of query about the statement.

"Yes."

I had decided to adopt a monosyllabic mode where possible.

"Er, can we offer you a coffee? Won't be of the quality you'll have had in Brazil and Colombia, of course. From a machine, I'm afraid."

"Machine will do. Black, no sugar. *Café solo.*"

"Very good. Barry?"

"Milk and sugar, thanks, Frances."

Evidently there was no discrimination in this office. Equal rights prevailed. She got up, went out. Henshaw and I stared at each other.

"Found the hit-and-run driver?" I asked.

He frowned as though I'd referred to something unknown. "I'm sorry? Oh, Lawrence Edwards. No, not yet."

"Yet?"

"We are pursuing a number of enquiries which we believe may lead us to the culprit."

"Ah."

So they were still up a gum tree.

He shifted in his chair. "What sort of vehicle do you drive?"

I steadied my natural reaction. "I do not own a car. I live near a railway station and come to London by train. When I do need a car I pick one up from a nearby hire-car company with whom I have a long-term contract. Pointless, the amount of overseas travel I do, to leave a car rotting on the seafront, quite apart from the depreciation. Much cheaper to hire. The same applies to airport trips. I have an arrangement whereby I leave it at the airport and they provide another one when I get back. Sub-contract, no overhead, no commitment. It's the way all business is going. I won't dwell on the obvious analogies with employment and modern life."

"Indeed." He sounded disappointed, which pleased me because I hadn't enjoyed the implications of his question, not at all.

Frances Parks came in with a plastic tray on which were three plastic cups of coffee.

"Here we are." She sat down. "As I say, I'm glad you could pop in."

"My pleasure." The coffee was terrible. Boiling hot dishwater. I put it down on the desk top, making sure there was a ring of moisture underneath it to attack the varnish.

I was starting to feel hostile. I didn't have to come up to London but it had been made clear that the DTI view was that I would be being unhelpful if I didn't.

"Our research into Lawrence Edwards's papers is complete." Frances Parks paused but I said nothing, so she went on. "It does seem that he was concerned about the theft of the microwave bean analyser. According to you, he asked you to research the market for this type of equipment in Brazil and Colombia?"

"Yes."

"Did he specify exact research contacts or correspondents?"

"No."

"Just left that to you?"

"Yes."

"But he did elaborate on the background to its creation?"

"Yes."

"I'm having just a little trouble, you see, in getting into his mind, so to speak. I'd appreciate any help you can give."

"Lawrence was much involved with the ICO over this fungus. Haven't they provided the answers?"

"Oh, they've been very helpful, very, but they are as mystified as us about the precise nature of Edwards's line of enquiry."

"Even after the market panic?"

"I beg your pardon?"

"The commodity panic. Market turbulence. Especially over Robusta beans. They didn't think that it might have been the cause, the anticipated cause you might say, of Lawrence's interest?"

"No, not at all. That was all a misunderstanding, they say. Normality has returned. I understand that Richard Keane has delivered his unit to Switzerland and that research into this, this toxin, is now proceeding in an orderly fashion, backed by reputable international organisations."

"Oh good."

A sharp glance at my mock-sincerity. "Do I detect some line of connection with Lawrence Edwards in your thinking about commodity prices?"

"Not really. I'm just curious. Not an expert on coffee commodities."

"Your research didn't give you any insights in that direction?"

"My research was terminated practically before it got under way."

"Yes. I realise that. But all the same."

"The few people I did talk to, in Colombia, denied that there was a problem at all. Not of any magnitude, anyway. Which wasn't borne out by events."

"Indeed not."

I frowned. "Have you investigated who were the beneficiaries of the coffee price turbulence?"

"As it happens, we have. There were a variety. A lot of people lost money of course, but some traders did very well. There appears to be no pattern, no particular strand, which links them, however. Most were abroad."

"And Tony Barnwell wasn't connected with any of them?"

At last I made impact. She looked up at me, flustered. "I—I beg your pardon?"

"The minister Tony Barnwell was in Brazil just before the crash. Did he benefit in any way, directly or indirectly, in the price movements?"

"That is not a question which has been asked to date. It is rather a shocking question."

"He knew about the bean analyser. He is a qualified scientist, as the political papers keep pointing out, as though that were an essential qualification for a trade minister. He must have known it could be used in reverse, to control output rather than input. He has been building up connections with Brazil for some time. Has indeed been congratulated on them. His connections with senior businessmen are well developed, they say. If Lawrence thought the scam came from the very top, it would explain his reticence to put pen to paper."

She had gone very upright. "That's no reason to suppose Mr Barnwell has in any way been involved in anything untoward."

"Forgive me. I have a suspicious mind. If I were you I should try to find a connection between payments from the Geneva office of a company called Kellerman International and any concern in which Tony Barnwell has an interest. Of any kind. You have lots of resources for that kind of thing. I haven't."

She stared at me in consternation. Henshaw had adopted his expressionless expression once again. Both pairs of eyes rested on me for several pregnant seconds before Frances Parks broke and began to jot notes carefully on a lined pad, the way she had when taking notes of my expenses at our first meeting at my flat. Then she shuffled papers on her desk and shot a worried look at Henshaw, who came in on cue.

"We were rather more thinking about the coincidence of your visit to Brazil and the subsequent turbulence. You too were conversant with the equipment."

"Only after it was stolen. I have no coffee interests. I never gamble. You will find no connection whatsoever with me and these events."

"But you did have the knowledge. A third party could be used. A broker, for example."

God, I hoped he didn't know about Betty. Or Maurice. I decided to brazen it out.

"Pah. You can't stick Barnwell's scam on me."

"If you have any evidence you know will lead to revelation of criminal fraud it is your duty to impart it."

"I've no documentary evidence. If I had, I'd do anything to impeach Barnwell."

He blinked. Frances Parks stared at me in surprise. "Why?"

"He deliberately destroyed my research visit to Brazil and his underlings reneged on my expenses. I rather liked Lawrence, too. Barnwell's Brazilian partner in this scam did his best to eliminate me. And other things."

"Have you any evidence for this? Any evidence at all?"

"Not written, no. I could, however, provide some very telling testimony. I am, it seems, the only person who can connect Edwards and Pulford in this matter. You will probably find that Kellerman International or one of its associates was a beneficiary from the coffee scam. Difficult, it may be, but you can check. I can't."

"These are serious allegations."

"You bet."

Henshaw recovered and continued. "Speaking of evidence, there is another matter on which you can perhaps help us."

"Certainly, if I can."

"You are involved with a machinery company in Milan. Run by a man called Mario Chiari?"

"I am."

"Can you tell us the precise nature of your relationship with this company?"

"Certainly. I sell their equipment."

"What is the nature of your contract with them?"

"An informal one."

"Do you act as principal or agent?"

"Both. Either. Depending on circumstances."

"I see. It's odd, you see, that you should be involved with them."

241

"Oh? Why?"

"Because we had a complaint, recently, about a documentary credit fraud involving a company in Brazil – a subsidiary of the very same Kellerman International you are accusing, oddly enough – who apparently bought a machine corresponding very closely with those made by this company and which you sell, but from Switzerland. A bank and the Brazilian authorities said that a very substantial sum – one million six hundred thousand dollars – had been the subject of this fraud. A substantial and respectable international group – the Kellerman Group – had announced this loss."

"Dear, dear."

"It was at a time when you were coming and going to this firm quite a bit. With one of the parties to this fraud."

Ah-ha, I thought, oh-ho, Barry Henshaw, you've given the game away. The spy Bernasconi outside Mario's factory was one of yours. And my God, someone has been researching my business and those of my phone calls they can get at. I must have been a prime suspect for some time.

"Have you any comment to make on this?"

"None at all."

"Oh, come on, Mr Barber. I'm sure you know what I'm talking about."

"I sold Mario's machine to Barranquilla. The transaction was entirely legal and the purchaser will confirm his satisfaction. I know of no other sale."

"Nothing to Brazil?"

"No."

"The details of the machine the subject of the fraud were very similar."

"There isn't only one baby diaper machine in the world."

"But you did show the machine to a man called Arochena?"

"Indeed I did. But I sold it to Descartables Serfaty in Barranquilla, who got in first. They will make the Bebé Seco brand on it. All this is perfectly verifiable. How could I possibly sell it again?"

"That's a good question."

"Arochena must have bought someone else's machine. Hasn't he received it?"

"No he hasn't."

"So is it he who is pressing for prosecution?"

Henshaw shifted in his chair again. "As a matter of fact, he isn't. We received a notification yesterday that there had been an error of some sort and the whole thing was now null and void. The money has been repaid from a Kellerman account in Switzerland. The Brazilian authorities and the bank are somewhat discomposed."

I nearly chuckled out loud. Carlos Guimares had faxed me a copy of the transfer instruction to repay the capital from his legitimate source while pocketing the money I'd sent him into the secret one in Lichtenstein. A useful way of laundering money. The parallels with Carlos and someone like Maxwell were getting even stronger, that is if a parallel can strengthen.

I said nothing, though. You can't afford to lower your guard in front of people like those.

"So if it's all over and done with, what's your problem, sergeant?"

"It smells, that's my problem. All of it. The company you used as principal in the transaction with this firm in Barranquilla – is that the only company you operate with?"

"All my companies are openly and legitimately declared. As I'm sure your investigations have established."

"It is an offence to conceal relevant information of this sort."

"My accountant will happily open any of my books you wish to examine." I leant forward in my chair and fixed him with a glare. "I'm getting very offended by all this. Let me remind you that the essence of any successful fraud is for the fraudster to disappear after the event and with the money. I have done no such thing. Indeed my profile here and in Brazil has never been higher. I have come here of my own free will to assist you. Lawrence Edwards trusted me implicitly. He's dead and you haven't the competence to nail his killer. Now you tell me that the fraud claim was all some incompetent mistake and yet you, despite your lack of success, sit here insinuating – what?"

It was Frances Parks's turn to shift awkwardly in her chair. "Look

Johnny –" Was that the first time she'd called me Johnny? – "we're not conducting an inquisition here. We're just trying to establish any facts that will throw light on this whole affair. I'm sure you want the same?"

"Of course I do. Lawrence and I had a very good relationship. I shall miss him. But you still haven't said whether he was murdered or simply killed by a hit-and-run lout."

Henshaw shook his head. "We don't know. And we may never know."

"Well my advice is to sniff around Tony Barnwell."

"I don't think you realise what that entails. Ministers are understandably protected from people like me."

"I thought we lived in a new age of open information?"

Henshaw smiled crookedly. Frances Parks looked abashed. For a moment I felt sorry for them, thought of telling them a good deal more, but of course that's what they always want, what they always hope for, the anecdote that fills the gaps between the data, the big gaps between the bare uncommunicative data they've collected and are scratching their heads over. It's the chat that gives the game away.

You simply mustn't let your guard down in front of people like that. Let them try to understand the tableau at Fort Zinderneuf for themselves.

"I – I think," Frances Parks said, "that I've asked all that I want to ask."

She looked hopefully at Sergeant Barry Henshaw. He looked grimly at me.

"I don't think we're in possession of the full details yet," he said, peevishly. "By no means."

"I'm sure you're not. But I'm also sure that the whole coffee commodity scam was the idea of Tony Barnwell, once he'd grasped the technology of the measuring device and how it could be used in reverse. The amount of money involved was enormous. The people who knocked down Lawrence and most probably blew up William Pulford were one thing. Those who tried the same with me came from the Brazilian end, where embarrassing stocks of Robusta

244

could be sold forward. I doubt if you can do much about that part of things. I've given you the lead to where you might investigate the connection, and I can provide some verbal testimony. It's all I've got. Otherwise, for me, the whole episode is over."

Silence. Then suddenly Henshaw grinned.

"You're a jammy bastard," he said. "You really are."

"I beg your pardon?"

"A jammy bastard. Hell, I thought I knew all about documentary credit games. The most common form of big-time robbery there is. And the most successful. An empty flat over a curry house in Clapham. And a really kosher-sounding company address in Zurich. A smashing set of bills of lading; really professional, they were. So were the packing specifications. But the money came back. Why?"

"I'm sure I've no idea what you're talking about."

"You said just now that the essence of a successful fraud is for the fraudster to disappear with the money. I can see why you wouldn't be able to do that without leaving this country pretty much forever. But why? Why transact the whole thing just to have it all repaid?"

"I'm afraid you're leaving me way behind."

"You've no further comment to make?"

"None. I'm completely at sea with what you're talking about."

Henshaw stood up, abruptly. His face moved from humorous to more serious. "I have to go. There is clearly a lot more work to do. I won't say that this has been a useful meeting because it hasn't. There are things to think about even if your allegations are, frankly, tenuous."

Suddenly I was irritated by his dismissive attitude.

"I may be able to produce some evidence," I said, peevishly.

"In that case, please do so as soon as possible. It should be more than hearsay, though. I'll leave you my card." He handed one across. "Get in touch with me whenever you have something. I have to go – now." He nodded at Frances Parks, said, "I'll be in touch again soon, Frances," and stalked out. She shook her head reproachfully at me as the door closed.

"It really isn't wise to antagonise the police, you know," she said.

"I know. I don't think I have, have I? Actually I feel quite sorry for him. Cracking Barnwell will be a very hard nut. But he should, rather than trying to pick on soft targets like me."

"You think you're a soft target?"

"Certainly. People like me are always easy to harass, like motorists. It's the top men who get away every time."

She looked at me curiously. "Why was the money repaid?"

But my remarks about top men had made me think about Carlos, and then automatically, Katie. Sadness steered me to silence. I really was very fond of Katie.

There I went again, using words she hated.

Frances Parks was watching my expression without speaking.

"Well," I said, managing to jerk my thoughts back to the present, "I expect you've much to do. I take it you've finished?"

"For the moment, yes."

"If you are taking over Lawrence's seat I hope I'll see more of you, will I?"

"Very probably. I hope so, too."

The reply startled me. Her face gave nothing away, just an open expression staring at me.

A quick response was needed.

"In that case, what are you doing for lunch?" I asked.

"Nothing," she said, smiling. "Or, actually, rather hoping you'd ask me that question."

40

After she'd been to powder her nose and make a quick phone call, I took her to a restaurant off Victoria Street, reasonably nearby. It was Italian, with a fairly broad menu and the dishes of the day were genuinely fresh. I had antipasto and veal, she had melon-prosciutto and Dover sole. We drank a light white wine.

Wonder was stifling my style.

There was a strange feeling about taking this investigative lady out to lunch, something odd but stimulating, a sense of wonder at why and other questions. Did she intend to deepen the relationship? Wouldn't that be dangerous in view of how I must be recorded in her office files? Was this just what Katie would call the frisson of the forbidden element? Was that all that I was in these cases?

Yet in the event the lunch was lightly dealt with, wittily conversed, part combative, the circling of performers or dancers awaiting an outcome. I had no illusions about her need for information, like Lawrence, but Lawrence was a dry old stick, pedantic, not a mature and attractive woman. We never lunched together. Whether it was genuine or not I didn't care, but she showed a lot of interest in my travels, where I'd been, what I'd done. Not in too probing a way, not seeming to look for evidence of Johnny the fraudster, or making those irritatingly suggestive remarks in which Lawrence had specialised. She asked about the places, not their businesses, the people in them, such as the folk groups playing music at Envigado outside Medellín in the old days, the *artesanía* of Brazil and Mexico, fossil stones in the market place off the Republica in São Paulo, emeralds, aquamarines, paintings, leatherwork, snakeskin shoes, beefsteaks – *bife a caballo* – in Buenos Aires, Chilean wine, *yerba mate*, many South American things, trips to the south of Chile where, by a glacier, you can drink 12-year-old whisky into which you put 1000-year-old ice. She'd obviously heard about a lot of them.

"Oh," she said, looking wistful as we finished the main course. "I'd love to see all those things, go to those places, one day."

How did she expect me to respond? Invite her on a trip at once? No, that was surely too obvious. Yet attraction needs action before time blunts its edge. If the lowering of that carefully clad, suited and bloused armour was to be accomplished it would be no good to play a cautious game, follow a patient agenda.

"It would be a pleasure to show you them," I said, gallantly but feebly, old-maidishly even, in what I could have kicked myself for being a pallid response.

Something was holding me back. Was it thoughts of Katie? Betty? Was it an imbued, boarding-school, puritan reticence that said no, things can't really be like this, things are never this easy unless she obviously takes the initiative? Do you really still think, for instance, that Carlos will let you get away with it? His money is in your bank but his tentacles must be long. His word could easily be invalid even though, as a gambler and dealer, he prides himself on honouring a commitment. Are you really no threat to anyone now? No one at all?

All the time Frances Parks and I were talking and beginning to flirt, a thin film of caution, a mental membrane, restrained my natural responses. The older you get the more you realise that there is a price for everything and for sex the price is usually highest.

"Oh, I'm sure you have many more glamorous ladies to show those sorts of sights, Johnny," she countered, roguishly.

"Not one," I protested, with a smile. "Certainly not one who I would rather take."

"Flatterer. I don't believe you."

"You have a totally mistaken idea of me. My existence is solitary. And I cannot think of any better relationship with the DTI except one whereby its investigator and I tour the *mis-en-scenes* of South American events together. It would be both educational and highly enjoyable. I can promise you that your expertise would become the envy of your department."

She laughed richly at that, taking the double entendre in her stride. The waiter interrupted us at that point, disturbing her modest but flirtatious disclaimers and the appreciation which went with this response. All the same, over black coffees, topical café solos, her encouragement was still subtly flattering. I began to feel that I was being slow on the uptake. Yet I knew so little about her.

Suddenly she looked at her watch.

"Goodness," she said. "Is that the time? I have a meeting at two-thirty. Blast the dear old DTI. Johnny, this has been great. The most enjoyable lunch I've had for ages. It's my turn next time. I'm sure we'll need to talk again – soon."

"It will be always be my pleasure."

She nodded, smiled, held out a cool hand. I shook it with care, holding it slightly longer than normal but not too long, and getting a warm look as she disengaged it.

Nonetheless, as she left, briskly smart down the street, I had a sense of *déjà vu*. It was almost a feeling of dismissal. As I paid the bill and called for a taxi to take me to the station it hit me where the sense came from: Carlos and my exits from Brazil.

41

I caught the three ten from Charing Cross, the fast train that misses several of the rural stations beyond Tunbridge Wells. It was fairly empty at that time of the afternoon and would be just ahead of the rowdy schoolchildren who pile on at Sevenoaks and Tonbridge around four o'clock. The carriage I got into was deserted. I sat at the platform window staring rather sightlessly across at other trains and a few people passing by, still thinking about Frances Parks and, now, how badly I'd handled that lunch. I hadn't got a grip on it at all.

What did she really want? A trip to South America? Something else I hadn't been advised of yet? My telephone might go at any time, with some summons or another instigated by her.

A man got in at the next door to mine and sat on the aisle end of the bench. The carriage was one of the older ones, with doors all the way down, two-seater benches on one side, three-seaters on the other. He was dressed in a windcheater with an open-necked flannel shirt under it, jeans, and striped trainers on his feet. His face was brown, perhaps from some foreign holiday, his hair dark. I put him at about forty, maybe a year or two less. He opened an early edition of the *Evening Standard* and his face disappeared behind it.

Along the platform came a suited man carrying a briefcase, walking from the front end of the train, not the entrance concourse, looking as though he had doubled back to search for a better seat or maybe a first class compartment. He passed me and, as he went by the next door, the wind-cheatered man shook his *Evening Standard* briskly, as though to straighten it. The suited one, passing by, glanced briefly into the carriage and went on without checking his stride. He disappeared from sight.

Two old ladies got in, talking volubly. I put them down as Orpington material. Quite a lot of the Orpington crowd like the fast, non-stop service out of London Bridge. One or two other people got in, opened up magazines and books, disappeared behind papers. The train moved slowly out of the station and I had time to look out over the river towards the Houses of Parliament. Somewhere in there, Tony Barnwell had an office, presumably with aides or assistants and a secretary to attend him. I thought of him, braying, with orange juice in hand at the São Paulo reception as the train moved cautiously into Waterloo East, then had an image of him talking to Carlos, glancing in my direction.

I think you'll find he has his own suit of armour, Carlos had said. Sergeant Barry Henshaw hadn't penetrated anybody's armour yet. Not even mine. What chance Barnwell's?

Coffee (which makes the politician wise…)

At London Bridge more people got in. A woman in a fawn raincoat sat opposite me and opened a copy of a woman's magazine. The train moved out, gathered speed, passengers slumped down for the sixteen minutes to Orpington. The woman opposite fell asleep. Suburban London began to streak past. I caught a glimpse of Canary Wharf, far off.

At Orpington, most of the people in the carriage got out, including the two old ladies and the sleepy woman opposite me. The man on the aisle at the next entrance continued to read his *Evening Standard*. We gathered speed again to rattle through Chelsfield, Knockholt, places between us and Sevenoaks.

The door at the far end of the carriage opened and the suited man with the briefcase came in. He started to move slowly down the aisle towards me.

It suddenly occurred to me that any minute now we'd plunge into the tunnel under the downs before you get to Sevenoaks. The man with the *Evening Standard* lowered his paper a little as he turned a page and glanced at me over the top of it.

I got up briskly, turned left, walked to the end of the carriage, through the connecting door, into the dark passage, went into the toilet and locked myself in. A couple of minutes later the train plunged into the tunnel with a whistling shriek and everything went black.

There were no lights in the toilet. I glanced quickly towards the window to find no reflected lighting against the tunnel wall. The lights in the carriage were off.

The tunnel seemed to last an age. I stood behind the door, holding the catch locked. Someone tried the door handle, shuffled, moved off. Another minute went by.

Bright light flooded the small lavatory compartment as we shot out of the tunnel, making me blink. I opened the door carefully, went back into the passage and looked through the connecting door window into the carriage. The wind-cheatered man was still reading the *Standard*. The suited man had seated himself about mid-way along the aisle.

Feeling a bit shamefaced, I went back to my seat. A few minutes more and we were into Sevenoaks. People got off. No one entered the carriage. After a pause and some shouting from a porter, we went off through another brief tunnel and began to gather pace again. After a long cutting, the familiar countryside, rather flat now, still with sheets of water from the heavy rain, stretched on either side of the speeding train, open land with farms and roads and trees. What had been small streams were swollen, overflowing into lower land.

The dark-haired, wind-cheatered man continued to read his paper. Busy Tonbridge came and went, then quiet Tunbridge Wells. Wadhurst next stop. There were only four people in the carriage now: me, windcheater, suit, and a middle-aged woman reading *Cosmopolitan*. As we neared Wadhurst, she began to gather her things together and stood up. She left us there. No one got on.

Sixteen minutes to Battle: the train began to gather pace again, through cuttings, a short tunnel, then it was going really fast.

Suddenly it occurred to me that, for an assailant, it was now or never. But how would anyone have known I was on this train?

The suited man got up and began to walk up the aisle towards me. Windcheater lowered his paper. The suited man still had his briefcase in his hand, walking head up, staring towards the end of the carriage as though heading for the toilet. As he went by, he dropped the briefcase, turned suddenly and was at the door beside me. One sharp grasp of the spring-loaded handle and he threw it open, hard, against the slipstream. It swung right back against the side of the carriage with a loud bang.

A great blast of roaring air hit me.

I reached up quickly and grasped the metal luggage rack above me rather than turning, unsecured, against them.

The wind-cheatered man had nipped round the seat behind the suited one. He grasped my jacket lapels and heaved upwards to try to get me off the seat. I came up towards him and brought my knee up hard between his legs. He gasped, but still held on, less tightly, pulling.

The suited man grabbed my knees to pull my legs off the seat. My feet almost went out of the door; beyond my shoes I could see a roaring blur of passing foliage, an upright post, other, solid things that I would hit if they succeeded in throwing me out. My fingers still gripped tightly to the rack. The suited man let go of my knees and reached over to prise my fingers off the metal rod. The carriage door swung back sharply in the slipstream, banging up against his back and my right shoe. I let out a shout of fear and drew my legs back to knee the suited man in the stomach. He staggered a little against the upright, put out a hand to steady himself, missed slightly, was off balance. I kicked at him again, not very effectively, let out another great terrified shout.

A stab of pain went through the fingers of my right hand. The wind-cheatered man had let go my lapels and was taking his turn to prise my grip off the rack. The door swung open again somehow. Now the suited one had a firm grip of my legs, was pulling me out off the seat, staggering with the motion of the train. It occurred to me in a blind, terminal snap of panic that if I let go of the rack now, the two of us would sail out through the doorway into the great bone-snapping, cracking beyond of the railway track, into God knew what post, stump, rock, iron implement to impact our broken bodies and heads. At least I'd have taken one with me.

Windcheater got my right hand prised off the rack. I grabbed his shirt collar with it, still holding the rack with my left. The other man, I thought, was reaching up to make one final heave that would bring me free, ready to be thrown out into the blast of air. Instead, he hit me a terrible blow on the side of the head. A sick numbness paralysed my whole body. My left hand let go of its grip.

I had reached the end.

The two of them stood me upright between them for one brief moment, the suited man almost in the doorway, the wind-cheatered one in the safer position inside. The suited man was on the point of turning so that the two of them would be side by side as they threw me out into the hurling void. The door had swung closed again but not on the catch and he reached out to push it open. There was a shout. The wind-cheatered one jerked violently once, twice, once again, and his knees buckled. He let go of me and fell onto the seat beside him. Into my fading vision came a view of a broken-nosed, stocky man shouting something as he hit the wind-cheatered man again, to the side of the head as he sat on the seat. The wind-cheatered man fell over sideways.

The suited man was still holding me with one hand, the other on the door sill. I managed, with a final effort, to push against him, hard. The two of us staggered at the door, which swung open again, revealing blurred ground falling sharply away from the edge of the track. A powerful hand gripped my collar from behind. The suited man let go of me to get back his balance and I managed to give him another shove. There was a scream as he swung out, still holding the door, against the slipstream. He tried to turn back but his centre of gravity had gone too far. The door moved out at right angles to the train. His legs swung under him like pendulums throwing a mechanism off balance. Another rending, despairing scream and he was gone, the door banging back in the wind.

I sat down suddenly on the floor, still gripped by the collar by someone from behind.

"Christ," said the educated voice of Barry Henshaw, above me. "You're not supposed to finish them off like that, you know."

I gaped up at him, vision clearing. Beside him another man with short-cropped hair was bending over the slumped, wind-cheatered assailant.

"You all right?" Henshaw asked.

I nodded dumbly. He released his hold on my collar.

"It certainly pays to follow you," he said, cheerfully. He reached out to close the carriage door properly. "Full of entertainment, you are. Sorry we left it a bit late. We thought they'd wait until you got to St Leonard's before making a move. Once the carriage was empty though, I suppose they decided to jump. We had to run like hell from the next carriage."

I was starting to shake; I could feel shock-unconsciousness coming on.

"But how on earth," I managed to get out, "did they know I'd be on this train?"

"They followed you. From the restaurant."

"How in hell did they know I was at the restaurant?"

Henshaw grinned broadly as he stooped over me. "I thought you were supposed to be an expert on mistresses of powerful men. Make a habit of cultivating them, don't you? What can you expect if you keep doing that?"

My head was still partly numbed. I shook it and was rewarded with a stab of pain.

"You mean – you mean – Frances Parks?"

He nodded.

"She's – she's – Tony Barnwell's –"

He nodded again.

"One of three, I believe, actually. But the only one of interest to me. I had an idea she wouldn't like your remarks at our various meetings. Particularly the connection with Pulford. Oh good, we're coming into Battle. I can start to make arrangements to scrape up your suited friend from the track. I say, take it easy; try putting your head between your knees."

But by that time darkness was descending.

42

My father died at the age of ninety-three. He was really angry about that. His grandmother had died at the age of ninety-nine and he wanted to get to be a hundred so as to go one better.

His grandmother came from Aston, like him. It was still a village outside Birmingham in her day. She told him that when she was a girl the family had an old gardener who did odd jobs for them. The gardener had been a drummer boy at the battle of Waterloo. My father really liked the idea of that.

"I have talked a lot," he used to say, "with someone who talked to someone who was at the battle of Waterloo."

It gave him a wonderful sense of continuity, of history at a personal level. Apparently the old gardener used to say that the battle was bad enough but when they got back to England the regiment was discharged at Dover. The drummer boy was given a shilling and had to walk all the way home. It took two weeks or more. He slept under haystacks or in barns and begged from kindly country folk who gave him milk and bread and cheese. My father always held this up to be typical of what the government did by way of gratitude to its loyal citizens. He had no opinion of authority except for the colonel of his squadron in Egypt and Palestine, an efficient ex-Gunner with a wooden leg who flew brilliantly and led from the front.

While he was training the Duke of York was assigned to his mess for a certain time. I think he was still called Prince Albert then. My father played snooker with him after flying, in the evenings.

"I played snooker with the future King George the Sixth," my father used to say. "Six times. And beat him every time."

It was a pity that his well-meant advice to me was obsolete. His experience was no good for the modern age. He came from a time when professionals could expect to work for one firm most of their lives, when loyalty and hard work would engender security and respect and honoured retirement. All that has gone now. People do not work for one firm for thirty or even forty years any more. We are all disposable at any time, in any takeover, any strategic revision.

Of course, other people must have seen him differently. They might say that my recollections are completely wrong. He was away a lot when I was young and he was still working, so I never had a lot of time with him. When he retired I was away a lot myself. I would like to have known him better when he was still active but it wasn't possible; his was mostly an offshore occupation.

When he died he was cremated. I should have scattered his ashes in Aston churchyard, but it is now right by a shrieking overhead motorway and I flinched from that. I was wrong. He wouldn't have minded the motorway; he liked anything to do with the building of things, the making of things, manufacture, progress, the forming of metal into useful, workmanlike objects, roads, bridges, beautiful ships and aeroplanes. He had blunt fingers and couldn't paint or play music very well but he was a draughtsman, an engineering designer. He was still very creative, even when he was mainly a commercial traveller and salesman of hard-travelling, exhausting days down in Rio Grande do Sul, or Bucaramanga, Warrington, Tucumán, Havana, Callao, Cali and Buenos Aires.

When South America beckons, he always comes to mind.

43

Sergeant Barry Henshaw was pleased with himself. I found him unreasonably cheerful as he organised everything that needed to be done after my train journey, including the collection of the dead body on the line and the despatch of his prisoner to a suitable police cell. I sat recovering in Battle station waiting room for what seemed like hours while droves of local rozzers came squeaking up in flash cars and scurried excitedly about as they talked into big mobile phones. Then I was removed to Battle police station.

You can stare death in the face every now and then, but not too often, without going out of your mind. Even if the face comes as close as the open door of a hurtling train, inches away, survival is a strong antidote to terror. There is a shaky rebound that sets in early, a nervous backlash close to euphoria. What is harder to absorb, or to find suitable solace for the flayed mind's raw wounding, is the knowledge of how ignorant, how gullible you have been. In a police waiting room, functional, antiseptic, the stupid susceptibility of my actions over Frances Parks, and what I should have known, locked me into a sort of coma as I stared at a blank, cream-emulsioned, fingermarked wall. After further delays, a cup of tea and much solo contemplation, Henshaw took me back up to London by car, to another grim waiting room where even weaker tea was served. By this time, after watching the changing scenery flick past, listening to a driver's caustic comments on the behaviour of traffic, absorbing the idea that no matter how dense you may have been, life always goes on, I was feeling marginally better. After all Henshaw's procedural part was over – it took hours and hours of form-filling and statements, statements about which I had to think carefully – I was allowed to go home.

No one offered to drive me; they didn't give me a shilling, either. It was back to Charing Cross station and the next available train, a slow late one, with plenty of time to relive the last, vivid journey. After an age of pulling into dark rural stations, we got to St.Leonards,

Warrior Square, and I could walk the shabby pavements of King's Road on my way to Marine Court.

There were no messages on the phone and only bills in the mail. If you're looking for symbolism, though, the clock was still ticking. And there was a really cheering typed sheet on the fax machine.

Johnny

Mario says thanks for the arrangements for him and Serfaty. He's glad to hear everything in Brazil was cleared up. He called from Amman to say that the machine in Jordan will be even better than Duvivier's. It's being put into containers to come back here. He wants to know where you are going to sell it when it's finished.

I look forward to seeing you again soon.

Best wishes

Chica Morelli

I poured myself a stiff measure of Scotch with something of a smile on my face. A new machine to sell. My pulse picked up. There was a guy in Panama and one in Chile who'd asked after machinery during my absence. That meant maybe Porto Bello and Valdivia, Vernon and Cochrane in one trip. There was a company down in Buenos Aires I should call as well, maybe get a *bife de churrasco a caballo* at the *Restaurante El Mundo* on *Maipú*, between *Lavalle* and *Tucumán*.

All the same, as I downed the whisky, an image of Carlos persisted uneasily. I wouldn't have put it past him to lie yet again. Once he'd got his money into Liechtenstein, once he'd laundered his Geneva funds, once he could tell Katie he'd paid me off, he could easily have sent a signal to Barnwell. Now, it would say, now you can get rid of Johnny Barber, whenever you like, but make it soon. He's best out of the way, where he can't give any evidence. If your suit of armour can manoeuvre him, set him up where he'll be vulnerable, do it. Carlos would be quite capable of suggesting that, despite the loss of quarter of a million dollars. Leopards don't change their spots.

I should have known. I should have guessed. When she and Henshaw arrived so suddenly at Marine Court, the line of communication direct to Frances Parks should have been obvious. The DTI probably knew nothing, whatever she told Henshaw; it was straight from the Carlos-Barnwell stable that the tip had come. I was too preoccupied with other thoughts to see it; she was still a strange outsider to me.

How gleefully I had believed they knew nothing of the background.

The shock discovery of Frances Parks's real motives turned my dismal, waiting-room thoughts back to Katie. In the past, no matter what rows had taken place, Katie would always return, reproachful but friendly, slightly mocking, tantalising, ever willing within her own terms. Give it a couple of months, I thought, give it another, inevitable girlfriend of Carlos's, give her a ring at home. Persistence pays. Next time a trip maybe to Argentina, the lakes, perhaps Bariloche for old times' sake. Or up to San Luis, keeping it in Brazil.

Then sense returned. Katie really had said goodbye to me. Like Betty. Closed doors were closed doors. If I came near again, Carlos would finish me off. I had to accept that it was all over. Really and certainly all over, between Katie and me, after ten whole years.

Matters needed taking in hand.

I arranged to meet Barry Henshaw a few days later, to buy him a beer as thanks for saving my life. We managed to get on pretty well after some initial reservations and cautious circling in conversation. It turned out he was an ex-boxer, amateur middleweight, quite apart from being a qualified accountant. Off duty, in a pub near Trafalgar Square, he had the sort of relaxed, breezy competence that might have got under some people's skin and he was a bit smug about his role in the whole coffee bean business, but who was I to complain? I preferred this breezy man to the cautious, watchful, rather snide fellow I first knew.

He told me they had arrested Frances Parks as an accessory and, technically, for conspiracy. She was almost immediately let out on bail. Her brief was an expensive, superior solicitor of the kind top people employ. Henshaw had a theory that she was the one who'd originally rumbled where Lawrence Edwards's investigations were taking him – close to Barnwell's scam with Carlos – but he'd need to work on that. Barnwell might have had other sources. My readily accepted Italian restaurant lunch was set up to provide time for the two train assassins to arrive but she was claiming she knew nothing of any murderous intentions. All her papers had been impounded even though Henshaw was sanguine about finding anything incriminating. Funny how instincts go; I might have made a real fool of myself at that lunch.

The wind-cheatered man, brought to London from Battle and undergoing what Henshaw called intense interrogation, wasn't admitting anything over William Pulford's caravan. Henshaw said that his team was assembling forensic evidence from under the dead man's car that could maybe just prove it was the one involved with Lawrence. There were indirect links with Barnwell coming in from all over the place, even though so far no transfers of funds from Brazil had been identified. Henshaw wasn't upset. He said that these things always take time; ask any accountant. Years might go by. Henshaw was used to playing a long game; he reckoned that, eventually, he would have Barnwell on toast.

I raised my glass to that.

Over more than one or two beers we talked a lot about documentary fraud. He had an accountant's fascination with it, in both theoretical and practical senses, and told me stories of computer frauds that were astonishing. He still tried to probe about why the money from Texteis Arochena was returned but I said I hadn't the faintest idea; it had nothing to do with me.

He grinned knowingly and gave me another of his penetrating, assessing looks.

"Some people," he said quietly, almost to himself, "will do almost anything to prove a point."

The remark startled me. I couldn't believe he knew as much as it implied. His experience was, clearly, considerable. Silently, I hoped that psychic powers didn't come into his repertoire as well as financial skills but, even as I thought, Katie and her repertoire of mystic beliefs came to mind. I had to suppress the concept with a mental wince, hoping he wouldn't notice any flicker in my expression.

The wounds were not healed yet.

Almost as soon as he made the remark he dropped the subject to talk of computer hacking pursuits. I have no doubt that bigger businesses, much bigger businesses quite apart from the pursuit of Barnwell were already occupying his time by then. I was small fry to him. But you must never let your guard down with people like that.

When he'd finished, he shook hands and said I'd probably hear from him in due course. The story wasn't over by any means. If I did move or anything, please to let him know but, and here he smiled again, I wasn't on his suspect list any more. Not for this affair, anyway. Then he left.

I walked out into Trafalgar Square and glanced back, just once, towards Northumberland Avenue, before I got the train home.

44

The lorries still made the shop shake as they went past. There was still the same tangle of electric wiring and electronics, bits of circuit boards, diodes, a glowing laptop and a monitor with a wobbly trend graph tracking across it. Still rugby-shirted, the proprietor looked at me with a grin.

"Like some coffee?"

"No thanks, Richard."

"I don't blame you. How are you? All right?"

"I'm fine."

He gestured towards his tangle of kit. "I got paid for the one finally delivered to Switzerland. Hell of a relief. Sally was starting to fret. Never mind the bank."

"Good. How's business?"

"Never better. Got an order for two more, different ones. Timber. There's a big potential there."

"Very good."

"I've had an idea for another development of the sensor, too." He smiled his most rueful smile. "It only needs money. Sure you won't have a coffee?"

"No thanks." I gave him a straight look. "Richard, have you given any thought to funding this business properly? So it can be developed commercially and pay you a living wage?"

His stare dropped. "Sally and I have discussed it. But there are always so many strings attached."

"I could fund you with a substantial sum in return for only a ten percent share. You could pay yourself and get some help. I'd look abroad for opportunities for you. No strings."

He licked his lips. "That's very kind. I much appreciate it, really I do. But Sally – that is, we – don't want to become someone else's puppets. It may seem silly to a businessman like you. But that's how we've seen it up to now. People who offered us money wanted too much in return."

"Well, I wasn't thinking simply of charity. I'm not a philanthropist. But I am really fascinated by this business. I'd be interested in investing and having a role to play. I think it has a great future."

"Thanks, Johnny. It's good of you to say so. But Sally and I have struggled for a long time and we're nearly there now. We're not interested in selling out after all the effort we've put in."

I shook my head. "I wasn't thinking of depriving you of control. I don't want you to sell out. You need finance to get going properly. The next steps are crucial to a business like this." I gestured round the shop. "You're ridiculously underfunded. A bank will burden you with debt, interest payments, demands for ridiculous forecasts, cash flows, explanations of what your development is about, all the time-wasting, documentary gubbins of the bullshit brigade. I wouldn't do that." I held up a hand to stop further objections. "Up to quarter of a million dollars is no problem."

"What? Wow. Why?"

"I need something to complement my existing business. My machinery brokerage, that is. I know that my trip to South America was a disappointment but it was a DTI thing and the DTI thing got in the way. You'd have to trust me and I you, if I put some finance in. We'd record the whole thing legally. Small companies like yours get screwed by financiers. I'm not a financier. I can help in other ways than just money. You'd still be your own boss. I'd be your outside man. Setting up deals and distributors. It's similar to an arrangement I have with an Italian engineer."

He stroked his jaw thoughtfully. "I don't know. I would like to try some other applications, I must say."

"Ah. That's development. You've already talked about one thing; what you'd do if you had more funds. Have you thought about any other ideas?"

He grinned broadly, looking round the office-shop. "All night, every night. All day, every day."

"Then let's do it."

He gaped at me.

I stuck my hand out.

"Is it a deal?"

"Quarter of a million?" His voice was incredulous.

"Only dollars, you know. Not pounds."

"For ten percent?"

"Ten percent. You can outvote me any time."

He laughed suddenly and grabbed my hand, quick, as though he thought I might take it away. "All right! It's a deal."

"Great." I returned a crushing, pumping shake. "I'll pay the legal costs. At least, one of my Swiss companies will."

He shook his head in disbelief. "You do realise, Johnny, that you're valuing my company at two point five million?"

"Technically, yes. Dollars, not pounds. Worth every penny, I'm sure of it. Every cent, rather."

"I can't believe this. I just can't."

"Richard, I know a good thing when I see one. I need a new product. Really I do. You'll be doing me a favour."

He shook his head again, as though to clear it. "If you won't have a coffee, how about going out for a beer to celebrate?"

"Good idea."

"Great. I'll lock up as we go."

He picked up a coat and stared round the shop-office carefully as he rummaged for his keys. He looked like a man taking leave of something, mentally as much as physically, memorising, as he did so, a scene he had been fond of but which, he suddenly felt, was about slip into the past. I went outside to let him savour the moment as he took in the transient sensation.

Another container-lorry blasted past as I stood on the narrow pavement, buffeting me with its trailing slipstream of noise, wind and spray. I grinned after its receding bulk as I watched it browbeat its unrelenting way through the crouching, congested village. What might it contain? Groceries, perhaps, or maybe coffee, or maybe even machinery.

Or maybe nothing at all.